LEANNE BANKS

footloose

HQN™

ISBN-13: 978-0-373-77128-8
ISBN-10:   0-373-77128-2

FOOTLOOSE

www.HQNBooks.com

Printed in U.S.A.

Special thanks to Alisa Banks, Rhonda and Bob Pollero,
Cindy Gerard, Cherry Adair, Traci Hall and
terrific editor and lifesaver Margo Lipschultz.

This book is dedicated to everyone who has ever been dumped
and eventually felt as if they'd dodged a bullet.

footloose

Dictionary Definition:
Heel: *Noun*. A solid attachment of a shoe or boot forming the back of the sole under the heel of the foot.

Amelia Parker's Definition:
Heel: *Noun*. A low-down dirty guy who steals your heart then stomps it into a thousand pieces.

CHAPTER ONE

AMELIA WAS SO EXCITED she could barely breathe, let alone eat the delicious dinner she would share in a short time with Will, his boss and his boss's wife at the fabulous restaurant in Buckhead.

Her ex-fiancé, William, was about to become her fiancé again and everything would be right with the world. She wished the two of them could have managed some alone time before dinner, but Will was arriving directly from the airport.

They would share a sweet reconciliation afterward. She had it all planned. Fighting butterflies, she walked down the stairs of the historical mansion that belonged to her recently married landlord, Aubrey Carter Elizabeth Roberts Gordon.

"You look beautiful, dear. He'll regret every minute he's spent without you," Aubrey said. "And if he doesn't, Harold will—"

"Pull out a can of whoop-ass like that boy has never seen," Harry finished.

Aubrey tried to pinch her lips together in disapproval, but a smile escaped. Polar opposites, the middle-aged couple provided a constant source of amusement and encouragement to Amelia. Harry was a rough rascal of a man who'd made a mint in mobile home sales and Aubrey was the quintessential perfect, proper, Atlanta-born-and-bred woman. Who would have thought the two of them would fall in love and marry within a month of meeting each other? Surely if Harry and Aubrey could make it work, then so could Amelia and Will.

"Do you have everything ready?" Aubrey asked.

Amelia nodded. "I've got candles waiting to be lit. I baked his favorite pie from scratch, bought his favorite wine and put his favorite country music CD on the stereo."

"You're going to knock him off his feet," Aubrey assured her.

"That pie smells awfully good. You sure you don't want me to test it?"

Aubrey gave Harry a playful swat. "Stop teasing her. Can't you see she's nervous?"

"Do I really look okay? This is his favorite dress. And I'm wearing his favorite perfume. He always said he liked my hair best this way." Amelia touched a hand to her carefully-straightened locks.

"You look gorgeous," Harry said, patting her

hand. "And more important than your hair or perfume, you're nice to be around. Remember that."

"Thank you," she said.

"We'll be way on the other side of the house," Aubrey said. "So don't worry about making introductions if Will comes back here tonight. We can save that for later."

Feeling a rush of gratitude, Amelia gave in to the impulse to hug Aubrey. "Thank you so much," she said again, and left for the restaurant.

Her mind whirled a mile a minute during the drive to the restaurant. She wasn't sure how she'd survived the last forty-five days of being in limbo with Will. She could hardly remember a time when he hadn't been part of her life. He'd proposed to her on the playground when they'd been in elementary school and they'd been together ever since.

Watching so many couples break up over the years, Amelia had always felt as if she must have been sprinkled with stardust. She and Will had found each other so early. What a relief to have that aspect of her life taken care of.

She felt a tiny ripple of unease at the thought, but refused to pay attention to it. Will had broken up with her twice during the last six weeks, then he'd turned right around and asked her to take him back, which she had. Two weeks ago, though, Will had told her he wanted to put their relationship on hold, and everything had felt off-kilter to Amelia again. She was ready to get back on track. Her only regret was that she would have to resign from the designer shoe company Bellagio, Inc. She would miss her new friends. She'd learned long ago, though, that true love required sacrifice.

Amelia pulled into the parking lot of the popular restaurant and walked into the entryway, hoping to see William, but he wasn't there. She checked with the hostess and was led to a back room of the restaurant where a couple and Will, looking more gorgeous than ever, sat at a small round table.

Will glanced up at her and stood. "Amelia, there you are," he said and lightly touched her back. "Mrs. Fitzgerald is dying to meet you. She's a big fan of Bellagio shoes."

That feeling under her nerve endings grew stronger when Will introduced her simply as Amelia Parker, not as Amelia Parker, his fiancée. He didn't kiss her or touch her hand during the meal. Although he was polite, he seemed detached.

Her stomach twisting into a knot, she still managed to make friendly conversation. By the end of the meal, however, she couldn't stop wondering why Will was acting so cool when he had been adamant about her joining him at this dinner.

He'd said it was important to him, so of course she'd come.

Feeling every tick of the clock, she refused dessert and wondered if she should excuse herself. Mrs. Fitzgerald saved her from her quandary when she received a call from the sitter saying that her child had a fever. The couple quickly excused themselves, leaving her alone with Will. Finally.

"Let me walk you to your car," Will said.

His silence as he escorted her to the parking lot made her stomach hurt even more. Amelia bit her lip. "I wasn't sure where you planned to stay tonight."

He shrugged. "I got a room downtown since I'm just here for the night. I guess we should talk," he said as he opened her car door for her.

Amelia had the sudden feeling of dread, the same, she'd bet, that someone being led to the guillotine would feel. She'd had this sensation when he'd broken up with her before. Amelia couldn't fool herself any longer. Will was going to dump her once and for all.

Maybe not, her hopeful naïve side argued weakly.

But deep down, she knew. He was going to give her the biggest heave-ho of her life and there was nothing she could do about it. She sank blindly into the driver's seat.

Will slid into the passenger seat and turned toward her. He sighed. That sigh was never a good sign.

"I don't know how to say this, Amelia, but I'm not in love with you anymore."

Her heart sank to her feet. No, lower—it had to be lower, lower than the bottom of her car and the paved parking lot. He'd never put it exactly that way before. She shook her head, her mouth opening, but she couldn't find any words.

"I don't know how it happened, but I fell in love with someone else."

Amelia's brain screeched to a halt. "Pardon me? There's someone else?"

He shrugged. "I didn't mean to fall out of love with you, bugaboo," he said, his pet name suddenly grating on her raw nerves. "It's just that I met Sidney and she knocked me on my butt. She's everything you're not."

She felt as if someone were shifting her internal gears without the benefit of a clutch. "She's everything I'm not," she echoed, confused. "I thought I was everything you wanted."

"I can't explain it. She's as ambitious as I am, always doing something that surprises me. She's impulsive, has a temper, but she makes me feel alive every minute."

Amelia couldn't digest it. She couldn't believe what he was saying. "Did you even notice that I fixed my hair the way you always said you loved it?"

she asked him. "I'm wearing your favorite dress. Did you notice that? I'm wearing your favorite perfume."

He shook his head. "I'm sorry, Amelia. I just don't feel that way about you anymore." He sighed again. She hated his sighs. "Sweetheart, I think I just outgrew you."

Outgrew her. Fury blasted through her fear. Some small bit of pride and self-preservation bubbled up from her desperation. She had made sacrifices for Will. She had traded a scholarship to a prestigious university for a state school where Will could gain admission, too. She had cut and colored her hair for him, dressed for him, put her career ambitions in the backseat for him. She had agreed to delay their wedding so they could be more financially stable. She had made sacrifices.

For the first time, she had the ugly feeling that she had made too many sacrifices.

"Would you mind giving me a ride to my hotel?" he asked. "I can tell you need time to think about all this. You can go ahead and give me the ring back, too," he added casually. "And bugaboo, we'll always be friends."

Amelia felt something inside her shift. She could almost hear the sound of stone platelets scraping against each other. It was monumental. She'd based most of her life on the plan that she and Will would be together forever. That plan had just been cancelled for good. After six weeks of waffling, she could tell that Will didn't want her anymore, even though she'd done everything she could to make him love her.

To be honest, she'd known it for a while, but had been too terrified to face it. Everything had changed. Everything would be different.

But her heart kept beating. She kept breathing. Her brain kept working. She was still living. She laughed in relief. Maybe the anticipation had been worse than the reality.

She looked at Will, really looked at him, without the gauze of love covering her eyes. He had a weak chin, he chewed with his mouth open and he rushed her during sex. He had chosen her engagement ring based on his taste, not hers, and he was cheap.

She removed her engagement ring from her finger and handed it to him.

Then she started her car. "Get your own ride and get another friend."

"But—"

"No buts," she said. "Get out of my car."

Looking at her as if she'd sprouted a third head, he complied. Still dazed, she headed back to her suite at Aubrey's house, where she smashed Will's favorite CD into a million pieces, poured his favorite bottle of wine down the toilet and gave his home-made apple pie to a sympathetic but appreciative Harry.

AMELIA HELD ON TO HER anger as long as she could. Anger, she decided, was loads better than sadness. Anger had energy and kept her from getting weepy. Anger was big and hot and bright. It filled up her bewildered insides like fireworks filled up the black sky on the Fourth of July.

The problem was that Amelia had never been able to hold on to anger that long. It had always seemed like a stupid waste of energy. So four days after Will had dropped the big bomb on her, the ache inside her overrode the anger. She felt so empty and so sad.

Her mother had always said the best way to deal with feeling sad was to bake a pie for someone. Focusing on someone else would help you feel better about yourself. Even the good book said, "It's better to give than to receive."

A lot easier, too, Amelia decided and began to bake some pies. She baked pies for thirty straight days, until her boss and friend Trina Roberts took her aside and gently referred her to a shrink.

The nice balding man listened and nodded his head and told Amelia she needed to experience herself more. Amelia didn't really understand what that meant.

During her next visit, the shrink told her she needed to be nice to herself. "You can't truly love another until you love yourself," he said wisely. "It sounds like maybe you lost sight of who you really are when you tried so hard to be what Will wanted."

He even quoted the good book. "'Love your neighbor as yourself' means you need to love yourself, too."

Even though Amelia was pretty sure her father would refer to the shrink as a flaming liberal, his advice made a little bit of sense.

When she couldn't quite figure out how to love herself, the shrink gave her homework. She needed to write down what she liked and what she didn't like, things she wanted to try. That was how she came to start the list. The first thing she wrote on it was that she'd like to live at the beach sometime. And studying what she'd written, Amelia decided it was time to get a life, her own life. At last.

CHAPTER TWO

Three weeks later

DRINKING HIS SECOND CORONA, Jack O'Connell watched the little blonde at the other end of the bar as she wrote on a cocktail napkin and sipped a drink with a colorful umbrella.

Amidst the tanned beach babes exposing yards of skin, she looked like a fish out of water as she kept pulling up the strap of her sundress. Her skin was alabaster white. Poor thing, he thought, she probably burned like a beast.

Her earnest intensity about whatever she was writing on that cocktail napkin made him curious. Which just showed he had too much time on his hands. Vacations made him edgy. He always felt that if he took time off, he would miss something. Even though he was down here to grease the skids on his biggest deal ever, he had a lot of dead time to fill.

He glanced at the blonde again, wondering what

her story was. He noticed a wallet on the ground by her feet and wondered if it belonged to her. Indulging his curiosity, he strolled toward her, picked up the wallet and straddled the stool beside her.

"This yours?"

She glanced up, her blue eyes wide with surprise. "Omigosh. Yes, thank you."

"Jack O'Connell," he said, introducing himself.

"Amelia," she said hesitantly.

"Amelia," he repeated and smiled. He liked the way the name sounded in his mouth. She reminded him of a white magnolia blossom. "What's a nice, well-bred southern girl like you doing at a tiki bar in the Florida Keys by herself?"

"It's the first time I've had a chance to get out. And my first hurricane," she added, nodding toward her drink.

"How do you like it?" he asked.

"It tastes like fruit punch. With some extra punch."

He chuckled. "One-hundred-fifty-one proof punch. And the cocktail napkin? Is that a new amendment to the Constitution you're writing? Looks pretty serious."

He watched in surprise and delight as pink color flooded her cheeks. A blush. He couldn't remember the last time he'd seen a female over the age of seventeen blush.

"Well, one side is a list of birthday gifts I need to get in the mail to my niece and nephew because I won't be home for their birthdays."

"And the other side?"

"It's a, uh, different to-do list," she said and took a gulp of her drink. "I recently had a big change of direction in my life, and so I'm making a list."

"Sounds like a good idea," he said. "Is drinking your first hurricane on the list?"

She hesitated, then her lips slowly stretched into a smile. "I guess it was on my mental list."

"You should put it on your written list, too," he said. "Because then you can check it off. And every time you check something off, it gives you a sense of accomplishment. Yeah," he added at her curious look. "I make lists, too. Down here the list includes watching as many sunsets as possible and missing the sunrises because I had such a good time the night before. Increasing my repertoire of memorized Jimmy Buffet lyrics and setting a new personal record for how many minutes I keep a Corona in my hand during a twenty-four-hour period."

Her smile broadened. "I'm not sure I can put all of that on my list because I'm not on vacation."

"You're working *here?*"

She nodded. "I work for Bellagio, the designer shoe company, and I'm down here on temporary assignment as an assistant to Lillian Bellagio. She's the widow of one of the founders of the company."

The mention of Bellagio made his heart rate pick up. The name always had. How ironic that she worked there. And how…opportune. "Sounds like a cupcake assignment," he said.

"Yes and no. Mrs. Bellagio is perceived as challenging and sometimes demanding. That's why they sent me. Before I became a full-time employee of Bellagio, I was a temp in almost every department. They always sent me to take care of the crisis du jour."

"So I bet you know a lot about the inner workings of Bellagio."

She shrugged and took another long sip of her hurricane. Jack noticed she was nearing the bottom of the glass. He gestured toward the bartender to bring her another and tapped his bottle of Corona.

"If you decided to go with Bellagio full-time, you must like 'em," he said.

She nodded. "I like the people there. They really pursued me. It's a relief to know that even if my personal life is in the toilet, I can still perform professionally."

"Personal life in the toilet," he echoed. "Is that the reason for the list?"

She looked self-conscious. "I guess."

"What do you have on there?"

She pulled the napkin protectively to her. "It's under construction."

"Come on. Give me a few hints. Maybe I could help."

She shot him a wary glance and took a sip of her fresh drink. "Please don't take this the wrong way. It was nice of you to get me a drink, but I don't know anything about you."

"And you're afraid I'm going to ply you with alcohol and have my wicked way with you."

Her cheeks bloomed with color again. "I didn't say that."

"Amelia, do you want to know the truth?"

She nodded.

"I'm bored. You looked more interesting than anyone else here."

She glanced around, then met his gaze again. "There are some very pretty girls here."

"Yep, but they don't look interesting. You look pretty *and* interesting."

She hesitated, clearly still uncertain.

"Listen, you're in the Keys. It's okay to have some fun."

She gave a big sigh and he could hear tension being released like air poured out of a flat tire. "I want to get a different car," she said, straightening her shoulders. "I want to travel. I want to start an

IRA. I want to get a different haircut, maybe change my hair color, buy some different clothes."

"Everything's gotta be different? What kind of car do you have?"

"A Honda."

"What's wrong with it?"

"My ex-fiancé picked it out."

"Oh," Jack said and kicked himself for not figuring that out earlier. She was recovering from a breakup. The classic signs were there—stiff drink, halter dress, distrust of the opposite sex. "A Honda's not a bad car."

"I know. It gets great gas mileage, doesn't break down frequently, has good resale value."

"Too practical for you? Are you more of a practical woman or do you like to take chances?"

She sighed again and frowned. "Up until now, I've been very practical."

She didn't sound happy with the revelation.

"That's Van Morrison playing," he said. "Wanna dance?"

She looked startled at his invitation, then hesitant, then a little defiant. "Yes, I would, thank you."

He led her onto the sand that served as a dance floor and coaxed her into the rhythm of the song. She stumbled a couple of times, laughing at herself. The breathless sound tugged at something inside him.

Her breasts brushed against his chest and he felt his blood sink to his groin.

Getting her into bed would be a piece of cake. She was vulnerable and he had Irish charm on his side. Another hurricane and a couple of slow dances were all it would take.

Jack was a shark by trade, but he didn't make a habit of taking advantage of wide-eyed, broken-hearted amateurs. Yet while she was innocent, she also seemed determined to get into the water. And with her knowledge of Bellagio, she could be useful. That, he couldn't resist exploiting. But her vulnerability was something else. So he would be careful with her, but he would get what he could from her.

After a couple more dances and half a hurricane, she loosened her tongue. At his gentle prodding, she gave him a new snapshot of the players, major and minor, at Bellagio, the corporate culture and the general attitude and mood of the employees. Tucking the information in the back of his brain for future use, he checked out what she'd scribbled on the napkin. "This list needs some work," he said.

She reached for the napkin, but he held it away from her. "That's supposed to be just for me."

"Don't worry. I'm just an anonymous guy you met at a tiki bar. I'll be the ghostwriter. If you really want to make some changes, then you need to climb further out on the limb."

"Changes such as?"

"I'll start you off small. Swimming in the nude," he said, taking her pen and writing it down.

Her eyes widened. "I don't think—"

"It's not as drastic as sex on the beach, but we can add that one if you—"

"No, and—"

"What about driving a convertible with the top down? Have you ever driven one?"

"No."

"Good thing to do at least once. Sky diving?"

"Absolutely not."

And so it went. He suggested. She countered. Egging her on to expand her list was the most fun he'd had in a long time.

TWO HOURS LATER, after Amelia had finished her third hurricane and Jack had extracted information about Marc Waterson, Bellagio's heir apparent, Jack did the honorable thing and returned Amelia to Lillian Bellagio's estate. She leaned against his shoulder and dozed during the short drive.

The thought occurred to him, again, that it would be so easy to take her back to the beach house where he was staying. She wouldn't protest. She reminded him of a little lamb without any protection. The wolves would get her in no time if she didn't shore up her defenses. At the same time, though, it would be a damn shame to see her toughen up. Her innocence was rare and appealing.

Pulling to a stop just outside the estate, he gave her a gentle shake. "Amelia, we're here. Time to wake up."

Her eyelids fluttered open and she looked at him in confusion. "Jack."

"Yep. I'll be at the gate in just a minute. Will you be able to walk to the house?"

She nodded. "Sure," she said and sat up, blinking.

"You're sure?" he asked.

"Yes, thank you." She looked at him. "You've been very kind."

He felt a sliver of discomfort at taking advantage of her hurricane-influenced state to get insider info on Bellagio. "It was a fun night."

She studied him for a long moment. "You're very good-looking. Could you do one more favor for me?"

"What?" he asked a little warily.

"Could I kiss you? I've never kissed a guy the first time I met him."

He felt a jolt of surprise. "Is this on your list?"

"Hmm. I guess it is."

"Okay," he said and leaned toward her.

She pressed her hand against his chest. "No. I have to kiss you. I have to start it."

Accustomed to taking the lead, Jack felt a startling punch of exhilaration. Damn, who would have thought...

Her eyes open, she leaned toward him and lifted her lips to his and rubbed from side to side. The soft texture of her mouth and the sensual movement provided the biggest tease he'd had in a long time. He was used to taking what he wanted. Sure, he knew the ways of seduction, but they were a means to an end.

She opened her mouth and he felt a lick of anticipation shimmy down to his groin. He could feel her indecision. To taste or not to taste.

He struggled with an instinct to take control, to plunge his tongue into her mouth, but her tentative explorations were too delicious.

He opened his mouth and barely brushed her lips to give her encouragement without guiding her.

She echoed his movement and rewarded him by sliding her tongue just inside his mouth.

White-hot lust raced through him. He wanted to devour her mouth, bury his face in her breasts and slide between her thighs until neither of them could walk normally. He couldn't remember feeling this hot since he was sixteen years old.

She lingered, rubbing just the tip of her tongue

over the inside of his lip, then against the tip of his own tongue. Then she pulled back and he again fought the urge to close his arms around her and kiss the breath out of her.

Something made him stop. He would figure out later just what that something was.

She looked up at him, her blue eyes smoky with a hint of arousal, and she smiled. "Thanks."

Over the pounding of his heart, he smiled back. "Thank *you*."

Driving to the gate, he pulled to a stop again, putting the car in park. He got out and opened her door. "You sure you'll be okay?"

"I'm sure," she said, her voice determined as she rose to her feet and stood for a couple of seconds as if to get her bearings.

He found an old paper receipt in the console and scratched his cell number on it. "Call me," he said, handing it to her.

She glanced at the paper, but just smiled enigmatically. "Thanks again."

He watched her walk down the driveway and wondered why he felt like he was the one who'd been hit by a hurricane.

CHAPTER THREE

OKAY, SO MAYBE the three-hurricane thing hadn't been such a good idea after all, Amelia thought the next morning as the sound of her alarm clock scraped like a thousand razors in her skull. She felt renewed sympathy for the state of Florida for the pounding of hurricanes it had taken throughout the years.

Images of the night before skittered through her brain. She'd started a list. It had begun sensibly, but then that hot guy had made suggestions. Had she really kissed the man she'd met last night? She pulled her sheet over her head in embarrassment. What was his name? Something that started with a J. John, Jim. *Jack.* He had been so hot, so good-looking and sexy, and she'd just bet he possessed little to zero ambition. She was lucky he hadn't taken advantage of her.

Or maybe not so lucky, she thought, as a kick of defiance raced through her. The advantage to being taken advantage of was that she wouldn't have to take responsibility for being a bad girl. Remembering how his biceps had felt beneath her fingertips and the contrast of his light eyes against his tanned skin, she closed her own eyes and relived the secret pleasure of feeling desirable. She wondered what it would take for her to find the nerve to have a fling with a guy like that.

A siege of protests stormed through her mind. She was starting to think that this sexual attraction thing was like a muscle and she needed to build up to it.

She might be ready in a couple of months, she told herself and pulled the sheet back down.

A hangover wouldn't keep her from beating Lillian Bellagio into the office. The one thing that had kept Amelia from dissolving into a puddle during her breakup was the knowledge that she was good at her job. She could make order out of mayhem on any day that ended with *y*. The love of her life may have kicked her to the side of the road, but the people at Bellagio thought she was all that and a bag of chips. Her boss, Trina Roberts, had even confided that several supervisors had engaged in little battles to keep her in their departments. Gingerly lifting her head from her pillow, Amelia eased out of bed and walked to the bathroom, wishing she could mainline ibuprofen.

She glanced in the mirror and saw the same old pale face staring back at her. Her blond hair rebelled at her meticulous efforts with the flat iron yesterday, sticking out in every direction represented on the compass. Will had preferred her hair super straight. That had been easy when she was young, but once puberty hit, her hair had turned wavy and more unruly.

She scowled at her reflection. She should cut her hair and dye it black. Add black lipstick and several piercings and she would look like a rebellious teenager.

Disgusted with her indecisiveness, she stripped off her nightshirt and got into the shower. After she lathered her hair and body and rinsed, she glanced down at her bright pink toenails in approval. One small step for independence.

Will had preferred neutral colored nails. But Amelia had learned that her brightly painted toenails gave her a little lift. One question about her preferences answered. Now she only had a million more questions about herself to ask.

Thirty minutes and three cups of coffee later, with her hair pulled into a low ponytail, she dressed in a cotton skirt and blouse and walked toward Lillian Bellagio's offices in the south wing of the house.

Knowing Lillian had ditched her last three assistants in record time, Amelia hadn't let the balmy climate and the sumptuous Bellagio estate fool her. Although Lillian's calendar was filled with garden club meetings and luncheons, Bellagio's grande dame had zero tolerance for sloppy staff, business or otherwise.

After confirming Lillian's usual breakfast of tea with cream, a peach scone and a small bowl of fresh fruit, Amelia turned on her computer and checked Lillian's e-mail for reminders and notices. Then she scanned her own messages and responded to her mother's daily e-mail, along with a note from one of her sisters. She printed off the tentative itinerary for the next board meeting and made a list of the most recent requests for Lillian's presence and/or the presence of her money.

Fifteen minutes before the planned time for their morning meeting, Lillian walked through the doorway, her perfectly groomed white hair smoothed into a stiff bob that Amelia was certain would defy gale-force winds. Lillian had arrived increasingly early each morning. Amelia wondered if the woman was trying to catch her off-guard. After taking care of several Bellagio disasters, Amelia wasn't about to let Bellagio's most demanding, fickle and finicky board member one-up her. It was a matter of pride.

"Good morning, Amelia."

"Good morning, Mrs. Bellagio. How are you?"

"Very good, thank you. Have you ordered my tea?"

"Yes, ma'am. I asked them to hold it until you arrived so it wouldn't get cold. Excuse me," she said and pressed the intercom button. "Beatrice, could you please bring Mrs. Bellagio's breakfast?"

"Yes, ma'am," the kitchen assistant said. "I'll be right up."

"Thank you," Amelia said and moved to a chair in the sitting area where Lillian preferred to plan her day.

"You're the most prompt assistant I've ever had," Lillian said.

"Thank you, Mrs. Bellagio."

"You're different from the others," Lillian continued, and thanked Beatrice when she delivered her breakfast tray. She prepared her tea. "You keep your belly covered and I don't see any tattoos. You're efficient to a fault. I like that. A little old-fashioned. I was like that at your age, too," Lillian said. "Perhaps I was a bit *too* old-fashioned. I understand you got out last night. As long as it doesn't interfere with your work, you should do it more often."

Amelia's stomach clenched. How much did Lillian know? Did the woman have spies everywhere?

"It's okay," Lillian went on, searching Amelia's face. "I know the only reason you were assigned to me is that I'm considered a pain and you're considered a magician. It's a shame I won't get to keep you. But I can tell you're headed for bigger things." She paused a moment. "I was told about your broken engagement. A couple of words to the wise. Never chase a bus or a man. Another one will be along in ten minutes. You may as well enjoy yourself while you're here."

Amelia stared at the woman in surprise. For the past ten days, Lillian had been polite, but reserved and impersonal. Now it was almost as if Amelia had passed some invisible test.

The older woman smiled. "I can see you must have believed the rumors. My reputation is notorious. It comes in handy sometimes. Can you imagine how many of those macho Bellagios would roll right over an old lady like me if I didn't cause a little fuss every now and then?"

Intrigued, Amelia smiled cautiously. "I can see your point of view."

"Good," Lillian said. "I suspect you and I will get along very well, but if you tell Alfredo or any of the others that I'm anything but a shrew, I'll tell them you're a liar." Her sugary southern accent didn't fool Amelia. She'd bet Lillian could gut any beast that caused her trouble, and that included a human male.

Lillian lifted her cup of tea to her lips. "I have a guest arriving next weekend. I'd like to host a small party. It's short notice. Can you plan it?"

Amelia felt a little kick of excitement. The party

presented a small challenge, but she loved pulling off the impossible. When presented with a professional crisis, her brain immediately began to supply her with a range of solutions. Planning a party under such short notice was no different.

"I'll need a guest list with phone numbers and addresses, your budget, any food preferences or allergies and the mood you'd like to create. I can have something preliminary for you this afternoon."

Lillian nodded in approval.

Amelia was thrilled with a legitimate excuse to procrastinate dealing with her trainwreck of a personal life. She could plan all of Lillian's social events for the next year in less than a week, but she knew that putting her own life together would be like building a house one brick at a time.

THE PARTY WAS A HUGE SUCCESS, with Lillian's guests begging to borrow Amelia. Lillian demurred, instead instructing Amelia to take two days off as a reward for her hard work.

The prospect of facing forty-eight empty hours nearly gave Amelia hives. Why was it so much easier to manage someone else's life than her own?

After Amelia showered, she slathered on SPF 50 sunscreen and changed her clothes three times because she couldn't decide what to do during her *free* time. Finally settling on a swimsuit that she covered with a skirt and top, she grabbed a straw bag and towel and plopped a pair of sunglasses on her nose.

She glanced at the cocktail napkin with the list she'd begun during her three-hurricane evening and felt it egging her on. Jack's bold scrawl contrasted with her softer print. She looked at some of his contributions to the list and noticed a common thread. Everything was to be done naked. Not sure whether to laugh or to panic, she grabbed the napkin and stuffed it into her purse.

She walked a half-mile down the road to a public beach and spread out her blanket. Reclining in the sun, inhaling the sea air, listening to the lapping sound of the waves, her mind strayed to thoughts of Will and the European honeymoon they'd planned. She'd turned down an opportunity to be a foreign exchange student in Italy for a semester because Will had wanted their first time in Europe to be together.

"Stop it," she whispered to herself. Rule number two for how to get over the love of your life was to replace thoughts of him with something else. Besides, she was supposed to be relaxing, clearing her mind.

She shifted on her towel and sighed. Why was relaxing such hard work? Flipping onto her tummy, she pulled her how-to book from her straw bag.

She lasted another fifteen minutes and decided to

take a walk on the beach. The stingy stretch of sand, which she now knew was common to the Keys, made walking more like pacing. Back and forth, back and forth.

So fidgety her skin felt tight, she gave up on the beach and walked into the small center of town to wander through the shops. She picked up a couple of books for her niece and nephew's birthdays, sent a postcard to her mother and eventually stopped at a popular breakfast and sandwich shop.

When no waiter showed up to take her order, Amelia considered leaving. After further observation, she overheard the owner, a frazzled but friendly woman with white hair, apologizing. Her cook had called in sick and the owner had to do everything herself until extra help arrived.

"I can pour coffee and water if you like," Amelia offered, and after a few half-hearted protests from the owner, Amelia began making beverage rounds.

Twenty minutes later, she put a glass of water in front of another customer, whom she noticed out of the corner of her eye was male. They'd started to blur together. "Good morning. Your waitress will be here in just a few minutes to take your order. Would you like some coffee?"

Silence followed. Then she heard, "Sure. New job?"

Amelia blinked, taking her first good look at the

customer. With amused blue eyes framed by a dark fringe of lashes that matched his dark hair, he could have been a heart-stealer. If she'd had a heart left to steal.

Jack. Recognizing him from her night of hurricanes, she felt a rush of self-consciousness. "Not really. The owner was in a little bind. I'm free today, so it was no big deal to pour water and coffee."

He looked at ease with himself in his t-shirt and shorts. Tanned, muscular legs and flip-flops suggested he had no problem kicking back and relaxing. She envied him that.

"You're off all day today?"

She nodded, pouring coffee into his cup. "And tomorrow."

"You want to take a day trip after you finish your shift here?" he asked, cracking a half-grin. "It's Jack, by the way."

"I remember," she said. "And I'm—"

"Amelia," he said before she could. His grin widened.

She hesitated a half-beat. She didn't really know him. However, if he hadn't taken advantage of her during her hurricane night, then he was probably okay. There had been the kiss, she reminded herself. But that had just been a kiss. A really really hot kiss, but…

She shook her head at her stupid debate. If she spent the afternoon with Jack, she wouldn't have to dream up twenty more things to do today. "Thanks. That sounds good."

He laughed. "Don't you want to know where we're going?"

"Oh, yeah. Where?"

"Key West. Sundown party at Mallory Square."

"I've never been to one of those," she said, feeling a ping of anticipation.

"We can change that," he said, lifting his cup. The way he looked at her over its rim made something inside her give a little jump, which surprised her. So maybe she wasn't dead after all.

Another employee showed up after thirty minutes, so Amelia turned in her coffee pot and water pitcher. The owner thanked her effusively and promised future lunches on the house.

Resisting the urge to return to the Bellagio estate to change clothes, Amelia freshened up in the restaurant's powder room. The humidity had her hair sticking out in twenty different directions. Without her flat iron, she would have to go au natural with her hair, which scared the poo out of her. Amelia had ironed her hair into submission for so long she didn't really know what it would looked like if she let it go free.

Sighing, she shook her head. It wasn't as if she was trying to impress anyone. She just wanted to fill some free time.

Jack tossed a few bills on the table and stood as she walked toward him. "Ready to go?"

She nodded and put on her sunglasses as she followed him to the small parking lot.

He stopped at a black Porsche and pulled a cap out of the back. "You might want to wear this. You look like you could burn in five minutes with the top down."

"Try three," she said wryly. "I don't remember this car."

He chuckled and opened the door for her. "I'm not sure you were in a condition to remember much of anything. The car belongs to a friend of mine. When I visit, he lets me stay at his place and use his wheels."

"Nice friend," she said, sliding into the passenger seat.

"Yep."

"Where are you visiting from?"

"Chicago, right now."

A roamer, she concluded. It didn't surprise her. He looked like the kind to travel light. If she'd been looking for a keeper, that would have put her off, but she wasn't so it didn't bother her.

"What do you do?" she asked. "For a living."

He shot her a smile that reminded her of a shark. "Whatever's profitable," he said, revealing nothing.

"Legal?" she pressed, because she had her limits.

"Clean as a whistle," he said, but his silence made her think he didn't teach kindergarten. He started the engine and backed out of the parking space.

"So, how's it been working for Bellagio's grande dame? She finally let you out of the cellar?" he said.

"Pushed me out," Amelia muttered. "She's not as bad as—" She broke off, remembering how Lillian had insisted she wanted to maintain her reputation. "She's quite a woman."

"Quite a woman," Jack echoed. "She's either won you over or you're being politely vague."

"Sort of like 'whatever's profitable,'" she shot back.

He glanced at her in surprise and looked back at the road, smiling. "So the sweet Georgia peach has been hiding a little kick."

Amelia hadn't really thought about having a kick. She'd pretty much relied on Will for most of the kicking. She adjusted her cap. "Who knew?"

"How long did you say you dated your ex?"

She winced, wondering how much she'd revealed during that night of too many hurricanes. "A long time," she said vaguely.

"Wasn't it twelve or thirteen years?"

"Nice of you to remind me."

He shook his head. "I bet you're just starting to find out who you are."

His insight surprised her. "Maybe, but one of the things I've learned is that I don't like to talk about myself."

"Unless you've had a few hurricanes," he said.

"A gentleman wouldn't continue to bring that up."

"I'm not that kind of a gentleman," he told her cheerfully.

"You were the other night when I was—"

"Smashed," he finished for her. "One-time thing. Everyone lives by their own set of rules. One of mine is to maximize whatever gets thrown at you. I'm a bastard."

Amelia digested that. He was an odd mix. He seemed laid-back. And not. She couldn't tell if he was a con man or a mooch. "Does that mean I shouldn't count on you if I drink too many hurricanes again?"

"I would get you home, but we might take a side-trip first," he said in a breezy voice with just a hint of sexy undertone.

Her stomach tightened at the warning. She looked at his large hands, one on the steering wheel, the other on the gear shift. The wind ruffled his dark hair and whipped at his shirt. His shoulders were broad and his pecs and biceps bulged from some kind of exercise. His abdomen was flat, his legs long. His thighs looked strong. Her gaze strayed higher and she looked away, embarrassed at the direction of her thoughts.

He was a hottie, so why had he approached *her?* She couldn't squelch her curiosity.

"There were at least a half-dozen females at that tiki bar who looked available and very attractive," she said. "I still don't understand why you didn't approach them." She paused. "Or maybe you did, and I just didn't notice."

He laughed. "No. I told you before that I approached you because you were the most interesting looking woman in the room."

Interesting looking. She narrowed her eyes. That could be a compliment. Or not. "Is that like 'quite a woman'?"

"No. You didn't look like the rest of the women there."

"They were tanned, beautiful and very thin," she said stiffly.

"You looked real and pretty. And I wondered what you were writing on that napkin."

"Well, now you know. The list," she said.

He nodded. "Have you added to it?"

"No," she said, feeling guilty and wimpy.

"Maybe you need a jump-start."

Amelia adjusted her sunglasses and felt another little leap of nerves in her belly. She suspected Jack wasn't the kind of man to provide just a little jump-start. He seemed more like a walking detonator. "Maybe," she said tentatively.

"I could make a lot of suggestions," he said in a wry, sexy tone. "But this is more about what you want. So, what *do* you want, Magnolia?"

Magnolia? She paused for a long moment and sighed. "That's part of the problem. I don't know."

"That's okay. The list is about experimentation."

"I don't really like to experiment unless it's connected with my job."

"So you want to just keep doing what you've always done? You don't need a list for that."

The prospect of being stuck in her current position forever made her want to scream. "No. You're right. I need to experiment. But I don't know how to start."

"Are you sure you don't want to sky dive?"

Her stomach clenched. "That's a little drastic, but parasailing looks interesting."

"Put it on your list. What else?"

"I've always wanted to sit in the front row at a concert," she admitted.

"Any group in particular?" he asked.

"I'm flexible."

"Write it down. Want to climb a mountain?"

"No, that's a guy thing. But I always wondered what it would be like to be someone totally different than me."

"So you'd like to switch identities," he said.

"Not forever."

"For a day." He grinned. "Write it down."

"But how could I do that?"

"Make up a person you'd like to be. Dress like her, talk like her, eat like her. Do whatever she would do that day. It's just an expanded version of Halloween."

"You probably think I'm nuts," she said.

"Nah. It's fun being part of your evolution."

"What about your own evolution?"

"I'm way past you. I know what I want."

"And that is?"

"To limit my commitments, always be ready to take the next step and not waste time looking back."

"That sounds a little cold. You never look back?"

"Only when it's profitable," he said with that razor grin. "I heard a football analogy that you can only make one play at a time. If you're thinking about an earlier play or a future play, then you're not focusing on what you need to do now."

"Hmm. Did you play football?"

He shook his head. "Not enough money as a kid

for me to do anything but work after school. My mother wasn't exactly a wise financial planner."

"And your dad?"

"Wasn't around," he said. "Let me guess your family situation. Mom and Dad sat down with the kids for dinner every night. You took a family vacation in the summer, visited grandparents at Christmas and you lived in the same house growing up."

His accuracy irritated her. Was she that transparent? That predictable? "My father wasn't at dinner every night because he worked out of town sometimes. Sometimes my grandparents would visit us. We moved once," she said.

"Bet you had some kind of music lessons, too," he said.

"Piano," she admitted. "What about you?"

"Air guitar," he said with a chuckle. "No money for that, either. Trust me, Magnolia, I didn't have the Norman Rockwell family experience. Let me guess again. You're not an only child."

"Right, I have—"

"No. Don't tell me. Sisters," he said.

A little spooked, she did a double-take. "Yes, three. I'm second out of four. How did you know I had sisters?"

"You're a girly girl and you don't seem comfortable with men."

She dropped her jaw at his assessment. "You don't know that I'm not comfortable with men."

"You're not that comfortable with me," he pointed out.

"Well, that's because you're—" She broke off because saying the next thought that came to mind would have made her sound ridiculous.

"I'm what?"

"Nothing," she said. "You're right. I'm a girly girl with sisters. My mother taught us to bake and sew and sent us to charm school so we could walk and talk like ladies."

"Did it work?"

"Mostly," she said. "My older sister is married with children. My younger sister is married. And I wouldn't be surprised if my youngest sister gets engaged soon."

"So you're the maverick," he said.

"I hadn't thought of being dumped as being a maverick."

"I've seen people do some crazy things after a break-up," he said. "Hell, even the courts tend to go lenient on a broken-hearted woman when she goes berserk."

"I have no intention of going berserk," she said.

"I'm sure you don't, but if you did," he said, "you've got a socially acceptable excuse."

"I'm not going berserk," she said again, as much

for herself as for him. "And for the record, Norman Rockwell was married three times. He was divorced from his first wife, so everything wasn't warm and fuzzy for him, either."

"Should have known. If it looks too good on the outside, there's probably something fishy on the inside."

"That sounds pretty cynical."

"Hard lesson that has served me well," he countered and pulled over to the side of the road. "I think driving a convertible is on your list."

"It is?" she said as he cut the engine.

"Yep," he said and got out of the car.

Amelia stared at the gear shift. He opened her car door expectantly. "I haven't driven anything but an automatic."

"Another thing to put on your list and mark off. Think of it as a test drive. You said you wanted a different car."

"But this isn't even your car. What if I leave the transmission in the middle of the road? This is a Porsche."

"Ian won't mind. He owes me a few favors. Scoot out, Magnolia. The secret to driving a straight is the clutch. No big deal."

Amelia got out and with no small amount of trepidation, she climbed into the driver's seat and adjusted it to accommodate her shorter legs. He put his hand over hers to familiarize her with the position for changing gears.

She had to force herself to concentrate on his tutorial instead of on the way his hand swallowed hers in a gentle but firm way. The gear shift, stiff with a bulblike head, reminded her of—well, something besides a gear shift.

Jack spoke to her in a low, coaching voice, and her mind took a side-trip. She wondered what his voice sounded like when he got hot and bothered. She wondered what it would take to get him hot and bothered. Her peripheral gaze snagging on the sight of his hard thighs, she was pretty sure she would faint before she could find out if she had what it took to get him hot and bothered.

Feeling hot from more than the sun, she pulled her hand away from the gear shift for a second to push back a strand of her hair. She took a breath, then grasped the shift again. "Okay, this is Neutral, this is Reverse, Neutral, First, Second, Third and Fourth. I press the clutch and ease out when I change gears or stop."

"When you stop, you hold in the clutch until you're ready to accelerate again. Otherwise, the engine will die."

"Okay, but if you need a whiplash collar after this, don't come crying to me."

"Go for it," he said, smiling a little.

She started the engine and after nine attempts, she succeeded in getting the car from Neutral into First gear with only a few sputters and coughs.

Thrilled at her accomplishment, she glanced at Jack. "I did it! I did it."

"Great. Now go for Second."

She did, and soon enough they were flying down the highway toward Key West with the radio cranked up to the sound of The Rolling Stones. Jack's choice, but she couldn't fault it. With Jack beside her and Mick coaching her from the CD player, Amelia felt like she was headed down the road to perdition. It felt a lot better than it should.

CHAPTER FOUR

USEFUL AND AMUSING. That was Jack's analysis of Magnolia. While he allowed Lillian Bellagio to wait for his response to her invitation, he wanted to gather as much information as possible about Bellagio's grande dame. Of course, when his mother was alive, she'd only had bad things to say about Lillian. Although he knew he hadn't escaped the bitterness she'd carried with her until she died, he'd moved on.

Having a mother addicted to meth had taught him early on that he wanted no part of the drug world. Instead of getting high after school or playing a sport, he'd worked. He'd wanted out of the bad neighborhood, away from the desperation and he would happily work 365 days a year to make it happen.

More than once before he'd graduated and left home, his mother had raided his earnings. It had taken him four years to earn enough money to buy his first business. Eight months later he sold it at a one hundred and twenty-three percent profit. Within a year, he'd caught the attention of Gig Marlin, a low-profile but highly profitable venture capitalist willing to share his knowledge, and Jack had started making money hand over fist.

Along the way, Jack had kept track of Bellagio and educated himself about the shoe business.

Every once in a while, he'd just gotten lucky, but most of his success had come from someone else's lack of foresight or ineptitude and his ability to buy out of their weakness and sell into someone else's greed. Fear and greed made the world go round, he'd discovered. Right now, Lillian Bellagio was probably sweating bullets from fear of what he could do to her and the Bellagio name.

Jack glanced over at Amelia as she fiercely gripped the steering wheel at the ten o'clock and four o'clock position, ever ready to reach for the clutch.

Her hair flying all over the place, she was so focused on the road ahead that she probably didn't know her skirt had ridden above her knees. The wind whipped at it, giving him peeks of her pale thighs. The tops of her knees were pink, probably from exposure to the sun. She had incredibly fair skin. Further down, he caught sight of her painted pastel toenails and flip-flops that sported a pink sunflower.

He could see her hearth-and-home upbringing

warring with ambition and desperation now that her marriage plans had fallen through.

Jack could tell exactly what she needed. She needed to untwist her panties and go a little wild, have some fun. Then she wouldn't feel so sad about her loser fiancé. Jack could help with that in exchange for information about the Bellagios. As long as she didn't ask too many pointed questions like she had earlier, both of them would enjoy the process.

Noticing that they were nearing Key West, he motioned. "Pull over, Earnhardt. I'll take it from here."

"Why? I like this," she protested. "I can keep going."

"You may not like it when you hit traffic, Magnolia. You'll be using the clutch a lot more."

Realization hit her face and she frowned. "In that case, you can have it," she said and pulled to the side of the road.

He got out of his seat and stretched as he walked to the driver's side of the car. Amelia stepped from the car and wove on her feet. He shot out his hands to steady her.

"Whoa. What's up?"

She grinned, exhilaration flooding her face. "That was so cool," she said.

Her eyes were glazed, her cheeks pink and she was licking her lips. She looked like she'd just had really good sex, he thought, and temptation rushed through him. He wondered how wild he could get her in bed. He might just find out after he'd gotten everything else he wanted from her.

To ease her into Key West mode, Jack bought her a margarita at an open bar, where they sat and did some people-watching. Afterward, they strolled through the Audubon House.

"Watches are outlawed down here," he said, pointing to her wristwatch as she dawdled in the Audubon shop. "But we don't want to miss the sundown celebration."

"Okay. I'm just going to get a few of these for my dad. He loves birds," she said and purchased several postcards.

She joined him in a fast walk to Mallory Square, passing by the sounds of Cuban and rhythm and blues music spilling from the bars. Food stands offered ice cream, drinks and hot dogs. A colorful array of characters filled Mallory Square, including a live tin man statue, a juggler and people hawking everything from hemp bracelets to hair braiding services.

"It's like a carnival," she said, doing a double-take when she spotted a guy with dreadlocks down to his hips.

"Yeah," Jack said. "Definitely not like your boss lady's genteel home. No cucumber sandwiches here."

Amelia smiled at his comparison. "She might be tough on the surface, but I think there's more to her than the grande dame."

"What makes you say that?"

"A few things she's said. I won't deny that she expects a certain performance level and good manners, but if you pass muster, I get the impression she can be a caring person."

"Madame Bellagio—caring?" he repeated in disbelief.

"You shouldn't be so prejudiced. Lillian really misses her son and hardly ever gets to see him. She doesn't want to intrude in his life, but I can tell that it hurts her that he lives so far away and visits her so rarely. Just because she's wealthy and she married one of the founders of one of the most successful shoe companies doesn't mean she's totally snooty."

"It doesn't?" he said, clearly fighting a grin as he rubbed his index finger over the edge of her nose.

"No, it doesn't. Haven't you heard that everyone is like a rainbow? More than one color? Some colors stronger than others?"

"No," he said. "Did you learn that in Sunday School or Girl Scouts?"

She rolled her eyes. "Oh, forget it. You're impossible."

"Impossible, but accurate," he said, slipping his hand around her elbow and guiding her toward the wrought iron fence at the edge of the Square. "Front row is standing room only, but it's worth it."

Leaning against the tall fence, she silently watched the orange ball of the sun dip below the horizon. She sighed at the beauty. "That was lovely," she said, glancing at Jack. "Thank you."

"There's a custom," he told her. "It's like New Year's Eve at midnight. You're supposed to kiss at sundown."

Quickly glancing around, she observed that no one else was kissing. She shot him a suspicious look. "And you also own some swamp land you'll sell me at a discount?"

He laughed. "Had to try." He circled her wrist with his thumb and forefinger. "Come on, Magnolia. Let's see if we can work off some of your tension."

"I didn't say I was tense."

"Trust me, babe, your body is screaming it."

She scowled at him. "I'm dressed in very casual, beachy attire."

"But your panties are in such a twist you can barely walk."

She felt her cheeks heat. "That's not nice."

"It's not terminal," he assured her and guided her into a bar. "What would you like?"

"I've already had a margarita," she said, her internal caution light blinking on at the devil in Jack's eyes.

"Then how about lemonade?" he asked. "I don't need help from alcohol to turn you upside down."

She opened her mouth in surprise, but couldn't think of a reply. His expression took her breath away. "Lemonade," she finally managed, much more breathlessly than she would have preferred.

He ordered two and they listened to the Lynrd Skynrd–style band for a while then got up to explore more. People from a jam-packed bar spilled into the street. She heard screams and cat-calls. "What's going on?"

"This may be too much for you," Jack said.

She frowned at him. "Too much?" she echoed and walked to the edge of the crowd. Inside the bar, five well-endowed young women were sprayed with water, turning their T-shirts to transparent strips of cotton.

"I warned you," Jack said and covered her eyes.

Morbidly curious, she brushed his hands away and stared at the spectacle. "Do they really not care that everyone can see…"

"Apparently not," Jack said.

"We have a winner!" a man joining the women on

the table called out. He lifted the buxom brunette's hand. "Sidney from Maryland!"

"Sidney," Amelia echoed, bitterness rising from the back of her throat as she recalled the name of the woman Will had left her for.

"You know her?" Jack asked in surprise.

"No," she said, shaking her head, wanting to brush off her sudden heavy feelings of inadequacy and discontent. "I think I want that margarita now. Is there another bar around here?"

"Only about thirty. You gonna tell me what this is about?"

"It's nothing. Can't a girl have a margarita?" she asked, meeting his gaze.

"Yeah," he said. "Except you're a terrible liar."

"Does that mean I should practice?"

He shook his head. "No. Come on. Does this have something to do with your ex?" he asked as they walked.

"I don't want to talk about it. This looks like a good place," she added and ducked inside another bar.

"Hey, wait," Jack called after her, but she disappeared into the crowd. Shrugging, Jack figured she needed her space, although he didn't see how she was going to find any space here. The place was packed.

Leaning against the bar, he ordered a Corona with lime. As he half-watched the baseball game on the television, he glanced around the bar every now and then for Amelia. A couple of beach bunnies approached him and he amused himself by chatting with them for a few minutes.

But he kept checking around for Amelia. Just as he began to wonder if she was sick in the ladies' room or something, he spotted her on the other side of the bar, cornered by two guys. The guy with a shaved head was touching her hair. The other appeared to be urging her to finish her drink.

When she tried to move away, the two men closed in even tighter. A surprising wave of protectiveness surged through Jack, and he wove through the crowded bar toward her.

"Hey, babe," he said, "I was afraid I'd lost you. We'd better hit the road soon."

One of the guys looked at him and shook his head. "You snooze, you lose. We've got dibs on this one," he said in a slurred voice.

The other guy nodded. "Yeah."

"Actually, I'm with him," Amelia said and tried to move toward Jack.

The first guy blocked her again. "But, honey, we were just getting started. Bo and I were telling you what a good time we could show you."

"She's not interested, Curly and Bo, so leave her alone."

The bald guy glared at him. "Butt out. If she'd wanted to be with you, then why was she alone?"

Growing impatient with the two, Jack cracked his knuckles behind his back. He'd knocked more than one drunk on his ass and he was pretty sure he could take these two, but he'd learned it was usually better to avoid fights if possible. Almost always less expensive.

"Sweetheart, you aren't drinking alcohol, are you? You know what the doctor said about that," he said to Amelia and watched her face turn blank.

The two men looked at him in confusion.

"I know you're not showing yet, but you will be in a month or two, and you shouldn't drink alcohol when you're pregnant," he continued, silently willing her to play along.

"Pregnant?" Curly echoed, looking slightly ill.

Bo stared at Amelia. "You don't look pregnant."

Meeting Jack's gaze, Amelia put her hand over her stomach. "Twins," she said. "Aren't we lucky?"

The bald guy swore under his breath. "Twins," he said in disgust. "You should wear a warning sign or something. C'mon, Bo."

The moment the men were swallowed up by the crowd, Jack snagged her wrist and tugged her toward the door. "I think we'd better go before I have to mess up my hands."

"Pregnant," she said with a small smile. "My mother would be horrified."

"Good thing she's not here," he said. "How did you get hooked up with those two?"

She shook her head. "All I did was walk out of the ladies' room and they ambushed me."

He sighed, stopping in the middle of the street. "It's the way you look."

"What do you mean?"

"Sweet, gullible, too polite to say no," he clarified.

"I said 'no, I need to go' repeatedly."

He shrugged, looking at her pink cheeks, blue eyes and angel blond hair. "You're gonna have to learn how to put some stink in it or no one will believe you."

"I shouldn't have to take up kickboxing in order to make my point," she said.

"No, but the pregnant scheme may not work all the time. And some guys are just too stupid to understand that a polite no is still a no. Pains me to say this, Magnolia, but one of the things you need to put on your list is learning how to be a little nasty when the occasion calls for it."

She lifted her nose in distaste. "I realize I'm not as experienced as you are, but politeness has served me very well."

"Like tonight?" he said.

She frowned at him. "This was an exception."

"Life's not a G-rated Disney movie. If anyone should know that, you should. Look at what happened with your Mr. Happily-Never-After. If you're gonna step out of your little cocoon, you're going to meet some people you like and some you don't. It'll go easier on you if you're prepared to handle the rough ones."

Jack stared at her for a long moment, feeling that unwelcome sense of protectiveness swell inside him again. He realized he'd just delivered a lecture. Swearing, he shook his head. "Hey, I'm not your father. Do what you want." He gave a short laugh. "Maybe I should have left you alone with Curly and Bo."

"No," she said and looked away. "I think I could have gotten out of that situation, but it was getting uncomfortable. I appreciate you—helping me."

"You're welcome," he said. "So who's gonna help you when *I* make you uncomfortable?"

She gave a soft smile. "Oh, Jack. You've given yourself away. You're a gentleman."

He shook his head. "No one has ever accused me of that before, so I wouldn't count on it."

She just continued to smile, which irritated the hell out of him. "Come on," he muttered. "You want to go to another bar?"

She shook her head. "Can we go in a few shops? I realize 'shop' is a four-letter word for most men—"

"I can handle it," he said. "If I get lucky, I can watch you get a tattoo in a special place."

"Not tonight," she retorted and wandered into a tacky beach shop filled with T-shirts plastered with suggestions for sexual experimentation.

Laughing at her rounded eyes and red cheeks after she'd read a few, Jack followed her as she hot-footed it out of the shop. "Didn't see anything you like?"

"No, thank you," she said, carefully studying the window display of the next shop before peeking inside the door.

"It's safe," he said, unable to keep a hint of mockery from his voice.

Rolling her eyes at him, she walked inside and looked at the jewelry. Jack had found the previous store much more amusing, so after five minutes, he excused himself and went to the bar across the street where he could catch more of the ballgame. After half an inning, he strolled back to the shop, amazed to find her still studying the jewelry.

"You're still here? You could have gotten a dozen piercings by now," he said.

She bit her lip. "I'm just looking. It's the first time I've shopped for jewelry without considering what Will would think."

Her revelation made a knot form in his gut. Why? He couldn't say. "What do you like?"

"I've always wanted an anklet, but I'm not sure I would wear it."

He shrugged. "It's not the Hope Diamond. Get it, try it. If you don't like it, it's no big deal."

"I don't know."

Her hesitation tugged at something inside him. "Which are your top three favorites?"

"Um, that one," she said, pointing to a sterling silver chain with tiny beads. "The one with the clam shells and the one with the daisies."

"Okay," he said and nodded toward the store clerk. "I'd like some anklets."

"What?" Amelia stared at him. "You can't get these for me."

"Yes, I can. It's not as if it they'll break the bank," he said.

"But—but—"

"Chill out, Magnolia. It's not an engagement ring. This is faster, that's all. At the rate it's taking you to decide, we won't get out of here until sundown tomorrow."

"Then I'll just take the one with daisies," she said to the clerk.

"We'll take all three," Jack corrected and handed the clerk several bills. "You sure you don't want to get that tattoo tonight? I can supervise."

"I'm not getting a tattoo," she said. "And I'm not

comfortable with you buying these. It's not appropriate for a woman to accept jewelry from a man she hardly knows."

It took him a few seconds, but then he got the reason for her discomfort. She was afraid he was bartering anklets for sex with her. "Don't you think a night of unbridled sex with you is worth more than forty-five bucks?" he asked in a low voice.

She sucked in a quick, shocked breath.

"I'm counting on it," he said.

"I never said I was having sex with you," she whispered.

Looking into her blue eyes and taking in the sight of her parted candy-apple lips, he made a decision. He was going to have Magnolia. Sometime, somehow and every way he could imagine. "But you will," he said, because in this circumstance he considered it fair to warn her of his intentions.

"That's very arrogant," she said.

"Confident. There's a big difference," he told her, accepting the bag and pocketing his change. "Thanks," he said to the cashier and turned back to Amelia. "You'll understand it after you get to know me better."

"What if I decide I don't *want* to get to know you better?" she asked as they left the shop.

He stopped and met her gaze. "Are you saying you don't?"

She opened her mouth and closed it, frowning. "Just because I find you interesting doesn't mean I'm going to bed with you."

"You will," he said. "But don't worry. Tonight's not the night."

DURING THE RETURN DRIVE to the Bellagio estate, Amelia's mind wouldn't stop whirling. She had hoped the rush of open air would clear her head and reduce Jack's impact on her, but she couldn't stop looking at his hands, and every once in a while when she inhaled, she caught a hint of his aftershave.

He was too cynical and too sure of himself. If that was all she knew of him, she could easily dismiss him, but the way he challenged her alternately bothered her and fascinated her. How could he be so wrong and so right at the same time?

"You're quiet," he said.

"I'm enjoying the ride."

"Pissed," he concluded, but didn't appear overly concerned.

"I'm not pissed," she corrected. "I'm uncomfortable."

"Afraid of what I'm going to do? Or what you're going to do?"

A sexy image of his hands sliding over her blew through her brain. She closed her eyes and shook off the picture. "Neither." She leaned forward and turned on the CD player.

"Stones to the rescue," he said when Mick Jagger's voice blared out the speakers.

But only for a little while, she thought and tried not to imagine all the good kinds of trouble she could get into with Jack.

By the time he pulled the car near the gate of the Bellagio estate, she felt as if she were in a convertible wind-induced stupor. Zoned out.

Jack slowed to a stop and looked at her. "You okay?"

She nodded.

"Before you go, give me your foot," he said.

She blinked. "Excuse me?"

"I want to see one of those anklets on you and I'm not sure how much longer I'll be in town."

Her stomach twisted and she felt an odd jab of distress. "You're leaving?"

He shrugged. "Depends on how a deal I'm working on shakes out. So give me your foot."

Reluctant but compelled, she shifted toward him and lifted her foot. He rested it on his thigh, drawing her attention to his crotch. She forced her gaze away, watching his hands as he pulled a chain from the paper bag.

He fastened the silver chain of shells around her ankle and looked at her. "Nice," he said. "How do you like it?"

The sight of his tanned hand over her pale skin made her stomach jump. "Uh, it's pretty." She met his gaze. "Thank you."

He eased her ankle down over his leg and took her hand, pulling her closer. "You can't blame hurricanes tonight. Are you going to kiss me?" He rubbed his thumb beneath her chin. "You gonna kiss a cold-hearted cynical sonuvabitch like me?"

"You're not totally coldhearted," she said.

"But I'm cynical as hell," he said, his gaze unwavering.

"Yes, you are," she conceded, his proximity stealing the oxygen from her lungs.

"And I'm a bastard," he continued, sliding his thumb down her throat to her collar bone.

Her mouth went dry. "I wouldn't have chosen that term."

He chuckled, then lowered his head. "Do I turn you on, Magnolia?"

She bit her lip.

"You turn me on."

She found that difficult to believe. "Why?" The question was out of her mouth before she could stop it.

"I like your mouth," he said, tugging on her lip with his thumb. "It's pink. I like your body. You're curvy."

"I'm not thin."

"I want to see you naked. I want to see your breasts. I want to see what color your nipples are and how they taste."

Her temperature shot up so fast she felt like she had a sunburn all over.

"I like the color of your skin."

"I'm too pale," she whispered.

He shook his head. "Not for what I have in mind." He lowered his head again, his lips just inches from hers. "I make you hot, don't I?"

She tried to turn away, but her body wasn't following her feeble mental instructions.

"When are you going to take what you want?"

The fact that he didn't push himself on her, but made himself oh, so available drove her a little crazy. It was like having a hot fudge sundae placed in front of her. All she had to do was pick up the spoon and that delicious dessert would be in her mouth.

One spoonful wouldn't kill her, she thought, and lifted her mouth. She rubbed her lips against his and lifted her arms to his shoulders, then the back of his neck. She slid her tongue over his bottom lip and he immediately responded by cradling her head in his palms and tilting her mouth to one side for better access.

Lightly massaging her jaw, he suckled on her lips and thrust his tongue inside her mouth. She felt as if she were being sensually devoured by him, as if the tables had been turned and she was the hot fudge sundae and he wanted more than a bite.

She felt the tips of her breasts tighten. He slid one of his hands over her thigh and she felt an edgy restlessness between her legs.

Unable to resist the urge to squirm, she heard him mutter his approval. "Oh, you're so hot. You feel so good."

He trailed his fingertip down her neck to her collarbone, then lower, to the open neck of her shirt. He fingered the strap of her bathing suit at the same time as he slid his hand higher up her thigh, all the while stealing her breath and her sanity with kisses that grew longer and more sexual.

His fingers dipped closer and closer to her breast. If he didn't touch her nipple, Amelia thought she would die. She arched against him, but still he didn't quite—

She lifted her hands to the back of his head and gave him a no-holds barred kiss. His finger finally glanced her nipple and she moaned.

He touched her again and she shuddered. She felt him slide his other hand further between her legs. He skimmed his finger beneath the edge of her bathing suit, just inside her, and swore.

"Damn, you're wet." He rubbed his finger inside her and she felt her heart pound in her head with arousal.

"I want to get inside you and…"

The combination of his sex talk and the way he stroked her took her into a different dimension. The tension inside her tightened with shocking speed and when he rubbed her sweet spot, she went over the edge in a ragged burst that took her by surprise.

"Omigod," she whispered, gasping desperately for a sliver of oxygen.

Jack swore under his breath. "Damn, you're good. If we weren't in this excuse for a car, I'd have you out of your clothes right now."

It slowly dawned on Amelia that she had just had the most intense climax of her life on the side of the road, in a Porsche, with a man she hadn't known more than a couple of days. Embarrassment seeped through her. "I don't know what to say. I didn't expect that. It just—"

"Don't apologize, Magnolia. Payback will be heaven."

CHAPTER FIVE

JACK RECEIVED a second royal invitation from Queen Bellagio herself two days later. It was almost as if she'd known he wouldn't cool his heels any longer to meet with her. When she'd cancelled their first meeting with a promise to reschedule, he'd debated heading back to Chicago, but had decided to give her a few more days. After all, he'd been waiting for this for thirty-one years. He could conduct business anywhere and Bellagio's grande dame could be useful.

She hadn't invited him to her home or to a restaurant in town. No. She still didn't want the public to know of his existence, but it didn't bother him. Jack was accustomed to being a dirty secret.

He researched the address she'd given him and learned it belonged to a cottage Lillian owned. She allowed a longtime friend to operate a catering business out of it.

Jack wore a Brooks Brothers suit that fit him perfectly due to his demanding tailor's specifications,

Bellagio shoes and a gold watch. Everything about the way he looked spelled success. He knew it because he had earned it, bought it and paid for it.

Arriving five minutes early for their appointment, he allowed himself to be led inside by a thin woman with iron gray hair and neutral gray eyes. She offered him tea, coffee or lemonade but he politely passed and wandered to the back verandah, where a table was set with a white tablecloth, fine china, crystal and sterling silver.

He couldn't help thinking the plastic placemats and veneer table his mother had bought at a yard sale were worlds apart from this. *He* was worlds apart.

He'd been a scrawny, skinny, illegitimate Irish-Italian kid with a mother who favored illegal drugs over feeding and clothing him. Swearing under his breath at the beautifully tended hedges that provided privacy, he felt a sudden tightness in his chest—a suffocating sensation he'd felt too often when he'd been a kid.

Glancing at his watch and noting that Mrs. Bellagio was now fifteen minutes late, he decided to leave. The old bag would have to get her fun jerking some other poor fool's chain. He headed for the front of the house in time to hear a car door close. Out the window, he saw the gray-haired woman embrace Lillian Bellagio and Lillian return the hug.

That surprised him. From what he'd heard about her, the southern belle who had captured the heart and bank account of Dario Bellagio would eat her young. Maybe that was why her son had moved to the west coast to pursue a career in research and education. Instead of joining the family shoe empire, Lillian's precious son had turned up his nose at the idea of working for Bellagio, much to the grave disappointment of both Lillian and Dario.

"Life's a bitch," Jack muttered under his breath. "And I'm getting ready to meet the top she-dog of them all."

He returned to the patio in the back and took a seat. Within a moment, Lillian, every white hair in place and dressed in a crisp navy dress, navy shoes and bag, stepped toward him.

He stood, but waited for Lillian to speak first.

"Jack, I'm Lillian Bellagio." She extended her hand. "Please forgive my tardiness. I had to address an unexpected matter at home."

He accepted her hand and gently shook it, looking into her eyes. She was warmer than he'd expected. His mother had always told him how cold she was.

"Forgiven," he said, because her tardiness was the least of her sins. "I've looked forward to meeting you."

She gave a slight nod, as if she wasn't sure she could say the same. "Please have a seat. Margaret will bring us tea. Or do you prefer coffee?"

"Coffee, thank you," he said, sitting down.

"Margaret, darling, would you please get Mr. O'Connell some coffee? Would you like a cappuccino or latte?"

"Black will work," he said, studying her. She had a fluid natural grace and at the same time she emanated good breeding and energy. Despite the fact that she was impeccably groomed, her facial features were anything but fixed. He would guess that she could be charming when she felt inclined.

He also knew she could get hostile when defending her turf. Talking with Amelia had given Jack a big advantage. He knew Lillian's sore spot—her crushing disappointment that the heir she had produced for Bellagio had thumbed his nose at the family company and headed west. Worse yet, from what Amelia had told him, Junior only visited Lillian every other year at the most.

Margaret delivered coffee, tea and pastries on a tray. "Thank you, dear," Lillian said and fixed her cup of tea. "That may still be a little too hot," she murmured, then looked up at him and took a deep breath.

He felt her gaze travel from his hair to his

eyebrows, lingering on his eyes, over his cheeks and nose, down to his mouth, chin and shoulders. Her expression was cool and assessing.

"You have the Bellagio hair, eyes and mouth." Her mouth twisted in a half smile. "You did better in the height department than your father."

"My mother's brother and father were both over six feet tall."

She nodded. "Then I suppose you can thank her for those genes."

"A little late for that since she's dead."

She nodded, her smile fading, her mouth tightening. "So she is. Please accept my condolences."

"I might," he said, feeling a nick of impatience. "If I thought you were remotely sincere."

She parted her lips in a half breath of surprise before she recovered. "My lack of affection for your mother is understandable."

He nodded. "Is it understandable that you kept me from meeting my father?"

She looked down at her lap for a long moment. "Understandable, perhaps." She picked up her cup and set it down. "Not forgivable."

That was when he knew he had her. Lillian Bellagio felt guilty and needed to assuage that guilt. Jack knew exactly how to help her.

She took a small sip of her tea. "From what I've

heard, it appears you may have inherited some of Dario's business acumen."

"I don't know much about inheriting anything, Mrs. Bellagio, but I do understand hard work."

"Jack, many people work hard. Very few reach your level, especially coming from your circumstances. Before I supported Marc Waterson's proposal to the board that Bellagio agree to your offer to provide venture capital for the redesign of the men's activewear shoe line, I made a few calls. I know your net worth, the deals you've made, your business associates, your friends and enemies and your real estate holdings."

"What made you decide to vote in favor of accepting me as Bellagio's money man?"

"Because I know you're not nearly as detached as you present yourself. You've bought and sold a South American shoe company, I suspect for learning purposes. You've purchased an accessory line that has the potential to complement Bellagio's existing products." She smiled. "You also attended a workshop on how to make shoes. How did yours turn out?"

He shouldn't have been surprised at her thorough investigation of him. "Not bad. I wear them around the house. Did you also learn how many cavities I've had filled?"

"If the gene gods were good and you brushed your teeth when you were a child, then you probably don't have very many. Bellagios have great teeth. I don't apologize for investigating you and your background."

"What do you apologize for?"

She looked down, and the life seemed to drain from her face. "I could apologize that you didn't benefit from the million dollars I gave your mother to go away. I thought she would give you up for adoption."

"A million?" he echoed in disbelief. He'd known his mother had been paid off for Dario's indiscretion, but he'd never known the exact amount. He vaguely remembered moving from a nice house to an apartment. A couple years later they'd moved into a worse neighborhood.

"She blew most of it the first three years, didn't she?" Lillian asked.

He nodded. "I think so. She had some bad habits."

"How did you manage to stay away from those habits?"

"I saw her crashing off the high often enough to know I didn't want any part of it."

"You could have announced who your father was a long time ago. Why have you waited? Why the secrecy?"

"Because I want to be more than an empty suit in those board meetings."

"You want respect," she concluded.

He shrugged because there was more involved

than respect, but it wasn't something he had ever said aloud.

"I'm ready to accept the consequences of the fact that my husband was your father."

"You sure about that? The questions, the gossip and speculation."

She lifted her cup of tea and sipped. "I don't spend a lot of time in Atlanta these days. Aside from my charity work and attending board meetings, I spend most of my time here."

"What about your reputation?"

She gave a wise woman's smile. "You're too young to know this, but upholding a reputation can be a strain at times."

At that moment, he almost liked her. Almost. "Why didn't you tell your husband about me?"

"I was young and terrified. Incredibly selfish. I couldn't see past my fear. In some ways, vision improves with age." She met his gaze. "What do you want from me?"

Part of him wanted to say nothing and let her simmer in her guilt for the rest of her life. But that wouldn't serve his purpose, and Jack had learned through observation and experience that things turned out better for him when he let logic instead of emotion rule his choices. "I want a chance. You have a reputation for allowing different members of the board to vote your shares, depending on your mood. I imagine Marc Waterson or Alfredo Bellagio call you up and state their case and you decide which direction you'll send your vote. I want a chance to win your vote."

She looked at him for a long moment. "Fair enough. You have your chance."

THERE WAS A DOMESTIC disturbance at the Bellagio estate and its name was Brooke Tarantino. The DD was currently in the bathroom suffering the effects of multiple lectures and a terrible hangover.

Before she'd left, Lillian had given Amelia her assignment. "Watch over her. Make sure she doesn't hurt herself." Amelia glanced at her watch. She hadn't heard any moans or groans for a few minutes.

Amelia wasn't exactly sure of the proper etiquette for watching over an heiress while she was in the bathroom. She knocked quietly on the door.

"Go away, Lillian!" Brooke yelled from the other side of the door. "If I get one more lecture from a Bellagio about what a disgrace I am, I'll disgrace you all even more by jumping out the window."

Whoooo, baby, Amelia thought. The DD was definitely alive. "Sorry," Amelia said. "Not Lillian. Just checking to make sure you're okay."

Silence followed, then the door opened and

Brooke, her auburn hair extensions matted on her head, mascara smudged beneath her eyes, her skin pale, stared at her. She looked Amelia up and down, her scowl softening only a millimeter. "Sorry, I thought you were Lillian."

Amelia nodded. "Can I get you something to eat or drink?"

Brooke made a face. "I won't be eating anytime soon."

"Some cool bottled water, then? It might help you feel better. You're probably dehydrated."

Brooke nodded. "That sounds good."

"If you wash your face and brush your teeth, that'll help, too," Amelia told her.

"Who are you? Some kind of Mary Poppins that's been assigned to me, the devil child of the Bellagios?"

"I'm actually an employee of Bellagio on temporary assignment as Lillian's assistant. She asked me to make sure you didn't die."

Brooke smiled. "Of course she did. Not good for the image for her great-niece to croak while under her care." She gave Amelia another curious glance. "You look kinda junior league. In the market for a husband?"

"Not really." Amelia wondered if she should be offended. My fiancé and I broke up recently."

"Oh. Well, congratulations," Brooke said. "I hear

it's always best to find out the guy's a loser before you say 'I do.'"

Amelia blinked. This was the first time she'd been congratulated for getting dumped. "I'll get your water."

"Thanks. I'll wash my face, brush my teeth and put on my jammies."

Amelia went downstairs to collect a couple of bottles of water from the refrigerator.

The housekeeper appeared and shot her a wary look. "I'll fix something for her, but I'm not taking it up to her room. The last time she was here, she threw a tray at me."

"She's not hungry," Amelia said, wondering about the tray incident, but almost afraid to ask.

"She wasn't hungry that time, either. Said she was on a hunger strike because her father wouldn't buy a resort in Mexico for a boy she met on spring break. She said it would contribute in a positive way to the global economy. And you know she left her fiancé at the altar. Very nice young man, too. If you ask me, she's a nutcase."

"Wow," Amelia said and gave a vague nod. She knew all about the way Brooke had left Walker Gordon at the altar because Amelia had worked with Trina, Walker's new fiancée. She'd gotten the impression that neither Walker nor Trina held a grudge against Brooke. Both were just thankful to have found each other.

After being dumped herself, Amelia felt a lot of sympathy for Walker, but he didn't seem at all unhappy with how things had turned out. She carried the bottles of water upstairs and entered Brooke's suite to find the socialite sprawled on her bed with the remote in her hand. With all the residual make-up scrubbed from her face and dressed in a nightshirt, she looked like a young teenager surrounded by stuffed animals.

"Here you go," Amelia said, handing Brooke one of the waters.

"Have a seat," Brooke said, patting the bed. "*E!* is replaying the top fifty worst red carpet moments. We can mock all the stars."

Amelia hesitated.

"Oh, come on," Brooke said. "Think of it as educational. You never know when your photo will be snapped for a gossip magazine."

Amelia tentatively sank onto the bed. "I'm pretty sure that's not something I'll have to worry about anytime soon."

Brooke chugged her water. "Well, I do. That's why I've been sent here to retirementville," she said with a scowl. "A hundred other females on the beach in Rio went topless, but that cameraman had to find me. Had to put my picture on the front of that Spanish gossip magazine. You know it's a slow day when they put my boobs on the front page."

Brooke glanced at Amelia and rolled her eyes. "Oh, don't tell me I just offended your delicate sensibilities because I went topless on a beach in South America."

Brooke lived in such a different world from hers that Amelia didn't know how to respond. She chose the rational approach since she suspected Brooke might suffer from a shortage in that area. "A, I haven't been to a topless beach. B, I'm not sure I would go topless because I burn like the dickens."

"Dickens," Brooke echoed and smiled. "I like that. Dickens." She turned her attention back to the television. "Oh, look. Now *there's* a role model for all women who have been dumped," she said, pointing to the starlet on the screen. "I heard she got dumped by her boyfriend and started dating a male model within two weeks. And the lesson is?"

Amelia had no idea. "Date male models?"

"No. If you've been dumped, always do the next cute guy you meet. It reestablishes the natural order of the universe."

Amelia opened her mouth, but couldn't think of a suitable reply.

Brooke chugged both bottles of water and offered various platitudes until, like a little kid who needed a nap, she hugged an extra pillow against her and fell asleep.

Amelia collected the empty water bottles, turned

off the television and quietly left the room. After she ditched the plastic bottles, Lillian's voice stopped her.

"Good evening, Amelia."

"Good evening, Mrs. Bellagio," she responded, turning toward her temporary boss.

"Did Brooke cause trouble this afternoon?"

"No, ma'am. She didn't eat anything, but I did get her to drink some water. She watched some television and fell asleep."

Lillian sighed and rubbed her forehead. "I just don't know what we're going to do with her. She doesn't seem to grasp the responsibilities of being a Bellagio. When she became engaged, we were hoping she would settle down, but that just wasn't to be."

"She's very personable," Amelia said, feeling the need, for some undetermined reason, to say something positive about Brooke.

"She didn't insult you?" Lillian asked in surprise.

Amelia supposed she could have been insulted by the topless comment or the junior league statement, but she'd been too busy trying to remain neutral. "She was friendly. She invited me to watch television with her."

"I'm sure that was enriching," Lillian said in a dry tone. "If she were just a little more levelheaded and practical, like you, I don't think she would get into so much trouble." Lillian studied Amelia for a long moment. "Perhaps if you could spend some time with her. Mentor her—"

"Mentor?" Amelia echoed, her self-protective instincts raging. "I don't think I would be a good person for that. I'm not sure I could teach her anything. Plus, mentoring suggests that the mentee actually wants to learn something from the mentor. On top of that, Brooke is much more worldly than I am."

"But that's part of the problem. She needs a different perspective. She needs to be with different people, sensible people."

"You fit that bill," Amelia said. "You're her great-aunt. You're the perfect person for that."

"In other circumstances. But Brooke thinks I'm an irrelevant old bag."

"After our first meeting, I don't think she views me as particularly relevant, either."

"I'll give you a bonus," Lillian said.

"Excuse me?"

"I'll give you a bonus if you'll help Brooke."

The woman was desperate. Amelia suspected that Lillian Bellagio was rarely desperate. Amelia also understood her own limitations. "Mrs. Bellagio, as much as I would like to help you, I absolutely do not want the future of my career at Bellagio affected or determined by Brooke Tarantino. I would be horrified if she did something on my clock that upset you or the rest of her family."

"How about if you just take her to lunch a couple of times, spend an hour or so with her a few afternoons? I won't hold you responsible for anything she does," Lillian promised. "This will just be part of your duties and I'll make sure you have extra time off. There, that's much better, isn't it? We can discuss it more thoroughly in the morning. Enjoy your evening, dear."

Amelia caught a wisp of Lillian's Chanel Number 5 as the woman whirled away. As she slowly walked toward her own suite, Amelia couldn't help feeling a big fat knot of dread in her stomach.

It was obvious that all the Bellagios knew that Brooke wasn't just a ticking time bomb. She was a truckful of ticking time bombs, a caravan of trucks of ticking time bombs.

Maybe this gig down in the Florida Keys hadn't been such a good idea after all. Amelia entered her bedroom and closed the door behind her. On the dresser, a light flashed from her cell phone. She picked it up and listened to the message.

"It's Jack. I'm still here if you want to get together. Give me a call."

Her heart jumped at the sound of his voice. Lillian's description of her echoed in her head. Level-headed, practical, sensible.

A woman who fit that description would never return Jack's call.

Amelia counted to ten for her sanity check, then dialed his number.

CHAPTER SIX

"I'VE DECIDED THEY'RE aliens," Amelia said to Jack as they walked the private man-made beach outside the condo where he was staying. She was ridiculously happy that he hadn't left and she'd nearly had to tie her hands behind her back to keep from wrapping her arms around him and hugging him when he'd driven up to the estate. He probably would have looked at her as if *she* were the alien.

Jack laughed. "Who? The Bellagios?"

Amelia nodded. "They look human, normal, even beautiful on the outside, but on the inside they're aliens. What am I supposed to do with Brooke Tarantino that someone else hasn't tried?"

"I don't know. Teach her something she hasn't learned."

"She's an heiress. What have I possibly done that she hasn't?"

"Stayed out of trouble. Lived within a budget."

Amelia threw him a dark look. "She doesn't

appear interested in learning how to do either of those things."

"Well, what about all that domestic stuff your mother taught you when you were growing up? Cooking, being polite, knitting." He snapped his fingers. "I'll tell you what you could teach Brooke that she hasn't learned. How to keep a low profile."

Amelia thought for a moment. "I don't know. Knitting," she said. "Do you really think it would be a good idea to give that woman sharp instruments?"

"Afraid the alien will come after you?" he teased.

"Or Lillian. They hate each other."

"Really?" he asked. "Strong word."

"Maybe not hate, but I am definitely not feeling the warmth from either of them. More like resentment from Brooke and desperation from Lillian."

"Desperation?"

"I know," she said. "I never would have associated that word with her, but I saw it in her eyes. I almost wish I could help, but this one is definitely beyond me."

"You'll figure something out. So what have you crossed off your list since the last time I saw you?"

"Nothing, really," she admitted reluctantly. "But it seems like I often cross off several things when I'm with you."

"So I'm your inspiration," he said, stopping to look down at her.

The intent expression on his face made her chest feel tight. "I'm not sure I would have chosen that description."

He leaned closer. "What description would you choose?"

She inhaled, staring at his mouth, wanting, but resisting. "I think my father would call you a rascal."

"He'd be offended because my motives toward you aren't pure," he said, his mouth lifting in just a hint of a wicked grin.

"Have you ever had pure motives toward a woman?"

"Good point," he said. "But it still doesn't take care of your list. Speaking of that... No one's around. It's a perfect night," he said, glancing toward the ocean.

For what? She bit her tongue to keep from asking.

"The clouds are hiding the stars. That should give you even more protection. Perfect night for a nude swim."

She blinked. "Are you sure that's on my list? Maybe that's on your list."

He shook his head. "You wrote it down. Swim naked."

"Yes, but you kept adding 'naked' to everything. Besides, I may have written down 'naked karaoke' after the second hurricane."

"Chickening out?"

Her pride kicked in. "I can't swim in the ocean. I'm shark bait. I'm wearing an anklet. See?" She lifted her ankle. "Sharks like shiny things. One might bite off my foot."

"You could just take off the anklet. But if you're afraid of sharks, there's always the pool at my friend's house. It's private."

A half-dozen lame excuses ran through her head.

"Unless you're afraid," he said. "Or you don't really want to try new things. And you'd rather keep doing the same—"

"Okay, I'll do it." She sighed. "But just for five minutes, and if there are lights you have to turn them off and you have to swear it's private."

"Five minutes doesn't count. You'd barely get wet. Has to be fifteen."

"Ten," she countered.

"Done," he said and snagged her hand. "Let's go."

Amelia immediately regretted agreeing to his dare. "I wonder if this would be easier after one little glass of wine."

He led her off the beach and across the street to a bungalow. "No. You don't want to use alcohol as an excuse every time you try something new."

"But I can't even blame this on a full moon," she said, following him to a side gate flanked with trees and shrubs. Just inside she glimpsed a small pool. The water was blue and inviting and the entire oasislike area was lit up like Christmas. "It's lit, Jack. I can't do this."

"I can turn the lights off," he said. "Buck up. Consider it a growth experience."

He left her side and she looked at the pool, then looked down at her clothes. She wore a cotton skirt, pink two-piece sweater set, a white bra and white bikini panties. She'd ditched her sandals on the beach. Amelia bit her lip, trying to figure out how quickly she could strip and jump into the pool. She tossed aside the cardigan sweater.

The lights went out and seconds later Jack returned, his gaze expectant.

"Well, you can't watch," she said. "You have to turn around."

"Amelia—"

"You have to."

"That's no fun," he muttered, turning around.

"No fun for you," she said, backing away and easing her panties down from beneath her skirt. "It's not supposed to be fun for you, remember? It's supposed to be a growth experience for me."

She unfastened her bra and pulled it off while using a few contortions to keep her sweater on. She moved to the edge of the pool. Taking a deep breath, she whipped her sweater over her head, pushed down her skirt and jumped into the pool.

The water felt like warm silk on her bare skin. With the darkness shielding her like a blanket, she sighed. "Oh, wow, this feels good."

"You sound surprised. It wasn't Lake Michigan," he said, turning around.

She moved closer to the side of the pool to keep her body concealed. "Stay right there. This is my little adventure."

"You don't have to be selfish." He pulled off his T-shirt, baring his impressive chest.

"Oh, no, you don't," she said. "This wasn't part of the deal."

"Consider it a bonus," he said and lowered his hands to the top of his shorts.

Swearing, Amelia closed her eyes. He was entirely too at ease with stripping in front of her. "I don't know why you're bothering. I'm not going to be in here that long," she said. "And it's already been at least three minutes."

"Try one, Magnolia," he said. She heard a splash and felt a slight wave.

Amelia turned the front of her body completely to the side of the pool. "I was almost starting to like this until you got in."

"I've got eight minutes to change your mind," he

said, his voice too close to her. He moved beside her, resting his arms on the side of the pool.

She took a deep breath and looked at him. "I'm not going to have sex with you in this pool."

"Okay," he said and slid one of his arms around the front of her waist, making her breath and heart stop. "We can just swim a little."

"But—"

"Your list said 'swim in the nude,'" he reminded her, prying her fingers loose from the side of the pool. "You haven't done any swimming. You're supposed to be enjoying this."

"I was before you joined me."

She felt his hand gently slide with sensual ease to the back of her head. Then…he…

Pressed her face into the water.

Amelia inhaled the pool water and sputtered, lifting her head and shaking it. The water burned her windpipe. She coughed so hard her eyes teared.

"Hey, you okay?" Jack asked, reaching for her.

She continued to hack, but managed to splash him. "No thanks to you." She coughed. "This was supposed to be a nice, peaceful—" she inhaled and coughed again, glaring at him "—swim. Not a drowning."

"You're not supposed to breathe the water," he said helpfully.

"Bite me," she retorted, still trying to breathe normally.

His gaze dipped and lingered, and it suddenly occurred to her that she'd forgotten about being naked and he'd just gotten a great view of her breasts.

Crossing her arms over her chest, she hunkered down into the water and scowled at him. "You're a—" She frowned and shook her head, unable to find the appropriate insult.

"Oh, come on," he said, his low voice full of sensual teasing as he paddled directly in front of her. The water on his broad shoulders was shiny in the moonlight. He had a strong upper body, not too bulky. She glanced downward at his flat abdomen.

He hooked his hand underneath one of hers and tugged her against him. "It's too late. I've already seen. Very nice peaches, Magnolia." He lowered his head and kissed her.

His mouth felt warm as he slid his hands to her back. The lure of his bare skin against hers was too much. Dropping her hands, she let him draw her more fully against him. The sensation of his chest against her naked breasts made her feel like she was ice cream melting on a hot July afternoon.

Lowering both of their bodies deeper into the water, he moved forward. His mouth still on hers, he slid his hand over her bottom and wrapped her legs around his waist.

"That's good," he muttered against her mouth.

The darkness and warm, soothing water made it all okay, safe. He felt so good she could almost forget that he was naked and so was she. Or maybe she just didn't mind so much.

She felt the poolside at her back while he continued to kiss her, making her feel like some kind of magic potion he was drinking.

She felt him drift against her, a suggestion of his arousal. An illicit thrill ran through her and he made it more intense when he slipped one of his hands between her legs and touched her intimately.

"Oh, you feel good." He slid his finger inside her and she felt herself sink into some kind of sensual oblivion. He rolled his tongue over hers at the same time as he played with her intimately.

He lifted his other hand to her breast and toyed with her nipple. Everything felt suddenly hotter—the water, his body, hers. She felt a twist of something inside grow tighter and tighter…

"Hey, Jack!" a male voice called from the porch that led to the pool. "Is that you?"

Panic slammed against her like an iceberg. "Oh, my—" She swallowed a yelp and lowered herself deeper into the water.

Jack turned around. "Yeah, Ian, it's me. Sorry, I didn't know you were coming."

"What the hell? Have you got somebody—"

"I do, and she's a little shy."

Ian laughed. "My apologies. I'm in town for a charity concert. Forgot to tell you." He cleared his throat. "I'll, uh, let you finish."

"Not much chance of that," Jack muttered. "Later, man," he called, then paused a moment. "You can come out now, Magnolia. He's gone."

Amelia was so mortified she wished she could disappear. "Maybe I'll just drown myself and get it over with."

"It's not that big a deal. At least he didn't turn on the lights."

Amelia groaned. "So he could have seen us nearly having sex. Omigod, I've lost my mind. This list is the stupidest thing I—"

"Hey, hey. You were doing fine before the little interruption."

"Little?" she echoed, glancing at her clothes, wishing they were closer. "My ten minutes are up, so I'd like you to be a gentleman and turn your head and—"

He laughed and shook his head. "I'm getting dressed. Feel free to watch." Before she could say anything, he lifted himself out of the pool, exposing his broad naked back and tight backside to her.

Her windpipe closed shut and she couldn't pry her gaze from him when he turned around. He took his time pulling on his shirt, leaving his hips, long, muscular legs and impressive package exposed. He finally pulled on his underwear and shorts and nodded toward her. "One minute, Magnolia." He clapped his hands then turned his back to her. "Better get moving."

"What do you mean, 'one minute'?"

"I mean I'll turn my back for one minute while you get dressed."

"That's not long enough," she protested, pulling herself up on the side of the pool.

"Fifty seconds."

She grabbed her skirt. "That's not fa—"

"Forty-five," he interrupted.

Scowling, she struggled with her bra. Everything was more difficult because her skin was wet. "This is ridiculous," she muttered as she pulled on the tank sweater.

"Thirty seconds."

She stepped into her panties and dragged them over her wet legs.

"Twenty seconds."

She felt a whisper of relief. At least everything

crucial was covered. She leaned her head to the side and wrung water from her hair.

He turned around, looked at her and smiled. "Pretty good. I'm impressed. Disappointed, but impressed."

"A few extra seconds wouldn't have hurt you," she said.

He made a sound of disgust. "Are you kidding? Every second was like a stab in my—" He stopped and allowed his insinuation to dangle like a treat.

Although it was tempting, Amelia decided not to play. She'd had enough insanity for one evening. "I'm sure you'll recover. I need to get back."

"To the aliens," he said.

She nodded. "Yes."

Grabbing her hand, he led her from the pool area across the road. "I'm a lot more fun than the aliens," he told her.

She couldn't quite swallow a smile. "I'm sure you are."

"You could stay with me tonight," he said as they drew close to his car.

Her heart jumped. "You and your friend," she reminded him *and* herself.

"Damn. I forgot about that." He opened the passenger door for her. "For a musician, Ian's got rotten timing."

Maybe, she thought. Maybe his friend had saved her from more than a nude swim. Jack got into the driver's seat and turned the ignition. The engine roared to life and he headed toward the Bellagio estate.

He stopped about a block before the gate, put the car in Park and turned toward her. He looked at her for a long moment. "I didn't realize your hair was so curly."

Hating to think how she looked, she ran a hand over her hair in a futile smoothing motion. "I'm fighting the humidity and it's winning."

He smiled. "So stop fighting." He leaned toward her and lowered his head, brushing his mouth over hers. "You should swim naked more often."

She laughed breathlessly. "If I do it once more in the next twenty-five years, that will be more often."

"Tell the truth, you kinda liked it."

"I didn't like being discovered."

"But you did like it before that."

"The darkness was nice and the water felt warmer than I expected." And she had loved the way he'd kissed her.

"You're welcome," he said.

"I didn't say thank you."

"You will," he said.

"Why?" she asked, thinking he was just a little too cocky.

"Because even though I would get a good laugh

out of it, I'm not going to let you walk into your employer's estate with your skirt inside out."

Amelia glanced down at her skirt and noticed with horror that he was right. "Why didn't you tell me back at the pool?" She unbuttoned and unzipped it. "You were going to let me walk past the guard in front of God and everyone—"

"Lillian Bellagio may be powerful, but she's not quite God," he corrected.

Amelia paused. "Are you going to look away?"

"No," he said.

A sound of disgust bubbled up from her throat and she shimmied out of the skirt, righted it and pulled it back on.

"You have to admit, if you'd walked in there with your skirt inside out, Queen Lillian probably would've changed her mind about shoving Brooke on you."

"Right now, I'm not sure which of you is worse."

He grinned. "I bet I kiss better."

Dictionary Definition:
Vamp: *Noun*. The part of a shoe upper or boot upper covering especially the forepart of the foot and sometimes also extending forward over the toe or backward to the back seam of the upper.

Amelia Parker's Definition:
Vamp: *Transitive verb*. To act and dress in a seductive way with the goal of creating hormonal havoc within a male which can result in fun or trouble. Or both.

CHAPTER SEVEN

"I'D LIKE YOU TO TAKE Brooke to lunch today," Lillian said after Amelia had worked a couple of hours planning a charity luncheon. "Preferably somewhere quiet, away from the bars and tattoo parlors. If she goes home with another piercing, I'll never hear the end of it."

Amelia met Lillian's gaze. "I thought you might want to join her."

Lillian's eyes widened slightly in surprise. "You wouldn't be suggesting that I'm not taking excellent care of my grand-niece, would you?"

"Not at all. I just thought that part of the reason she's here is to be under your guidance and influence."

Lillian's laugh sounded like glasses tinkling against each other. "Brooke won't accept my guidance or influence. She was sent here because it's harder for her to get in trouble. We keep hoping that she'll settle down after a couple of weeks here in Geriatric Village. No, I can't influence her, but I bet you can."

Amelia shook her head. "I really don't think I'm the best one for this job."

"Of course you are. You're the kind of young woman I would sponsor for membership in our Junior Charity Guild."

Amelia wasn't sure that was a compliment. "I'm not perfect. And after my recent—" She hesitated saying the words. "Breakup, I may be wanting to have a little fun of my own."

"Trust me," Lillian said. "Your idea of fun is nowhere near Brooke's idea of fun. If you can keep her out of prison and out of the tabloids, I'll be thrilled." She reached into a tiny file box and pulled out a card. "Here. Lovely restaurant for a luncheon. I'm sure you'll enjoy it."

TWO HOURS LATER, Amelia left with Brooke for their luncheon. Two minutes into the drive, she knew she was in trouble.

"Let's stop for a margarita," Brooke said.

"It's only one o'clock," Amelia protested.

"So. Haven't you heard it's five o'clock somewhere?" Brooke argued.

"Let's stick to our reservations," Amelia said and continued toward the restaurant.

"Oh, for Pete's sake, don't tell me you're going to treat this like a field trip for a kindergartner,"

Brooke said and studied Amelia. "Great," she muttered. "She's already poisoned you against me."

"*Poison* is an exaggeration."

"What would you call it?"

Amelia considered diplomacy, then decided Brooke would appreciate honesty more. "'Trouble magnet.' She didn't use those words, but that's what I would call it."

"I just like to have fun. What's wrong with that?"

"Against-the-law, make-the-tabloids fun."

"I don't break the law," Brooke said. "Not that often, anyway. No more than a lot of other people."

"A lot of other people don't have your name."

"Don't tell me you're going to give me the lecture on my responsibility as a member of the Bellagio family."

"No. But if you want to have fun, then you really do need to keep a lower profile. The way you look and dress attracts a lot of attention."

"I like attention. I didn't get enough as a child," Brooke cracked, but Amelia heard a ripple of truth behind the joke.

"Unless you want to keep pissing off your family, you may need to make a choice between flashy or fun. You can't have both all the time."

"So what you're saying is I need a disguise."

"That wasn't exactly what I said, but it's close enough."

Brooke's eyes lit. "Let's go shopping for my disguise."

"Let's eat lunch," Amelia said.

"Why?"

"Because your great-aunt will check to make sure we were here, and unlike you, I need a job."

"Sorry. Bet that sucks."

Walking into the plantation-style restaurant, Amelia soaked in the genteel ambiance of attentive wait staff, classical music and an array of menu choices that made her mouth water.

"This place is so dull I could die from it," Brooke said.

"I love it. It's peaceful and wonderful. Relax, enjoy the food and listen to the music."

"It's harp music," Brooke said, tearing apart her corn muffin. "Harp music is what they play when you die."

"Brooke, you're stuck. You've done the crime, so now you have to do the time. Just make the best of it."

"I'll die of boredom."

"Have you considered that this is an opportunity for you to enjoy some quiet activities such as yoga or reading? You could even do something artistic."

Brooke rolled her eyes. "Let's talk about my

disguise. If I need to look more average, do I need to make myself look like you?"

Amelia stopped mid-bite and swallowed hard over the bite of muffin that suddenly felt as dry as dirt.

It took Brooke a full moment of silence before she realized she'd offended her. "Oh, I'm sorry. I didn't mean it as criticism. You just have a little of that Stepford junior league look." She tilted her head to the side. "With a different haircut, different make-up and new clothes, I bet you could stop some traffic. Hey, maybe you could show me how to ditch some of my flash and I could help you get some." She smiled. "Fab idea, isn't it?"

Fab wasn't the first description that came to Amelia's mind. "I don't really have a problem with the way I look," Amelia said. "It's professional, a little conservative, maybe, but—"

"A little?" Brooke said with a snort. "Do you have a boyfriend?"

Amelia paused. Will was no longer her anything. Jack wasn't really anything either. "I did. We broke up."

Brooke's gaze turned sympathetic and she reached over to pat Amelia's hand. "A new look and a hot guy will totally cheer you up. Trust me, I know. I've dumped a lot of guys."

Amelia bit her lip. This girl had no idea. "I was

engaged," she said. "I told you the other day, remember? He broke it off."

Brooke's eyes widened. "Ohhhh," she said. "That may take a little more. A new look and *two* hot guys."

"Let's just enjoy our lunch," Amelia suggested as the waiter delivered their entrees. "I love crab-cakes."

"You can have crabcakes anytime," Brooke said and turned to the waiter. "We'd like some to-go boxes and the check, please."

Amelia stared at Brooke. "Not yet," she said firmly, then turned to the waiter. "We'll eat first, but we'll take the check anytime, please."

The waiter left and Brooke began to argue. "We're wasting time."

"Your great-aunt will find out if we bolt out of here. Do you want to deal with that? Wouldn't that mean you'd be stuck in your room even longer? Eat your lunch. And let me eat mine in peace."

As soon as the waiter returned with the check, Brooke pulled out her credit card and smiled. "My treat."

With Brooke tapping her foot the entire time, Amelia barely finished the last bite of her crabcake. No sooner had she swallowed than Brooke stood. "Okay, can we go now?"

Amelia wondered what she'd gotten herself into as

Brooke directed her toward a small center of shops. "The shopping here really sucks unless you're like eighty, but maybe we can find something. If not, maybe you can talk Lillian into letting us drive to Miami."

Brooke shook her head as she parked the car. "I don't think there's any chance Lillian is going to let you anywhere near one of *Forbes*' top ten topless beaches, South Beach."

Brooke rolled her eyes. "How long will it take for them to get over those photos?"

"They will live in infamy," Amelia murmured. Until Brooke did something even more spectacular. "Maybe we should save this for another day."

"No, no. You're here. I'm here and eager to learn how to be boring. You can teach me."

Amelia pulled to a stop and cut the ignition. "Brooke, you really need to go back and read *How to Win Friends and Influence People*."

Brooke looked at her with a blank expression, then winced. "I offended you again? You're not boring. You just don't get into trouble. You're *safe*."

Amelia thought about her recent nude swim and felt her skin heat with embarrassment. "I wouldn't swear to that."

"Well, you don't get into trouble when you're not safe," Brooke said. "And that's what's important. Let's go find my DL outfit."

"Down-low outfit," Amelia murmured to herself as she watched Brooke sashay out of the car with a toss of her long, red mane. She wore skin-tight white pants, a jeweled turquoise deep-plunging top and sky-high heels, and flashed so much bling she could cause cornea burns. Amelia knew she was good, but she wasn't sure she was *this* good.

Amelia and Brooke toured two shops that Brooke deemed "too old lady." Growing impatient, Amelia took charge and made a list. "You need jeans."

"I have jeans," Brooke said. "Seven jeans. They're great. Super low rise with crystals. They show off my belly ring."

Amelia shook her head. "Conservative jeans that don't show off your body," she said, sifting through a rack of denim and pulling out a couple of pairs.

"And T-shirts," she continued, heading to another rack.

"I wear extra-small, small at the absolute largest," Brooke protested when Amelia grabbed T-shirts in medium and large.

"Not for your down-low outfit," Amelia said and grabbed a medium jean jacket.

"Eww," Brook said. "We really are going for ugly here, aren't we?"

With her arms full of clothing, Amelia looked at Brooke. "We need to do something about your hair and shoes. You definitely need to ditch the jewelry and those designer sunglasses."

Brooke looked appalled. "But I love these sun—" Her face fell and she sighed. "Okay, but I'm not cutting my hair and I'm not wearing old lady shoes."

Amelia grabbed an elastic band, a cap and a pair of tennis shoes, then hustled Brooke into a dressing room.

Moments later, after Brooke donned the clothes, she stared into the mirror in dismay. "Omigod, I look like the 'before' picture of a makeover."

Amelia approved of the transition. "This look doesn't scream for attention. It somewhat conceals your figure and—"

"Somewhat?" Brooke echoed with a grimace.

"You still need to ditch the rings and bracelets," Amelia added.

Brooke looked at her in disbelief. "Are you telling me I can't show an ounce of style or even an inch of flesh?"

"Not for your DL outfit."

Brooke sighed again. "This is going to take a major adjustment."

"Or you can just keep doing what you've always done and keep getting what you've always gotten."

"Trouble," Brooke said grimly. "Okay, I'll take everything but the ugly tennis shoes. That's where I draw the line."

"A true Bellagio," Amelia said and smiled at Brooke in the mirror.

"Maybe," she said, smiling back. "Now for the fun part. We're going to give you all the flash we took away from me."

Amelia shook her head. "Oh, I don't think that's a good—"

"No backing out," Brooke said, stripping off her new outfit. "You helped me, now I get to help you. I think we should start with a belly ring."

"Absolutely not," Amelia said. "I have a professional image."

"When you're working," Brooke said. "We need to get you some hot play clothes."

Amelia felt a knot of resistance in her stomach. "I really don't think—"

Brooke snapped her fingers outside the dressing room door. "Could I have some help please? I want to buy this." She turned back to Amelia. "Fair is fair. I'm buying all these ugly clothes. The least you can do is let me pick out a few things for you."

"But I didn't really ask for your help."

"That doesn't mean you don't need it," Brooke said and thrust her clothes into the arms of a store clerk. "You never told me why your fiancé broke up with you. Did he think you were a little too conservative?"

"I was conservative because that's what he

wanted. I was trying to please him," Amelia blurted out, surprising herself.

Brooke stared at her for a long moment. "Then he decided he wanted something a little wilder, right? Prick," she muttered. "Well, that settles it. You have to get some wild stuff and make him regret leaving you."

"He doesn't live in Atlanta anymore."

"But he visits, doesn't he?" Brooke asked.

"Yes, but—"

"There you go," Brooke said.

"But I'm not wild," Amelia said. "Not really."

"Everyone's a little wild," Brooke said. "We all start out that way, then our parents try to make chickens of us."

"I can't say I've heard that particular philosophy before. Have you ever thought that our parents just try to keep us safe?"

"I'm right about this. I had a boyfriend one time who was a baseball player. He told me that you never make it to second base if you always play it safe."

Amelia stared at the wacky, worldly heiress. Damn if there wasn't a seed of wisdom in Brooke's thinking.

THE FOLLOWING AFTERNOON, Jack left a message on her voicemail telling her he was taking her out for the evening and to be waiting for him outside the gate. Her feminist side chafed at the notion that he thought he could order her around. On the other hand, she found him too appealing to resist. The fact that she never knew if this was the last time she would ever see him made her reluctant to turn him down.

With Lillian taking a quick overnight trip to Atlanta and Brooke safely esconced in front of *E!* and suffering from menstrual cramps, Amelia felt safe slipping out of the house to meet Jack at seven-thirty. She even wore the outfit Brooke had talked her into buying the day before—silk skirt that dipped below her belly button, aqua halter top and strappy sandals.

As she stood outside the gate, a truck slowed down. The driver leaned across the passenger seat and lowered his window. "I'll take you anywhere you want to go."

"That's okay," she said. "I'm waiting for my, uh—"

"Bet I could give you a ride you wouldn't forget," he continued.

Uneasy, she backed toward the entrance of the Bellagio estate and waved him on. "No, really, I'm—"

A car horn beeped and she jerked her head to see an unfamiliar car. Was that a Jaguar?

"Magnolia," Jack's voice called from the vehicle and she felt a rush of relief as she ran toward it. He got out of the car, she supposed to help her in, but she pulled open her door and slid inside before he had a chance.

He got back in and looked at her. He gave a low whistle. "In the mood to stop traffic?"

"Not really," she said, twisting a wayward strand of her hair. "I just came outside a little early. Curse of being prompt."

"You look great," he said, surprised at the change in her dress. The skirt hugged her hips and the shoes did great things to her legs. He wondered if she was wearing a bra underneath her top. Her hair was a mass of waves and her expression was uncertain, maybe even a little nervous, as if she weren't sure this was such a good idea. "Looks new."

She took a breath. "Thanks. It is. I kinda got talked into it, but that's a long story. You know, it's really against the rules to order a woman to meet you for a date."

He smiled. "If that's true, then why are you here?" He decided to save her ego. "I know. Because you were bored and didn't have anything else to do."

She shrugged. "And maybe a little curious."

He liked that about her, the mix of curiosity and restraint, her inability to be cool and aloof. Her warmth eventually leaked out.

"But you still shouldn't assume that I'll take orders."

He heard a hint of injury in her voice, and suspected her ex had given more than his share of orders. Jack was starting not to like her ex.

"Okay, you want to give the orders for the rest of the night?" he asked.

She blinked in surprise. "Me?"

"No one else in here," he said. "I had something in mind, but—"

"What was that?" she asked.

He smothered a grin. "I got front seats to Ian's charity concert tonight." At her blank look, he added, "Ian 'Snake' Grant. Remember him from the beach house the other night? He's the one who almost caught us—"

She blushed. "You're telling me that Ian 'Snake' Grant almost saw me naked?" She closed her eyes a moment. The man was a legend in the music world. "And that you're staying at his house?"

Jack smiled. "Sure am. I'll even take you backstage tonight if you promise not to throw yourself at him."

She opened her eyes and snuck a look at him. "Backstage with Ian 'Snake' Grant?"

Hearing the note of awe in her voice, he shook his head in disgust. "I don't know what it is that makes chicks go nuts over a guy with a guitar."

"It's a fantasy," she told him. "That he's singing just

to you, just for you. Even though a crowd of women are crazy for him, you're the one he's crazy for."

"Does this mean you're going to drool all over him when I introduce you for real?"

"Of course not, but I would like to get an autograph."

"On your breast or your ass?" he mocked her. "You should've asked him the other night, if that was what you had in mind."

She gasped. "Neither of those possibilities had occurred to me."

He laughed, enjoying her indignation.

"But now that you mention it," she retorted. "How did the two of you become friends anyway?"

Jack remembered the deals he'd done for Ian and the sponsor he'd referred his way for one of Ian's early tours. "I did a couple of favors for him when he was still low-profile. He's the kind to remember."

"That's nice."

"Yeah, he's a good guy."

"No, I meant it was nice that you did a couple favors for him," she corrected.

The sincerity in her words oozed into a raw space inside him that he kept well protected. "It turned out to be profitable."

"And that's the bottom line, isn't it?" she asked, the admiration in her voice fading. "Profitability."

"Yes, but profitable doesn't have to equal dollar value. Although it usually does."

"If that's true, how in the world is it profitable for you to spend time with me?" she asked.

He felt a faint slice of discomfort, but dismissed it. "You're fun. Enough about me. To keep things fair, since I ordered you to meet me, you can give the orders for the rest of the night."

"I don't have that much experience giving orders," she said.

"Consider it practice. I predict you're going to end up in a position where you'll be giving plenty of orders."

He felt her looking at him silently and glanced at her.

"I think that may have been a compliment," she said. "If so, thanks."

"You're welcome. Think about what you want to do after the concert. You give the orders. I'll take them."

"I haven't gotten the impression that you're the kind of man who is good at taking orders," she said.

"Try me and see."

CHAPTER EIGHT

SHE LIKED THE WAY he looked at her. She liked the way he touched her, closing his hands over hers briefly when he handed her a glass of wine. Behind the café table, he slid his chair next to hers so she was aware of his scent and every move he made. His shirt gaped slightly, teasing her with a quick glance at his chest. She remembered how he had felt against her bare breasts. From her peripheral vision, she saw him take a drink of wine and remembered how dizzy she'd felt when he'd kissed her.

The sound of Ian's guitar and soulful singing added another layer of seduction. Even though Ian was in the spotlight, Amelia's attention was centered on Jack.

Odd things kept popping into her head. *Be good to yourself. Do the cute guy.*

Give me the orders and I'll deliver.

That last thought played over and over in her mind, and each time, she felt a shot of adrenaline. The air was heavy with humidity, steamy with anticipation.

The crowd applauded, tugging Amelia out of her fog, and she instinctively clapped.

Jack lowered his mouth to her ear. "That one's on his latest album. You like it?"

She nodded, looking up at him.

He studied her for an extra half-beat. "What's the name of the song?"

Amelia hesitated for a second. "No idea."

He smiled and took her hand, sliding his fingers through hers. "Where's you head tonight, lady?"

Her heart raced even faster and she picked up her wine. She wasn't going to answer that question. Not now, anyway. She wondered if she could muster the nerve to answer later.

Ian played another song and Amelia allowed herself to drift back into the delicious haze. The darkness seemed to give her permission to lean against Jack. He responded immediately by sliding his arm around her back and touching her hair.

Amelia closed her eyes and sighed. A second later, she felt his mouth rub against her ear. "You smell good," he murmured in a low voice.

"So do you."

"You feel good, too."

"You do, too," she said and gave in to the urge to slide her mouth against his neck, then away.

His quick exhale was this side of a groan. Moving

his arm from behind her, he slid his hand down her arm to her own hand and brought it to rest on his thigh.

It wasn't the most intimate touch, but a laserlike heat rushed through her. Her breasts felt heavy, and between her legs she felt swollen. And she wanted to lick him.

The song ended and everyone applauded except for Jack and her. He met her gaze and she saw a blatant hunger in his eyes.

Amelia wanted to rip off her clothes. She wanted him, intimately, as soon as possible. The urgency felt like a hot poker jabbing at her.

If she were someone else, she could do it. She could give the orders. She could say, *do me now.* Through the thick haze of lust, she realized she still could. She just wouldn't be Amelia. Tonight, she would be someone else, a woman who could get hot and bothered and do something about it. A woman she'd never really been before.

The notion terrified and liberated her and she decided not to think again. She lifted her mouth to just under his ear. "Now," she said.

He drew back slightly to look at her. "Now what?" he asked.

Mustering her nerve, she took a quick breath. "I want to go now."

His eyes widened for a microsecond and he took

a quick chug of his wine, then stood and tugged her with him, not pausing until they were far from the stage. Pulling her against him, he took her mouth with his, sliding his tongue over hers.

"Are you sure about this?" he asked, drawing back.

"Do you have a condom?"

"Yes."

"Then I'm sure."

"Do you want me to take you back to the beach house?"

"I don't want to wait that long."

Jack's gaze darkened and he swore under his breath. Glancing around, he squeezed her hand tightly and pulled her into step with him.

Amelia's heart was beating so fast she couldn't think. She didn't even know where he was taking her until she found herself climbing the stairs to the small house that served as headquarters for the event's caterers.

Jack flashed a backstage pass at the man at the door and they were waved inside. They walked down a corridor and Jack led her up another stairway to a darkened hall. Tugging on one door that appeared locked, he pulled out a credit card and unlocked and opened the door. He led her inside and closed the door. And locked it before she even had time to look around.

"How did you know how to use that credit—"

"Later," he said, moving toward her until her back was against the door and he was against her front. "Are you sure?"

"You already asked."

"No regrets? This isn't the Ritz," he warned her. "Not your usual style, Amel—"

She put her hand over his mouth. "Don't call me Amelia. Don't call me Magnolia. Not tonight."

A second passed and realization crossed his face. "Your evil twin," he said. "What's her name?"

She closed her eyes and tried to think. "I don't know. Something wicked. Jezebel," she said.

"Okay, Jez, give me an order."

She took a breath and remembered Brooke's words. "Do me now."

He immediately took her mouth and she felt her skirt and panties pushed down her hips in a pool on the floor. French-kissing her so thoroughly she felt dizzy, he unfastened her top and cupped her breasts.

She sighed at the sensation. He toyed with her nipples, making them hard and taut and sending shimmering tingles throughout her body.

She groped at his shirt, fumbling with the buttons, relief rushing through her when her hands encountered his bare skin, bare chest. Her relief vanished, though, when he lowered his hand between her legs and found her already wet, already swollen.

"You feel like a flower in the morning," he said. "Wet and soft…." He plunged his finger inside her and she couldn't bite back a moan.

She tugged at the button on his slacks and managed to slide down the zipper. When she slid her hand over him intimately, he groaned.

With her equilibrium turned upside down by his kisses and caressing hands, she was distantly aware of being guided away from the door. Within seconds she found herself lying on her back on a hard surface while Jack pulled something from his pocket and pushed down his slacks and underwear. His unbuttoned shirt spread over his chest like an open invitation.

"You sure you want—"

She closed her eyes and her mind to any second thoughts. "I already answered that question."

Hearing the sound of a cellophane wrapper tearing, she opened her eyes and met his gaze. "And you don't mind the fact that you're on a desk?" he asked.

"Either make me forget it or make me like it," she told him.

He put on the condom and pushed her thighs wide apart and thrust inside her. Amelia felt a little shock at the invasion. It must have shown on her face.

"Too rough?" he asked.

"No," she said, inhaling as her body adjusted to his. "I just—" A laugh bubbled up from her throat. "I just didn't expect you to be that—"

"That what?"

"Big, I guess."

He gave a rough chuckle. "You feel pretty damn good to me. Jez," he added as an afterthought and began a pumping rhythm that rubbed her in all the right ways.

When he slid his hand between their bodies to stroke her at the same time that he was inside her, she felt herself zoom. All she felt was him, all she heard was her breath and his, and someone's moans of pleasure. Were they hers or his?

Just as she felt herself go over the top, he covered her mouth with his, absorbing her sounds with a kiss. A second later she felt him stiffen and groan into her mouth. He moved his mouth from hers and dipped his chin into her shoulder, breathing hard.

He swore. "You feel so good. It's a damn shame the people out in that hall could discover us in here any minute."

Amelia blinked, holding her breath and trying to hear above the rapid beat of her heart. Sure enough, she heard voices in the corridor. And she was naked with a man between her legs. "Omigod. Get up. I've got to get dressed."

"Does this mean Amelia is back?" he asked in a teasing tone.

She pushed at his chest. "Help me get dressed. Look at you. You're already practically dressed. Me? I'm naked."

Jack rose and she scrambled to her feet, trying to locate her clothes in the dark. "Looking for these?" he asked, retrieving them from the floor.

Her hands shaking, she pulled on her panties. Jack steadied her when she threatened to lose her balance. She stepped into the skirt and he helped her pull it up, then he worked her top over her head.

"I don't even remember taking this off," she muttered.

"You're welcome," he said. "And just for the record, you weren't totally naked. You were still wearing those sandals. And sweetheart, it will be a long time before I forget what it was like seeing your sexy white legs with those sexy sandals in the air while I—"

"That's enough," she whispered, feeling her entire body blush. She might as well be a walking tomato. Thank goodness it was dark in here. But not so dark that she couldn't see how pulled together he appeared. *He* didn't look like he'd just had sex on a desk.

Amelia raked her fingers through her hair in vain. "I just had sex on a desk with a man I don't love. I'm officially a nymphomaniac slut."

"I'm devastated," Jack said in a deadpan voice. "Does this mean I was just a boy toy? Besides, *you* are not a nymphomaniac slut. Jezebel is."

Amelia felt an odd sense of relief mixed with something else. Something she would think about later. "This is so easy for you. So easy for you to be casual about this." She looked at him, and the secret she'd wondered about from the beginning wouldn't stay inside one second longer. "Are you a gigolo?"

He looked at her in disbelief, then laughed aloud. "You're joking." He paused. "Oh, you're not," he said, covering his mouth as he laughed harder. He shook his head. "I don't know which was more flattering—that I was bigger than you expected or that you thought I was a gigolo. I can honestly say I've never had my ego stroked to this degree by anyone who wasn't trying to influence a business decision."

His response made her curious. "Business decision?"

He shook his head. "Too long a story. We need to get out of this room before one of those security guys finds us in here. It's quiet in the hall. I'll go first. If I don't knock on the door after I leave, then come on out. Okay?"

For one sliver of a second, she felt strangely reluctant to leave the room. Even though she was bombarded by a dozen emotions, predominantly embarrassment, Amelia had cut loose tonight in a way she'd only dreamed of. She glanced around the room, lit only by moonlight shining through the window. A small cramped office with a large desk that had been swiped clear by Jack. Unable to fight the urge to return it to its proper order, she picked up a sheaf of papers and placed them on the corner. Spotting a notebook a few steps away, she bent to pick it up.

Jack bent also. "What are you doing?"

"We made a mess. I was just trying to straighten things up a little bit," she said, setting the notebook on the desk. "Do you think we should clean it or something?"

Jack snagged her hand and led her to the door. "Chill, Amelia. The condom protected you, me and the desk. Remember, if I knock, don't come out. Otherwise, move fast."

She nodded and watched him leave. She waited, counting to ten for his knock. The door whipped open and he extended his hand. "Come on," he said and she followed him down the hall, fiddling with her hair.

"How bad is it? Do I look like a total slut puppy?"

He turned to look at her and brushed a finger beneath each of her eyes. Mascara, she guessed. He rubbed his thumb over the top of her lip and surveyed her hair. "I like your hair this way. You should always leave it wryly."

She shrugged. "Will liked it straight."

"Will was wrong. You look beautiful. Stop thinking about what you did and maybe you can stop blushing," he told her and lowered his voice. "But that blush is really sexy."

She felt her cheeks heat even more. "Stop," she whispered. "You're not helping."

"Okay. Let me introduce you to Ian. Just remember, no drooling," he told her. "I know he's got a guitar and can sing, but I'm the guy you came with, not him. And I mean that in every sense of the word."

She couldn't help laughing and really appreciated his ability to smooth over her awkwardness. "No drooling," she said. "My mouth's too dry."

"We'll take care of that," he said and led her down the steps. His broad shoulders shrunk the space in the stairwell and she was reminded again of the power in his body...and his personality.

At the bottom, he took her hand and headed toward the back of the house and down another hallway. The roar of voices carried throughout the building.

"The concert must be over," he said. "I don't want to be at the end of the groupie line." He flashed his sticker at a big beefy buy outside a room where a line of people stood waiting. "Tell him Jack is here."

The guy gave Jack and Amelia a hard look, but went inside the room. A minute later, he returned. "You can go on in."

In a flash, a woman appeared at her side. "Amelia, there you are. Who's your date? Isn't it fab that we ran into each other here?"

Amelia did a double take at the woman in slouchy jeans and denim jacket. Diamond studs adorned her ears, but a ball cap partially covered the trademark red mane, which was pulled into a ponytail.

It took three seconds of staring before Amelia recognized her. "Brooke, what are you doing here?"

Brooke pulled her aside. "Shh. Don't call me Brooke. Call me Anna. I heard Ian was going to be here and I couldn't miss it. I've been wanting to see him forever."

"How did you get out of the house? You're supposed to be on house arrest."

Brooke shrugged. "Pillows on the bed. It wasn't hard. Remember, Lillian is gone and the staff thinks I'm a candidate for an exorcism."

"Brooke," Amelia said, feeling an ugly fore-shadow of disaster.

"Anna," she corrected. "Come on. I've been wanting to meet this guy for years. You're not going to blow it for me, are you?"

"Amelia," Jack called. "Come on. I want to introduce you to Ian." He glanced at Brooke. "Who's your friend?"

"Anna," Brooke said, extending her hand. "Nice to meet you. I work at the yogurt place in the square."

"Jack," he said, shaking Brooke's hand and studying her for an extra second. He turned to Amelia. "Should we ask Anna to join us?"

CHAPTER NINE

AMELIA LOOKED AT BROOKE and felt a bolt of sheer fear in her stomach. She knew Brooke had an unerring ability to find trouble and she definitely didn't want to be part of another Brooke-style explosion.

Clearly sensing her hesitation, Brooke smiled widely and pulled Amelia aside. "Amelia, come on. I just want to meet Ian. He's an awesome musician."

"And that's why you want to meet him," Amelia said skeptically. "Because he's an awesome musician. Luciano Pavarotti is an awesome musician. Do you want to meet him, too?"

"Okay, Ian is beyond hot and he doesn't hit the party circuit. He writes intelligent lyrics and he's not all ego. How rare is that? C'mon Amelia, you have to do this. Your hot guy is staring at us."

"You have to swear to keep all of your clothes on and not to break or bend any laws," Amelia told her. *"Swear."*

"I swear," Brooke said, a little too easily for Amelia's comfort. "Let's go."

"Okay?" Jack asked, meeting Amelia's gaze.

She nodded and he led them inside the room to bedlam. The small room was crammed full of fans pushing to get closer to Ian.

"Maybe this wasn't a good idea," Amelia murmured when she watched a young woman jump on a table and start singing one of Ian's songs.

"Jack," an unmistakable male voice called from beyond the throng. "Jack, are you here?"

"That's Ian," he said and pulled Amelia through the crowd to where the rock star stood behind a table, frantically signing autographs and flashing a grimace at a camera. Another beefy bodyguard stood beside him, preventing the scores of fans from throwing themselves across the table.

"Hey, Ian," Jack called.

Ian glanced up with a wild expression on his face and motioned Jack closer. "They're animals," Ian said. "This was supposed to be a civilized charity gig. My handler assigned the security job to someone who didn't show up and the charity rep got sick. Save me."

"Price of fame," Jack said. "I have a couple of friends I'd like you to meet. Amelia Parker and Anna—" He paused. "I'm sorry, I didn't catch your last name."

Brooke stared, speechless, at Ian.

"Jones," Amelia invented and gave Brooke a slight nudge. "Anna Jones."

Brooke blinked and nodded, but still seemed unable to produce a sound.

"Amelia," Ian said, extending his hand and studying her for a long moment. He grinned wickedly. "Would this be Jack's shy pool guest from the other—"

Jack elbowed him. Amelia blushed.

"Sorry. Sensitive subject, I guess." Smiling apologetically, Ian met Amelia's gaze and said, "Lovely. Lovely spirit." He glanced at Jack again. "What's she doing with a cynical bastard like you?"

Jack laughed. "She sees past my rough exterior."

"To your heart of stone," Ian said and extended his hand to Brooke. "Nice to meet you."

Brooke stared down at his hand and just nodded.

The noise in the room grew louder and Ian winced. "I've got to get back to it. I'll never get out of here. But if I do, I'm firing my handler."

Amelia's fix-it instincts began to churn inside her. "Would you like us to help?"

"How?" Ian asked. "It's out of control."

"I think we could get it under control," Amelia said, already constructing a plan.

"We?" Jack said. "I thought we had other plans for the rest of the evening."

"It wouldn't be nice to leave your friend alone here in chaos."

"I like her," Ian said. "If you can improve the situation, then have at it."

Jack sighed. "Okay, Mary Poppins, what did you have in mind?"

"Groups of four for a maximum of three minutes. We just need to get their attention…"

Jack gave a loud whistle. One more and the crowd quieted. "Listen up. If you want a face-to-face with Ian, you have to follow instructions. Otherwise, you'll be escorted out of the room."

A few low grumbles followed, then Jack glanced at Amelia. "Your show."

"You'll meet Ian in groups of four. Please have your cameras ready along with one item for autographing. Jack and Anna here will divide you into groups of four."

Brooke tore her gaze from Ian and stared at Amelia. "Damn," she said. "You're good."

"We'll see," Amelia muttered, but they cleared the room within an hour. Two hours later, Ian signed his last autograph and slumped back in his chair. The only mishap occurred when Jack had to help a security guy haul out two inebriated college guys who were apparently jealous because their girlfriends wanted to get their boobs autographed by Ian.

Ian looked at Amelia. "Name your price. I have to have you."

Amelia blinked. Brooke gasped. Jack stepped in front of her. "Not in a million years. Her company loves her and everyone knows you shed PR people like a snake sheds skin."

Ian frowned. "I would have appreciated a different analogy. I would pay her well. Why don't you let the pretty lady answer for herself?"

Jack, Brooke and Ian looked at her expectantly. She cleared her throat. "I'm technically not trained to do this sort of thing," she said. "I'm flattered, but I'm very happy with my current company. May I have your card if that should change?"

Ian sighed and pulled a card from his pocket. "What incredible manners. Of course you can have my card. Where on earth did you find her?" he asked Jack.

"Making a list in a tiki bar as she was drinking a hurricane," Jack said, his gaze just plain wicked. "I helped her with the list."

"List," Ian repeated and shook his head. "I'm sure there's a story."

"Not worth telling," Amelia said, feeling her cheeks heat. "Boring, very boring."

"Where did you say you work?" Ian asked.

"For Bellagio," Brooke said. Surprisingly enough,

Brooke's usual loose tongue had seemed to freeze whenever Ian glanced her way, which he did now.

"Bellagio what?"

"Shoes," she said with a hint of appalled censure that he didn't know the name. "Bellagio shoes are the best shoes money can buy."

Ian met her gaze. "Then why haven't I heard of them?"

Amelia could practically see a chemical reaction taking place between the two of them. She wondered what Brooke would say next.

Brooke tossed her hair. "Because you've been too busy being your obscenely talented, productive self and creating amazing music and avoiding the pitfalls of celebrity."

Ian's lips twitched. "Maybe, but it sounds like I may need a new pair of shoes."

"Pancakes would be a better choice right now," Brooke said. "I know just the place."

Less than an hour later, the waitress delivered platters of blueberry, apple, buttermilk and chocolate chip pancakes. Each of them argued the merits of their favorite flavor, and the carbohydrate fest was totally devoured.

"I'll need to run an extra mile for the next week, but it was worth it," Ian said.

"Ah, the life of a rock star. Your public doesn't

want to see you busting out of your jeans, do they? Average guys like me have the freedom to get a gut."

"Average?" Amelia echoed in disbelief. "I thought I was the only average person at the table, and I'll have to run two miles a day to get this off my...derriere," she finished as delicately as she could.

"Your derriere is just fine the way it is, and you don't have an average bone in your body," Jack said.

Amelia felt a little thrill at his praise. She'd always felt incredibly average.

"I received an average grade in chemistry in high school," Brooke said.

"So did I," Ian told her. "And I flunked my third year of Spanish."

"Not me," Brooke said. "Spanish was the one class I didn't skip. The professor was a major hottie."

"And you got straight A's," Jack said to Amelia, daring her to deny it.

"I got a B every now and then," she said. "But not on my report card."

Ian lifted his coffee cup. "Cheers to misfits. When you don't fit in, you have more time to study, practice guitar or make money."

Amelia noticed that Ian glanced at Jack during that last one—making money. She wondered about that. She wondered exactly what Jack did for a living. He insisted it was legal, but he was so secretive about it.

A large group of teenagers burst into the pancake house. "There he is!"

"We've been discovered," Ian said, clearly disappointed.

Jack glanced around. "Take the emergency exit. I'll pick up the bill."

"I'll owe you," Ian said.

"You'll always owe me," Jack replied.

"I'll go with you," Brooke offered.

"Great," Ian said.

Amelia felt a sharp twist of panic. "Remember your oath, Anna."

"Yeah, yeah. I remember." Brooke slid a glance at Jack. "You remember that you didn't make the same oath, and also the rule about hotties."

Ian and Brooke raced for the exit, disappointing the teenagers. As promised, Jack paid the tab. Afterward, he walked Amelia to the Jag. "What's the oath? And what's the rule about hotties?"

"Nothing, really," Amelia said as he opened the door and she stepped inside, grateful the darkness would cover her rising color.

"That's a lie," Jack said after he climbed into the driver's seat.

"It's a girl thing," she told him, hoping that would end the discussion.

"Then let's try a different question. Is Brooke Tarantino's middle name Anna?" he asked, starting the car.

She bit her lip. "How did you know?"

He pulled out of the parking lot. "I've seen a few publicity photos. She looked like she dressed down tonight."

"That was her down-low outfit."

"Almost worked, but those diamond studs in her ears didn't match. Neither did her Bellagio heels."

"I tried to convince her to wear tennis shoes, but she wouldn't listen."

"What's the oath?"

"She has to keep her clothes on and can't break any laws," Amelia said, full of doubt.

"Good luck," he said, his voice husky with laughter. "And what's the hottie rule?"

"I told you, it was a girl thing."

"Humor me. Educate me."

She sighed. "Brooke has this philosophy that after a woman has been dumped, she needs to do a cute guy. Then the world returns to its proper alignment."

He paused a half-beat. "I guess that means the world is a better place, since I did you on a desk tonight."

Amelia closed her eyes in a wave of self-consciousness. "If you buy into Brooke Tarantino's order of the universe," she said.

"Do you?"

"Of course not." But her complete denial had the same effect as a rock in her shoe. "Okay, underneath some of what she says, there's a bizarre thread of truth."

He pulled to a stop outside the Bellagio estate and turned to her. "It was pretty fast tonight."

She nodded slowly. Amelia had tried not to think about the quick, passionate coupling and what it meant. Or didn't mean.

"Don't be embarrassed," he said.

"I'm not," she said. "Okay, maybe a little bit. It wasn't like me to do something like that."

He leaned toward her and brushed his cheek against hers. "I could have sworn I was told I was with a woman named Jezebel."

She smiled at his reminder, at his playful way of letting her off the hook.

He dipped his mouth to hers and took a long, leisurely kiss. "If one time didn't take care of the natural order, I'll do my part to keep at it until the universe is back in proper alignment."

I just bet he would, Amelia thought. When he kissed her again, though, she felt her sense of gravity turn on its side.

AMELIA WAS SO EXHAUSTED she fell asleep as soon as her head hit the pillow, despite a few lingering worries about Brooke. Where was she? Would she end up in the papers in the morning? Would the police or the fire department be calling?

Her last thought before she drifted off was that she had a back-up job offer from Ian if she got fired.

Amelia awoke to something bouncing on her bed. "What—"

"It's me," Brooke said. "Wake up! We have to talk."

Amelia glanced at the clock and groaned. "Brooke, it's four-thirty in the morning."

"I know, but I'm too excited to sleep," she said. "Ian and I walked on the beach and talked for hours."

Amelia pushed her hair from her eyes, one of which refused to open. "Tell me you didn't take off your clothes," she said.

"No, we just talked and talked—"

"And you didn't smoke anything illegal," Amelia said, propping herself up on her elbow.

"No! Amelia, this is important," Brooke said, grabbing her arm. "I have to tell someone or I'm going to bust."

"What?" she asked, trying to keep dread from her voice.

"I've finally found my soul mate. I'm in love."

Amelia sank back on her pillow and groaned. "This is great. I help you meet a rock star and you think you're in love with him."

"I don't just *think* it. I have instincts about these things," Brooke insisted.

"How often have you had these instincts?"

"A few times," Brooke admitted. "But never like this."

"Brooke, you just met him. You can't be in love with him. You can be infatuated." Amelia had a gut sense she was also talking about her own feelings for Jack. "But you can't be in love. Love takes time."

"Okay, well, maybe this isn't like tenth-anniversary love, but I do believe you can know when you've found your soul mate. I could tell Ian loved talking with me as much as I loved talking with him. He liked the real me, the me that didn't need to dress up, the me that's not related to the Bellagios."

Amelia rubbed her forehead. "Wait a minute. I thought this was the down-low look for Brooke. The real you likes the flash. And the real you *is* a Bellagio."

Brooke thumped the bed in frustration. "I shouldn't have told you. No one believes I can have a meaningful relationship. No one."

"I didn't mean it that way," Amelia said, feeling a twist of sympathy for the heiress. "I just don't want you to be hurt or disappointed. It's okay to take a little time to get to know someone before you dive into the water, isn't it?"

"Maybe." Brooke sighed. "But I have this feeling that Ian is a once-in-a-lifetime guy and I don't want to miss him. Be happy for me, please?"

Amelia sighed and smiled. "Okay. I'll try very hard to be happy for you. Just remember, keep your clothes on in public, don't break any laws and try to stay out of the tabloids. Avoid video cameras at all cost. Think low-profile."

"Okay," Brooke said, nodding. She got up from the bed and danced in a circle. "He's asked me to lunch before he heads to New York. Do you mind covering for me with Lillian since she's supposed to be back this afternoon?"

"Brooke," Amelia began.

"Oh, come on. It won't be that difficult. You can tell her you're taking me to lunch and then go do some shopping or hook up with Jack the hottie."

Trouble. Amelia smelled trouble. She groaned and tunneled her head under her pillow, hoping sleep would chase away the bad feeling she suddenly had.

CHAPTER TEN

LILLIAN BELLAGIO CALLED Jack again, apologizing for asking him to meet her on short notice. He agreed, figuring he didn't have anything to lose but a little of his time.

She requested the same meeting place as before. The same woman greeted him and poured a cup of coffee and served him on the patio. This time, however, Lillian didn't keep him waiting. She joined him within two minutes of his arrival.

"I'm sorry again for the short notice. Thank you for coming," she said, carrying a leather portfolio and putting it on the table as he stood and offered his hand.

"No problem, Mrs. Bellagio. It's good to see you again. How are you?"

She paused and exhaled. "A little rushed from my flight, but fine. Thank you. Please sit. I won't keep you long," she said, sitting down and pulling a folder from her attaché. "It occurred to me that since you never met your father you might like to see some of his photos and learn about the health issues common among the Bellagio family. And I've put together a DVD of professional and personal video of your father." She gave him the folder. "Most of it's self-explanatory, but I added a few notes."

Surprised, he looked at her. She seemed more restless than last time, more ill-at-ease. "Why did you do this?"

She shrugged. "I thought you would be interested. Was I wrong?"

"No, you were right. But I've been interested for a long time. Why now?"

She paused. "It's the right thing to do."

"And it wasn't twenty years ago?"

She pursed her lips and looked away, tapping the table with her well-manicured fingernails. "I didn't get pregnant easily. I was threatened by my husband's affair with your mother. I was afraid he would choose her over me even after we had a child together."

In that sliver of a second, he glimpsed a young, frightened bride. "Did you love him?"

She smiled. "He pursued me first. I always thought the way you start out is the way you continue. But somewhere along the way, I fell totally in love with Dario and our relationship flipped from him needing to pursue me to him being the center of my life, having my undivided attention. The conquest was gone for him and your mother provided a new challenge. She was exciting. I had been conquered."

"What about when you found out about the affair?"

"I ranted and raved and cried. He didn't stop seeing her until I moved out." She closed her eyes. "That was the hardest thing I've ever done in my life, next to getting out of bed after he died." She bit her lip. "He decided he wanted me after all. We negotiated and I moved back in."

"The negotiations included sending my mother away," Jack said flatly.

She nodded. "With a payment to be disbursed over a period of ten years. The goal was to provide for the child without—"

"Interrupting your perfect family life or getting your hands dirty with an illegitimate child."

"Don't be deceived. Our family life was far from perfect. Dario had other affairs. He was just more careful, more discreet. He was moody and could have a terrible temper."

"Why did you stay? Public image?"

"No. I loved him. Yes, I know it's crazy, but I did. I loved the way he filled up a room with his personality. His laughter was so big it bounced off the walls and his passion could keep a woman warm for two lifetimes. He was the father of my only child. It wasn't easy allowing Damien to be close to his father and at the same time protecting him. In the end, I'm not sure I provided the best balance. He's in California and rarely visits."

"Does he have a job? Support himself? Does he seem happy?"

"Yes."

"Then you must have done a pretty good job."

Her lips lifted in a half smile. "Then why doesn't he visit?"

He shrugged. "Most guys are bad about visiting their mothers. He probably felt like he had to move to the other side of the country because of his domineering father and over-nurturing mother. You could always visit him."

"I don't like to intrude."

Jack gave a short laugh. "I would have given my eye teeth for my mother to intrude—when she wasn't trying to score some money for her dirty little habit."

"It's amazing that you turned out as well as you did."

"Bellagio genes?" he asked wryly.

She tilted her head to one side. "Maybe. That stubbornness gene may have served you well, but I sense you have something more, although you try to hide it. Heart. You fight it, perhaps even deny it, but you have heart."

Jack felt as if the well-coiffed woman of his nightmares was looking deep inside him. It should have been ridiculous, but she had captured the attention and ultimate devotion of Dario Bellagio. He would have been a fool to expect a slacker. She would clearly love absolution, but it didn't suit him to grant it to her yet.

"Thank you," he said. "I'll look this over later tonight. I craved this kind of thing when I was eight. I used to fantasize that my father would come and rescue me from the life my mother had chosen."

Her eyes crinkled with guilt. "I'm sorry about your childhood. I can't fix that. I tried to make sure you were provided for."

He cracked a grin. "I'm a helluva complication, aren't I?"

She looked at him for a long moment, as if she still hadn't decided if he was a good complication or a bad one. "Yes, you are. I need to get home." She stood. "If I think of something else you need to know, I'll call you."

Standing, he gripped the folder. "Thank you, Mrs. Bellagio."

"You're welcome." She paused. "Are you certain

you don't want the board members to know that you're a Bellagio? They think you intend to be a silent board member. They won't be happy to learn you plan to get actively involved."

"I'll let you know if I change my mind. I'm ready for this. I've been preparing for it for years."

She nodded. "Good luck."

"Thanks again. I'll be in touch."

He let her leave first because he suspected she preferred it that way. Watching her walk away, he set down his barely sipped coffee, picked up the folder and slowly walked to the Jag.

The folder was like a quarter burning a hole in his pocket when he was a child at the candy store. Although he had his own collection of photographs and a couple of video snippets of his father, Jack couldn't wait to look at Lillian's file.

On the way back to Ian's beach house, he stopped at a liquor store to pick up some good Irish whiskey. He didn't drink the hard stuff very often, but every once in a while, an occasion called for it.

Pulling into the driveway, he used the remote to open the garage door and saw Ian's Porsche parked. His buddy had told him he planned to grab lunch then get a Towne car to the airport, so Jack had the house to himself. He could view the photos in private.

Changing out of his coat and tie into shorts and a Tommy Bahama shirt, he took the folder and his laptop out to the lanai. He looked at the photographs first.

Jack hadn't spent much time assessing whether a man was good-looking or not, but based on the photos, he could tell that his father had been handsome. With a head full of black wavy hair, lively blue eyes and great bone structure, Dario Bellagio had been the kind of man to garner attention from men and women. Men revered him for the power and charisma he exuded. Women gravitated to him for his power and sex appeal. He wasn't that tall, but he'd been muscular.

In the formal portraits, Dario looked directly into the camera as if he were talking to you. In the wedding picture with Lillian, Dario looked proud, almost cocky, as if to say *look what I got*. Other photos showed him at the office, standing beside a massive mahogany desk, on the golf course with the governor, shaking hands with President Reagan. Lillian's choice of photographs showed her pride in Dario.

Jack slowed at the sight of the picture of Dario holding his infant son in his arms with Lillian beside him, one of her arms around Dario, the other around their son. She'd been the glue that held their little family circle together. He drank in the sight of Dario with his son, playing soccer, swinging a bat, sailing.

Jack felt a tightening sensation somewhere between his gut and his chest. He absently rubbed at it.

The son grew into a skinny teen with glasses and braces, standing with his father, awkwardly posing with a golf club. Although Dario looked heavier, he still stood with pride beside Damien, who held a diploma. Then another diploma....

Jack couldn't help thinking how much he would have loved to have a father who played baseball and soccer with him. His mother had often brought home pretend uncles. Unlike his real uncle Thomas, a navy corpsman who had visited when he could but who was often away, every once in a while a pretend uncle would play catch with him or watch a ballgame with him. Usually, though, they were more interested in sex, weed and his mother's drug of the moment. The nice guys hadn't hung around very long.

He flipped through more of the photos, seeing streaks of white thread through Dario's hair. His chin grew softer, but his eyes never lost their fire or intensity.

At the last page, two small faded photos grabbed Jack's attention. He wondered where Lillian had found them. His mother, young and clear-eyed with long red hair, stood with several other people behind Dario in an office. In another photograph, the two of them stood talking to each other. His mother, wearing a cocktail dress and high heels, stood toe-to-toe with Dario, meeting him eye-to-eye. He could almost sense the sizzle between them.

His heart hurt. She looked so young, so pretty. Thomas had always told him that Sara pushed things a little too far. She was a little too wild. Life couldn't happen fast enough for her.

Unscrewing the top of the bottle of whiskey, Jack poured a shot and drank it straight down, wanting the burn to replace the ache. He was the result of an illicit office affair and his mother had used him as a meal ticket.

Part of him had always wondered and sometimes secretly feared that he was a bad seed. His mother had always said he was the best mistake she'd ever made, but he'd never been sure if that had been her heart or the money talking.

He poured another shot of whiskey and swallowed it, looking around. Restlessness ate at him. Unable to sit still, he stood and wandered around the backyard. A small shed stood in the far corner. It needed work. He needed something to do. Fortunately, he found the supplies he wanted right there in the shed.

He pulled out the rotten boards and replaced them with new, then primed and painted them. In between coats, he ate half a pizza and slid the DVD into his laptop and watched his father come alive.

The photographs hadn't done him justice, Jack thought. The man had been so charismatic he could have been president. His personality was so large and powerful it seemed to light everyone in the room up like candles.

Jack wondered what it would have been like to have Dario for a father. It might not have been easy. It might have been pretty damn intimidating. *I still would have liked to have the opportunity,* he thought and downed another shot of whiskey.

He gave Amelia a call in hopes of distracting himself, but she didn't pick up. He left a message, watched the DVD one more time and drank one more shot of whiskey.

He was starting to feel the effects of the alcohol now, thank God. He stowed the file in his laptop case along with the computer, planted himself in front of the TV and slid into a dreamless sleep.

AMELIA FROWNED AT HER cell phone for the fiftieth time in ten minutes. Jack had left her two voice messages and he hadn't sounded like himself in either of them. She'd called back, but there'd been no answer.

He wasn't her concern. He was a fling.

She was worried.

She should have climbed into bed over an hour

ago. Since Brooke had lost an entire night of sleep from her soul mate convention with Ian, she'd hit the sack early. Amelia was tired, too, but she knew she couldn't sleep.

Still dressed in her skirt and silk tank, she played with the idea of going to the house where Jack was staying. But what if he was introducing some nubile thing to the wonders of nude swimming?

The prospect made her gut twist.

He had sounded so strange on the phone, down, almost lost. Almost like he had needed her? *Ridiculous,* she thought. Glancing at the clock, she made a face. She would be breaking at least five rules by showing up at a man's house after ten o'clock without an invitation.

So maybe she would just drive by the house and make sure he was okay. Maybe she wouldn't even need to get out of the car Lillian had told her that she could use anytime.

It was insanity for her to even consider going to see Jack. Pure insanity. She grabbed her cell phone and purse and headed downstairs and outside to collect the car keys from the security guard.

Ignoring the sound of her mother's chastising voice running through her mind, she drove to Jack's and passed in front of his house several times. Unable to tell if anything was wrong, she parked the car, deciding to jump into the deep end of insanity and knock on the door.

She knocked lightly, but there was no response. Biting her lip, she banged on the door and counted to ten. Just as she reached fifteen, Jack opened the door and looked at her with a blank, sleep-weary expression.

"Amelia?"

"I can't explain this without sounding like a weirdo, but you didn't sound right in the messages you left me. I don't—" She broke off, feeling like an idiot. "You just sounded like something was wrong."

He stared at her silently for a long moment.

Feeling more like an idiot than ever, she shrugged. "I can see you're okay, so I'll just leave now. Sorry for bother—"

He reached out and took her hand. "No," he said and paused. "Can you come inside for a while?"

She nodded slowly. "Sure." She followed him into the house, which was furnished in beachy casual décor. A ceiling fan swirled in the front room and she heard the sound of a television in the back.

He led her to a den flanking a small kitchen. He pointed to the sofa. "Have a seat. I don't have a lot to offer. Beer, soda, water. Sorry, no wine."

"Water is fine."

"Oh, and whiskey," he said with a wry smile as

he brought a bottle of water to her. "I put a dent in that this afternoon."

She studied him, noticing paint stains on his shirt and arms. She touched his hand. Was that blood? "What in the world have you been doing?"

He glanced down and swore. "I forgot. I haven't even taken a shower. I did some work on Ian's shed this afternoon. I guess I scraped myself a couple of times."

"I hope it wasn't from rusty nails. Are you current with your tetanus shots?"

"Probably," he said with a shrug.

"Where's your first aid box?" she asked.

"It's just a scratch. You don't need to go all Florence Nightingale on me."

"Someone docs. Where's the kit?" she asked.

"Under the sink in the kitchen, but—"

"Sit down. I'll be right back," she said and collected the kit. She opened a few drawers and pulled out a cloth and ran it under the faucet, then returned to the den.

"Okay, give me your hand," she said.

"Amelia."

"Really," she said. "Give me your hand."

Sighing, he relented. "It's not that big a deal."

"Probably not, but it could be if you get an infection." She gently cleaned off the bloodied scrapes, then opened the first aid kit.

He watched her dab antibiotic ointment on the

scrapes and put a Band-Aid on the worst of them. It occurred to him that he couldn't remember the last time someone besides himself had taken care of one of his scrapes.

She looked up at him and he felt her search his face. "What happened today that upset you so much?"

"Nothing happened."

She continued to look at him expectantly, as if she didn't believe him. "If nothing happened, then why did your voice sound the way it did? Why did you drink a lot of whiskey? And why did you mutilate your hands?"

Her insight bothered and comforted him at the same time. "Nothing happened. You ever take a walk down memory lane that you should have skipped?"

She paused and nodded. "I've done that more than once lately, but there are roads and there are valleys, ravines, craters." She paused. "The black hole."

His chest tightened into a knot and he looked away. "My mother wasn't married when she had me. She was young and wild. She was always looking for the next big rush. She died of an overdose. I always wondered if I could have done something to make her stop. There were times I tried. Found her stash and flushed it when she wasn't looking. I always wondered if I could have done something else to make her stop, or if I was the reason she started."

Amelia touched his bandaged hand gently. "You were a baby, then a kid, not Superman. I don't want to blast your mother's memory, but I bet she was looking for the next thrill long before you came along."

"Yeah," he said. "Maybe." He glanced down at his paint-splattered clothes. "I'm a mess. You mind if I take a quick shower? Would you stay a little longer?"

She nodded. "I can stay a little while."

He saw something deep in her eyes he wasn't accustomed to seeing. "Thanks," he said and headed for the bathroom, surprised at himself for asking her to stay. He usually avoided trips down memory lane, but when he took the occasional fruitless look back, he preferred solitude. He had too many weird feelings about his upbringing to sort them all out. The important thing was that he'd made a decision early on that he wouldn't go down the same road his mother had traveled and he wasn't going to be poor.

He turned on the jets and stripped off his clothes while the water temperature heated, trying to clear the crap from his brain. Climbing into the shower, he stood with his face directly in the spray. After a minute or so, he lathered himself from head to toe.

Feeling a quick cool breeze from the back of the tub, he glanced around and nearly fell on his ass.

Amelia, naked, stepped into the tub with him. "I

thought you might like some company," she said, her expression a little unsure.

His body responded immediately. "You thought right," he said and took her hand. "You're gonna get wet, though, Magnolia."

"That's okay."

He pulled her against him and groaned at the sensation of her breasts against his ribs. Lowering his head, he pressed his mouth to hers and dipped his tongue past her lips. He felt her arms slide around the back of his neck and her response was so sweet it made him hard on the outside, achy on the inside.

He slid his thigh between hers and she deepened the kiss so that he felt as if she were devouring him. Slick from the water, their bodies slid sensually against each other.

Caught in the erotic, steamy haze, he wanted to take her in a dozen ways and have her do the same to him. He played with her wet nipples and lowered his head to take one into his mouth while he slid his hand between her legs and touched her.

She slipped her hand over him intimately, distracting him. She moved her hand, slippery from the warm water, in a heart-stopping rhythm.

"Uh, Amelia," he began.

When she sank onto her knees and replaced her hand with her velvet mouth, all thought left his brain.

The sensation of her mouth on him was an insanity-inducing combination of heaven and hell. Heaven, because she looked and felt so good. Hell, because he couldn't do everything at once.

Allowing himself a few more strokes from her tongue, he pushed her gently away, cut off the shower and pulled her outside with him. He grabbed towels from the shelf, wrapped one around her and pulled her down the hall to the bedroom.

Jack lowered her to the bed and ran his tongue over her throat. She gasped and he slid down her body to take her with his mouth. She felt as soft as a rose petal against his lips, and the sounds of her quickly escalating arousal grabbed at something primal inside him.

She was sweet and warm and good, and being with her made him feel…better, as if some of her good might rub off on his bad.

He felt her climax ripple through her and rose, grabbed a condom from the bedside table and thrust inside her.

"Oh," they both breathed at the same time. Allowing himself to sink into her gaze at the same time he sank into her body, he knew he couldn't last long. When she lifted her hand to touch his cheek, the tenderness took him by surprise and he went straight over the edge. Rolling over, he pulled her against him and put the extra towel over her. "You're still wet," he muttered. "And I wrecked your hair."

"You're not supposed to notice that."

He smiled, but struggled with an odd combination of feelings. He was sated, but he felt more, something he couldn't identify. It was too unfamiliar. Comforted? Cherished? Feeling a rising tide of discomfort, he shook his head at himself.

"Should I be speaking to Jezebel?" he asked, kissing her shoulder. When she didn't respond, he slid his arm around her waist. "Was it on your list to seduce a man in the shower?"

Silence followed. "No. It wasn't on my list. And that wasn't Jezebel. That was just me."

His chest squeezed tight from another weird feeling. Damn, they were coming at him like five o'clock traffic in Chicago. "'Just you' was pretty fucking amazing."

She turned slightly and looked into his eyes. "I could say the same about you."

"Except you don't use the F-word."

She laughed. "If I really wanted, I could put it on my list."

"Just make sure I'm there when you say it. I want to hear it and see you turn red as a cherry."

She lightly punched his arm, then turned around and cocooned herself in his arms. "Shut up and hold me."

Jack wrapped his arms around her a little tighter and felt her sigh. Holding Amelia was no chore, no chore at all.

CHAPTER ELEVEN

AMELIA MADE IT BACK to the Bellagio estate just after one a.m., thanking her lucky stars that she didn't run into anyone on the way to her room. After joining Jack in the shower, she was a total mess. She washed off her smeared mascara before she left the house and pinned her impossible hair into something resembling an abandoned bird's nest on the back of her head.

The next morning, her alarm clock tortured her out of a dead sleep. She took a shower and would have loved to climb back into bed, but she refused to be late, especially for Lillian. Pulling her hair into a French twist so tight it almost made her eyes water, she followed with extra blush and concealer in the hopes of making herself appear perky.

Taking a final look in the mirror, she scowled and rubbed off that extra blush, which had made her look more feverish than healthy.

Although she felt jittery, she gulped down a cup

of coffee on the way to Lillian's offices. She wasn't cut out for this. Not cut out for a wild, no-strings affair. She was a nervous wreck.

She didn't know how other people did it, getting naked with a man and being as physically intimate as two people possibly could, but remaining emotionally detached.

Trying to push aside unwanted thoughts and feelings about Jack, Amelia sat down in her office chair and ordered Lillian's breakfast. She booted up the computer and replied to e-mails from her mother and sister Valene. She checked Lillian's e-mail for invitations and pressing issues.

Lillian entered the room. "Good morning, Amelia. I want to thank you again for spending some extra time with Brooke. I know she can be challenging, but it looks as if you've already had a good impact on her. She's much calmer than when she first arrived."

Because she's learned how to keep a lower profile, Amelia thought, feeling a twinge of guilt. "I can't take credit. I think retreating from the partying has helped her feel a little more relaxed. Underneath it all, I think she has a good heart."

Lillian stared at Amelia in disbelief. "Brooke? Heart?" Lillian laughed. "You're seeing something I've never seen. Brooke has always been blinded by whatever she wants at the moment. A new boyfriend.

Money. Travel." She waved her hand. "But enough about that. Anything pressing for me?"

Amelia gave an update on the e-mail and other correspondence that had arrived during the last two days while Lillian's breakfast was served.

With a faraway expression on her face, Lillian stirred her tea. "I wondered…are there any Bellagio corporate needs or events taking place soon in California?"

Amelia heard an odd undertone in Lillian's voice. "I don't know that information offhand, but I'm sure I could find out. Did you have something particular in mind?"

Lillian sipped her tea. "Not really. I was just curious." She shrugged. "Don't worry. It's not important."

But Amelia sensed it was. "Okay. I'll just send an e-mail to Trina in PR so we'll have the information if you change your mind."

Lillian gave an absent nod. "In the meantime, I've given some thought to your suggestion that I spend some time with Brooke. I've decided to take her to lunch, followed by a visit to the local artists' museum."

Amelia blinked, picturing Brooke's lack of enthusiasm over the outing. But she bit her tongue. Who knew? Maybe the two of them would have a terrific time together and bond. "What time did you want to leave?"

"Not too early. Eleven-thirty should be fine. Please make reservations at The Pelican Café."

"No problem," Amelia said, thinking she would need to rouse Brooke since the young woman rarely lifted her head from the pillow before eleven a.m. "Is there anything else I can do for you?"

"One of my bridge groups is meeting here next Tuesday. I'd like you to plan a light menu with finger sandwiches, fruit and vegetables and a couple of fabulous desserts, one chocolate and one not. Other than that, you can take off early this afternoon. You've earned it."

By mid-day, after she'd coaxed Brooke out of bed and out the door with Lillian, Amelia wrapped up making the arrangements for Lillian's bridge meeting and checked her cell voicemail. There was a message from Jack. He wanted to meet her this afternoon.

JACK ROSE FROM HIS chair in the coffee shop when he saw Amelia walk through the door. She wore a skirt that swayed just above her knees. She almost always wore a skirt. He liked that about her. Sure, he liked looking at her legs and those slim little ankles, but her girliness appealed to him, too.

Sweet southern girl with a kick. She was just a little too sweet for his comfort. He saw her gaze slide to his and felt her search his face. She'd gotten closer than he'd expected. It was good that he was leaving.

She walked to him and slid one of her arms around him and brushed her mouth over his cheek. "You okay?"

Resisting the urge to pull her closer, he stepped back and gestured toward her seat. "Yeah, I'm just in a hurry."

Sinking into her seat, she crossed her legs and he spotted one of the anklets he'd given her. He felt a weird sensation under his ribcage and rubbed at it.

She looked at him expectantly.

He had the same feeling he got when he was going to turn down a request for an extension on one of his deals. Even though he'd been clear as glass that he would ultimately leave and there would be nothing between them, he knew she was going to be hurt and it put a bitter taste in his mouth. Better to do it fast.

"Something's come up and I have to go back to Chicago."

"Oh," she said, her gaze unwavering from his. "How soon?"

"Tonight."

Her eyes widened. "Oh, wow. That's soon." She glanced away and folded her hands together. "Well, thanks for letting me know. I hope you have a good return trip." She paused again and looked at him, smiling with effort. "And, uh—" She bit her lip and appeared to search for words. "It's been—" she cleared her throat "—an adventure to spend time with you." She rose to her feet. "Take care of yourself."

Jack gaped at her. He'd expected shock, hurt, tears, maybe an accusation. Not *take care of yourself.* "Hey," he said, rising as she had. "I've got time for coffee."

He saw a flicker of indecision in her eyes, but then she shook her head. "No. That's okay. Thank you, though."

She turned to walk away. Feeling as if he'd just taken a right hook, but needed to get up before the bell rang, he went after her. "Amelia," he said, snagging her hand. "Are you angry?"

She looked at him in surprise. "No. Why should I be angry? I knew you were leaving sometime. I was prepared for it."

He felt a trickle of suspicion slide through him. "Was that your prepared kiss-off speech?"

She hesitated a half-beat. "I like to be prepared."

"So it *was* a prepared response," he concluded. "Nice job. Polite, brief, not at all sticky." He should be thankful, relieved. He wasn't. "Just out of curiosity, where are you putting me in your file drawer?"

"T for temporary," she said without batting an

eye. She lifted her lips in a soft, wry smile. "Thanks for helping me with my list." Then she leaned closer and kissed his cheek. "Don't be too hard on yourself. You've got some good stuff inside you," she whispered and pulled back.

If only she knew, he thought, feeling the faint threat of guilt that he quickly banished. At the same time, he wondered how he could have been so prepared to tell her he was leaving her behind, yet so *un*prepared for her to tell him the same. Weird as hell.

He wondered what she would think when she returned to Bellagio headquarters and found him there. It wouldn't be pretty, he thought, but that wouldn't stop him from what he planned to do. He'd spent too much of his life preparing for this to let a sweet little southern magnolia get in his way.

STANDING TALL, AMELIA walked out of the coffee shop with her pride intact. She hadn't whined, asked him to call or—heaven forbid—cried. She cringed at the thought. Maybe she was getting good at this dumping thing.

Her hands were shaking and freezing cold despite an outdoor temperature of eighty degrees. Pulling open the car door and slipping inside, she felt her heart race. Her chest felt tight, making it difficult to take the deep breaths she needed to keep her head clear. She felt like a little boat on choppy water. She had started to care about Jack. She would die if he knew, but she couldn't help caring for the lost child inside him.

Closing her eyes, she finally caught her breath, determined not to drown. No one was the villain here. In a way, she was thankful he was leaving before she became too attached.

Turning her cell phone to silent, Amelia blew the rest of the afternoon strolling through shops. She bought a pair of earrings, a halter top, a toe ring and gave serious consideration to getting a tattoo. For at least thirty-eight seconds.

After stopping by the grocery store, she returned to the Bellagio estate and went to her room. Brooke pounded on her door just as Amelia stepped into her pajama bottoms.

"Come in," Amelia called, hanging her skirt.

Brooke burst into the room. "Where have you been?"

"Out. Shopping," Amelia added.

"Why didn't you take me?" Brooke demanded. "I need a distraction with Ian gone."

"It didn't start out as shopping. Jack left today."

Brooke's eyes widened. "Oh. So you're devastated, too?"

"Not totally. I knew he was temporary. This wasn't a real relationship. I mean, I don't really even know what he does for a living. I don't know where he lives in Chicago. He doesn't know where I live in Atlanta."

Brooke cocked her head to one side. "Are you trying to convince me or yourself?"

Amelia sighed. "I don't need to convince myself. I'm just reminding myself. He was temporary, transitional."

Brooke nodded. "His purpose was to restore the earth to its proper alignment by providing great sex. Did he fulfill his purpose?"

Amelia couldn't help chuckling. "Yeah, I guess he did."

"So you're okay and I'm not," Brooke concluded with a pout.

"Not totally. I'm a little past bummed," Amelia admitted. "But I have a temporary solution as long as I don't get carried away."

"What's that? Tequila?"

"No. Pie," she said, heading out her bedroom door and down the hallway. She heard Brooke's footsteps behind her.

"We're going to eat a pie?"

"Bake," Amelia corrected. "I'm going to bake a pie. My mother's philosophy is when you feel down to bake a pie and give it away."

Brooke made a face. "Why can't we just eat it our-selves?"

Amelia led the way downstairs. "Because the theory is that doing something nice for someone else will make you feel better about yourself."

"Depends on what kind of pie we're making," Brooke said. "If it's chocolate, then charity begins at home, with me."

THREE WEEKS LATER, Amelia awoke at the usual time and conducted her usual routine of ordering Lillian's breakfast and prioritizing correspondence.

"Good morning, Amelia," Lillian said.

"Good morning, Mrs. Bellagio. How are you?"

"Depressed," Lillian said.

Amelia did a double-take. "I'm sorry. Is there something I can do?"

"There is, but you shouldn't," she said. "Person-nel called yesterday. They insist that Bellagio needs you more than I do. They want you back in a position created just for you. Executive Support Spe-cialist. To start, you'll have one person working with you."

Amelia gaped at her in surprise. "What will I be doing?"

"Some of what you did before. Putting out fires started by incompetents. When you're not fixing the crisis du jour, you'll train support staff to perform their jobs more efficiently. Oh, and your salary," Lillian said and pulled out a piece of paper. She named a figure that made Amelia blink.

"Omigoodness, I can't believe this."

"So I can tell them you said yes."

"Yes!" She stood. "Definitely yes. When do I leave?"

Lillian's lips twitched. "Really, Amelia, a tiny pretense of regret would be appreciated."

Oops. Amelia sat down. "I don't want you to think I'm ungrateful to you. This has been a dream job. Living in the Keys on a beautiful estate."

"You've been bored out of your mind," Lillian said.

Amelia winced. "I haven't been bored at all. You're just already such an organized person, there's not much left for me to do."

Lillian nodded. "Lovely spin."

"It isn't spin. It's the truth."

"Well, I shall miss you. Brooke will be devastated. *I* shall be devastated if I have to entertain her."

Amelia studied Lillian for a long moment. "I wondered if it might do Brooke some good to take a trip," she said. "With you."

"Me? I'm not going to dance on tables in martini bars or go topless at the beach."

"No, but you both enjoy fashion and shopping.

You could expose her to other things that may interest her."

"But where on earth?"

"I thought California might be a good idea. It would give the Bellagio west coasters an opportunity to have some face-time with you, which I'm sure they would love. And Brooke could see another part of the Bellagio business."

Lillian looked at her for a long moment of indecision. "I'll think about it."

She would need another nudge, Amelia thought, and knew just how to do it. As she was packing her suitcase after lunch, Brooke burst into her room.

"Lillian just told me. You traitor. You're abandoning me to Lillian. I'll die of boredom and it will be nearly impossible for me to get out to see Ian if you're not around. How could you do this to me?"

Amelia couldn't quite swallow a chuckle. "Thank you for your kind congratulations and good wishes on my promotion."

Brooke scowled. "Congratulations. Now what the hell am I supposed to do to get out of here? I thought they would let me go at least a week ago, but my father says no." She plopped down on the bed. "He's planning to keep me here until I turn eighty."

"I've thought about it and I have some suggestions, but you'll really have to be motivated to leave."

"I'm motivated," Brooke said. "I'm desperate."

"Desperate enough to take action?" Amelia asked. "Mature, grown-up action?"

"Yes."

"Get a job."

Brooke swore. "I can't get a job. How can I meet Ian during his tour if I get a job?"

"Getting a job is a very grown-up thing to do, Brooke. That would convince your father that you've changed and he can count on you not to do anything crazy."

Brooke sighed and shook her head. "I just don't see how I can get together with Ian if I have a job. And being with Ian is the most important thing to me."

"There are a couple other things—"

"Which are?"

"I think you should try to get Lillian to take you on a trip to California."

"Why on earth would I want to do that?"

"Because her son lives there, and she misses him because he doesn't visit her very often."

Brooke crossed her legs and pumped her foot. "Is this like making a pie? Doing something nice for someone?"

"Something like that," Amelia said. "I think she might see you in a different light if you did something nice. If she's grateful to you, then—"

"Then she might talk my father into letting me the hell out of here."

"Yep, but it would help if you had something you wanted to do once you left Lillian's."

"I do. I want to be with Ian."

"Is that what you want to tell your father? That you want to leave Lillian's to be with a rock star?"

Brooke grimaced. "I guess that wouldn't go over very well. I need a secondary mission."

"If you won't get a job, maybe you could volunteer—"

"There you go," she said, slapping her thigh. "If I volunteer, I can do it on my schedule, not someone else's."

"Yes," Amelia said slowly. Brooke still didn't get it. She still didn't understand about being a grown-up. *Still evolving,* Amelia thought. *Aren't we all?*

TWO DAYS LATER, with hugs and good wishes from Brooke and Lillian, Amelia left the Bellagio Estate. She would miss flip-flops and the beach, but she was ready to work on her list. First stop after checking into the hotel Bellagio had booked for her was a whirlwind tour with a realtor. The next day, Amelia found a two-bedroom condo to rent. The company was paying for the move, so she arranged for what little furniture she had to be transported from storage to the new place.

She spent the next few days updating her wardrobe to reflect her new position at Bellagio, buying living room and bedroom furniture and getting situated in the condo.

On Monday, her first day returning to the Bellagio offices, she received warm greetings as she walked through the hallway. After taking care of the necessary paperwork, she was briefed on her new position by the personnel administrator. She felt on top of the world, confident, strong and ready to enjoy her new job and life.

Her hands full of files about three departments in crisis, she headed for the elevator to go to her new office. Just as the doors started to close, a man's hand stopped them.

"Hold on," said a familiar voice. Amelia watched in shock as Jack walked into the elevator. The small space shrank even more. She inhaled a draft of his dizzying aftershave and stared, wondering if her mind was suddenly playing tricks on her. Nope. He might not be wearing a Tommy Bahama shirt and cool shades, but the cocky attitude was there, wrapped in what looked like a Brooks Brothers suit tailored to perfection over his athletic frame.

"Amelia."

"Jack."

The doors swung closed and they both spoke at the same time.

"What are you doing here?" she blurted out.

"I like your hair," he said. "Looks nice."

She'd thrown her flat iron away. "Thanks, uh—"

"And how're you doing with your list?" he asked, his mouth curving with a sexy smile that called to mind wicked images of what they'd shared.

She felt her cheeks heat. "Okay, but—" She shook her head. "What are you doing here?"

"I'm on the board."

Confused, she waited for the rest of the joke…or the story. "New board members don't just pop out of the woodwork. How?"

"They needed some capital for a redesign on the activewear line. I provided the cash. My position was part of the deal."

The doors swung open at the floor where she needed to exit, but her feet seemed rooted to the floor. "I just don't understand how…" An ugly realization crept past her shock. "Did you know about this when we first met?"

He paused a half-beat. "Yeah, I did. Sorry. I just couldn't tell you."

Her insides agitated so much that if she'd been a bottle of wine she would have popped her cork. "You what?"

The doors started to close and Jack stuck out his hand again. "This your floor?"

She gave a vague nod.

"You and I, we should get together. I can explain the deal. We can work on your list."

She looked at him in disbelief as two people entered the elevator. He'd used her for inside information and was offering to work on her list, which was his way of saying he'd like to take her to bed.

She shook her head. "I don't think so," she told him flatly. "Not unless I'm adding murder to my list."

CHAPTER TWELVE

AMELIA WAS SO UPSET she thought she was going to explode. Her stomach churned, her pulse pounded in her head. "A stroke," she muttered to herself. "If I don't settle down, I'm going to have a stroke."

Forcing herself to take deep, calming breaths, she pushed open the door to her new office.

"Surprise!" Trina Roberts called, lifting a plate of cupcakes.

At the sight of her friend and former boss, Amelia's spirits immediately lifted. She flew toward her and hugged her. Then she smiled, catching sight of the welcome sign hanging across the window on the back wall and the balloons and flowers. "What a sweetheart."

"I wanted you to feel welcome even though I'll never forgive you for not coming back to work for me," Trina said. "How bad was the Dame Bellagio? Is she really the devil in paradise?"

"She can be demanding," Amelia said, remember-

ing that Lillian wanted to maintain her tough reputation. "But I got along with her."

"You look great." Trina clasped her hands
together. "Please tell me you didn't spend the entire
time working. You managed to have a little fun,
didn't you?"

Amelia though of Jack and a bitter taste filled her
mouth. "It was a beautiful place. I got a few
sunburns, drank a few hurricanes, drove a convertible…"

"Are you better about—"

"Will," Amelia finished for her and smiled. "Yeah.
Much better. I've started getting a life."

"Meet any men? Just for fun?"

"No one worth remembering," Amelia said,
clenching her teeth. "What about you? How's
Maddie? And Walker?"

"Maddie is walking, God help me. She's wonderful. Walker is wonderful. We're getting married after
Thanksgiving."

Amelia saw the joy in Trina's eyes and could only
feel happy for her. Trina had been through a lot on
her own. "That's fabulous."

"My mother wants to do the wedding. I want to
elope. She says I already did that, so I can't do it
again."

"And Walker?"

"He says he'll take me any way I want. He'd just like to stay away from the whole reality TV show thing if possible."

Amelia laughed. "At least he has a sense of humor about being dumped on national television by Brooke Tarantino."

"He feels like he dodged a bullet."

Amelia nodded, thinking of how Brooke still had some lessons to learn. "I can't disagree. She was visiting Lillian when I was there and she still doesn't seem to have a handle on the concept of adult responsibility. On her behalf, though, I'll have to say that when you're born a princess and spoiled nearly to death, your view of yourself and the world have to be skewed."

"True," Trina said and frowned. "She was visiting Lillian? That doesn't sound like her. Maybe South Beach, but not Lillian's quiet place in the Keys."

"I got the impression it was more a forced visit," Amelia said.

Trina raised her eyebrows. "Oh. Got into trouble again?"

"She seems to have an instinct for it. Anything new around here that I should know about?"

Trina gave a short laugh. "Just the war of the worlds." She moved behind Amelia and closed the door. "You know they had to redesign the activewear line."

Amelia nodded, feeling her stomach tighten. She wondered what she had unwittingly done to Bellagio by telling Jack everything.

"Well, cash is temporarily tight, so they decided to get some money from a venture capitalist. I hear they got great terms. The kicker was the guy wanted a seat on the board and a position with the company. This guy's history is that if he gets a seat on the board, he's pretty quiet, so no one was worried," Trina said. "Until he showed up and wanted office space and started attending meetings. Marc Waterson is freaked over this, totally freaked. Poor Jenny," Trina said, speaking of Marc's wife. "Plus, the new guy isn't stupid and he seems to have a *lot* of insider information about Bellagio. Some people are afraid there's a mole, so the paranoia is raging. It's a little creepy. This guy even knew stuff about me."

I can explain that, Amelia thought. *The mole is me, but I didn't know I was being a mole.* She bit her lip. "Sounds weird," she said. "Does anyone know what this guy wants? Does he want to take over Bellagio?"

"Nobody knows. And that's why we're all creeped out. Especially Marc. Plus, Alfredo had to take some time off because his heart has been acting up."

Alarm shot through Amelia. "Alfredo? I thought he was totally healthy."

Trina nodded, her mouth turning down in sadness. "Me, too. He was pushy, but he had good intentions." She sighed. "I don't know what's going to happen. Marc walks around like he going to explode any minute. When he and the new guy are in the same room, you almost feel like you're looking at two Greek gods getting ready to throw fireballs and lightning bolts at each other. And here's the wild thing. They even look a little bit alike."

"No, they don't," Amelia automatically said. Jack didn't look like Marc except for his dark hair and his height. Well, come to think of it, they had a similar body type. She hadn't really studied Marc's face up close the same way she'd studied Jack's. Besides the fact that Marc was happily married, Amelia hadn't felt a desire to study his face. She felt Trina watching her and realized her mistake. "I mean, do they look alike?"

Trina nodded. "The Bellagio gods may strike me dead for being disloyal, but this guy's a total hottie. If he weren't the equivalent of the son of Satan around here, I would tell you to take a look at him."

"He doesn't sound like my type."

"He's every woman's type."

Amelia lifted her chin. "Which is why he wouldn't be my type."

"Tell me that after you get a good look at him. But how does it feel to be a big whoopty-do specialist with your own office? You've got to feel great that they created a position for you when everything's in an uproar."

"Ask me at the end of the week," Amelia said, feeling a swarm of butterflies in her stomach.

AMELIA DECIDED NOT TO think about Jack because every time a tiny image or thought of him snuck into a corner of her mind, it ruined her mood. This was supposed to be a fabulous day. She'd received a promotion and she was taking huge steps toward getting a life, her very own life.

Her decision might have worked if Jack hadn't walked through the door of her office after a perfunctory knock just as she was getting ready to leave.

Standing there looking so sexy in his suit, he took her breath away as he closed the door behind him. "Hey." He glanced around. "Nice. I like the balloons."

She fought the image of him in shorts and a Tommy Bahama shirt. "Trina gave them to me."

"I thought you and I could get a drink after work."

She felt her blood begin to heat again. "Sorry, I'm busy."

"What about tomorrow night?"

"I'm busy then, too." She hesitated a half-beat

and decided to speak her mind. Something, she recalled, she'd always had trouble doing with Will. "Actually, Jack, I wouldn't go with you if I had the time. I don't want to talk to you. You used me to get information about Bellagio."

He smiled a little. "You say that like I put bamboo sticks under your fingernails or slipped truth serum in your drink. You were more than willing to talk about Bellagio."

True, but she was still so furious she could barely contain herself. She wouldn't have talked to him if he'd given her half a clue about his intentions. "You didn't tell me that you were planning to get involved with Bellagio."

"Why are you pissed, Amelia? Because you underestimated me and thought I was a gigolo?"

She swallowed the urge to scream. "Every time I asked you a question, you gave me a vague answer," she said, knowing her voice was clipped. "You didn't give me a chance to do more than guess. You deceived me so I would talk to you."

"You're making a big deal out of nothing. You didn't spill state secrets. You told me about personalities within the organization and a few trouble spots. Did you ever stop to think I could make things better around here because of what you told me?"

No, and she still felt betrayed. "I trusted you." Her

eyes filled with tears, appalling the living daylights out of her. "I need to leave," she said, grabbing her purse and a stack of files as she headed for the doorway. "Please close the door behind you."

JACK FELT A BREEZE from the speed and force of her exit. Whew. Magnolia was *mad*. Just seeing her made him feel like he'd been slapped awake with a splash of cold water. He'd been surprised at how many times he'd thought of her, how often he'd wanted to pick up the phone just so he could hear her voice. Hell, a couple of times he'd called her cell at odd hours just so he could hear her voicemail message. Which was stupid as hell.

He snorted at himself and raked his hand through his hair. He'd never needed to work at getting a woman's attention before. In fact, he'd had more trouble getting rid of them when they decided they wanted something long-term and he didn't.

Inhaling the lingering whisper of her scent, he walked to her desk and glanced at the photos already arranged on top. Family. He remembered seeing photos of her mother and father and sisters, along with a few nephews and nieces, when she'd dropped her wallet at the tiki bar. He spotted a recent photograph of Amelia with Lillian Bellagio and Brooke Tarantino. He shook his head. Hell, if she could get those two to make nice, maybe Amelia should be in charge of negotiating peace in the mideast.

He would bet Lillian had hated to see Amelia leave. Brooke, too. Giving Amelia this job had been one of the few recommendations he'd made that had been accepted, and he'd done that one on the downlow with the director of personnel.

Adding up how many times he'd thought about her since he left the Keys made him restless. Walking out of her office, he closed the door behind him and headed for the elevators. The doors opened and Jack saw Marc Waterson standing beside his wife, Jenny, one of Bellagio's hot designers. Marc gave a curt nod. Jenny smiled uneasily and slid her gaze to her husband.

"Hi. How you two tonight?" Jack asked.

"Fine, thank you," Jenny murmured. "And you?"

"I'm good," he said. "Not quite done for the day. I guess you aren't, either."

"Alfredo asked me to bring the latest progress reports on the redesign by his house tonight," Marc said, adjusting his tie and directing his gaze to the elevator doors.

"Nice of you," Jack said. "You think it's a good idea for him to stay so involved with the business while they're trying to get his treatment planned for his heart problem?"

Marc threw him a cold look. "Alfredo is as strong as an ox. The only reason he agreed to take a short leave is because his wife has threatened to haul him off to Italy."

Jack shrugged. "Please send him my best wishes. By the way, Jenny, I got a look at your latest wedding designs. They're so good we're not going to be able to meet the demand. Great job."

She beamed. "Thanks. I'm always trying to top what I've done before."

"You succeeded this time."

"How would you know?" Marc demanded. "You've only been around a couple of months."

"As you know, I've been studying the company for years. Jenny, I'd love to see Bellagio introduce a more cost-conscious, streamlined version of your designs for the mainstream buyer who can't afford our couture designs."

"Like Isaac Mizrahi," she said, unable to conceal her excitement. "I mentioned the same thing to Marc a long time ago."

The doors opened and Marc narrowed his eyes at Jack. "Jack has brought up this idea several times. No one on the board considers it a viable option. We don't want to dilute our designer impact."

"Just hate to see all those dollars from the average American going to someone besides Bellagio," Jack said and walked into the hallway. "Good seeing you both. Take care now."

He could feel Marc Waterson shooting daggers into his back at the same time as he heard Jenny whisper, "Do you have to be so hostile?"

Jack shook his head wryly as he ducked inside his small office. Even though he'd called ahead and announced his intention to be actively involved with Bellagio, Marc had tried to keep him off the executive floor.

Jack had insisted and he'd been given a small, narrow room with a tiny window and unmatched furniture. Jack suspected it had previously been a file-storage room. He'd expected hostility and resentment, but not to this degree. Marc Waterson didn't trust Jack one iota and Jack could tell that Marc was poised for the possibility of Jack taking over. Like a pure-bred Doberman guarding the prize.

The problem with Bellagio was that some of their archaic business practices were biting into profit potential. Everyone in a significant position of power was either a Bellagio family member or bowed completely to Bellagio tradition. Plus, they were all male. In fact, with the exception of Trina Roberts and the personnel administrator, all the managers were male.

Bellagio management needed a kick in the ass, and Jack was just the guy to do it. He glanced at his desk and pressed the Power button to his laptop. A mug with the dregs of his afternoon coffee sat beside it. Several files were placed on the other side.

No pictures. No family, except his uncle who sent him monthly e-mails. It was strange. He'd waited most of his life to join to the Bellagio side of his family, to feel like he was good enough to contribute something to the company. Instead he felt like a trespasser, someone who didn't belong. He might have the blood, but he didn't have the history.

Shaking off the depressing thoughts, he turned to his computer and got down to work.

CHAPTER THIRTEEN

WITH HER NEW JOB, new office and new condo,
Amelia didn't have time to think about Jack and
what a prick he'd been, so she decided to pretend he
didn't exist. It shouldn't be that hard. His office was
on a different floor and she couldn't imagine any
reason she would need to interact with him. Except
in the elevator, and using the law of statistical
averages, that shouldn't happen very often.

She almost believed the plan would work—until
she received flowers, roses in every color. The
enclosed card read, *Which color do you like best?* No
signature.

That seemed like something Florida Jack might
do, but since he hadn't signed his name, she couldn't
exactly take the roses up to his office with her
grateful message attached: *Sit on these. Hope you
find a thorn the hard way.*

Despite her suspicions, she couldn't help
enjoying the perky buds and the yummy scent they

exuded. Amelia spent the morning reviewing the file for her first disaster assignment. The mailroom was a mess.

Near the end of the day, she met with the mail clerks, two college drop-outs who spent more time sending text messages on their cell phones than sorting mail. Unfortunately they shared their supervisor with the shipping department, which meant they weren't actually supervised very often.

After working with them throughout the afternoon, she feared she may have had more success retraining the guys from *Dumb and Dumber*. Deciding to give them one more session, she told the clerks to be ready to be tested on their training by tomorrow afternoon.

She spoke with the personnel administrator and their supervisor regarding previous performance reviews and was told they were both distantly related to family members already working for Bellagio.

Amelia downed some headache medication she'd put in her desk drawer for emergencies, collected the files and headed for the elevator.

Despite the statistical improbability, when the elevator doors opened, she saw Jack inside. She hesitated.

"You could always take the stairs," Jack suggested with a sly smile that said he knew she wanted to avoid him.

Goaded, she stepped inside opposite him. "Everything will be fine if you don't talk to me."

He nodded. "No problem. Looks like your second day back wasn't a trip to Disneyland."

"I'm fine, but I work best with people who care about doing a good job," she said, hugging her files to her chest and willing the headache medication to hurry up and take effect.

"People don't care about doing a good job at Bellagio?" he echoed in mock disbelief. "Bellagio couldn't have substandard employees especially since the personnel department's decisions are usually overridden by the good old boys' network."

She cringed at his accurate evaluation. "I didn't say that in Florida, did I?"

"Magnolia, it doesn't matter if you said it or not. The question is, is it true and is it best for the company to continue this way?" The doors opened and he lifted his hand for her to proceed in front of him.

Disturbed by what he'd said and his presence in general, she practically ran toward the exit. In Florida, she'd found him exhilarating. Now, he just pissed her off.

The next day, after she spent a fruitless morning with Mr. Don't Care and Mr. Couldn't Care Less, she wrote a report recommending their dismissal. She suggested Ballagio either replace them with quali-

fied applicants or outsource the mailroom responsibilities. She took a peek at her next file and saw that
it involved training a space cadet receptionist in the
legal department. Her last name was Bellagio.

Amelia took a late lunch at her favorite deli four
blocks away from the office. The walk cleared her
head and she ordered her favorite, half a club
sandwich on rye with an extra pickle spear, and salt-
and-vinegar chips on the side. She headed for the
back of the deli, where a few tables were arranged for
customers. A couple sat at one table, a man read a
newspaper at another. She grabbed the last vacant
table, sat down and took a big bite of her delicious
sandwich.

"You must have had a busy morning, Magnolia.
Why the late lunch?"

Jack's familiar voice caused her food to stick in
her throat. She swallowed hard to get it down and
blinked at him. "Why are you here?"

He smiled and moved to her table. "Don't you
remember? You told me about this place. Great
sandwiches."

She frowned, trying not to notice how good he
looked in a black suit. "Why don't you go to the
Italian place down the street with the rest of the big
dogs?"

His eyes flickered briefly. "Aside from the fact

that I haven't been invited, I miss my favorite Chicago deli and this is as close as I can get to it. They even make Chicago-style hot dogs."

It occurred to Amelia that he was a fish out of water in Atlanta and at Bellagio. She felt a sliver of sympathy, which she quickly dismissed. He wasn't a fish out of water. He was a shark. "You sound like you're terribly homesick for Chicago. Why don't you go back?"

His eyes widened. "Whoa, where's that famous southern hospitality?"

"Hospitality is about pleasing your guest. In your case, you sound as if you would be much happier somewhere else. Need a lift to the airport?"

"Ouch. Are you still holding a grudge against me?"

Amelia had always advised against holding grudges. Holding a grudge made a person bitter and ugly. She'd probably even been a little preachy about it, so she didn't want to think of herself as a grudge-holder. "I'm still upset that you tricked me. I don't like being made the fool."

"I'm sorry," he said, meeting her gaze. "But you're not a fool, Amelia. You're one of the smartest women I've ever met."

Flattery, she thought, squelching the surprising little rush of pleasure. He was just trying to butter her up so he could get extract more secrets from her. "Flattery won't work."

He nodded. "What about my sincere apology? What are you going to do about that?"

His unswerving gaze bothered her. "I'll have to think about it. Right now, I'd like to eat," she said, giving him a broad hint that she wanted him to leave.

"Don't let me stop you," he said cheerfully, leaning back in his chair and watching her. "I finished my food ten minutes ago."

"I'd like to eat in peace," she added. "Alone."

He looked affronted. "You would banish a lonely visitor from your table, a man who craves a few crumbs of your compassion so he can feel a few minutes of human connection in a hostile environment?"

"Aside from the fact that you just gave me a bunch of bull," she said.

"The Irish call it blarney," he corrected.

"Whatever," she said. "You created your own hostility."

"Actually, I didn't, but that's a story for another time. Aside from a few guys on the Atlanta Falcons football team, you're my only friend in town."

"I'm not your friend," she said, wondering about both of his statements.

"Okay, lover," he conceded.

Her heart stuttered. "We're not lovers," she whispered, glancing around to make sure no one had heard him.

"We were," he said.

"I'm sure you could find feminine company without too much trouble," she said.

"Thank you. I prefer you."

Exasperation rushed through her. If there was a quick thrill at his words, too, nobody had to know about it but her. "Why?"

"I trust you," he said. "And I like you. Is it really too much to ask to sit with you while you eat a sandwich?"

Amelia was unable to look away and unable to deny that he wasn't asking for much. It wasn't as if he was asking to kiss her or make love with her. He wasn't the kind who would need to ask. He was the kind to take. *And give,* a little voice inside her reminded her. The thin silver chain around her ankle added to the evidence.

She sighed. "Okay, just this once." Looking away from him, she told herself to pretend he wasn't there. She savored every bite of her half-sandwich, interspersing it with salt-and-vinegar chips and bites of pickle that gave her a puckering sensation.

She left a few crusty crumbs of the bread on her deli paper and started on her second pickle spear. Crisp and juicy. She licked her lips after each nibble until she sucked the last bite into her mouth.

Hearing Jack's audible intake of breath distracted her. She glanced at him and found him staring at her lips. "Do I have mayonnaise on my mouth?"

He shook his head.

"Then why are you staring at it?"

"Do you know what you looked like when you were eating that pickle? Your eyes were closed, you made sounds."

It took her a few seconds, and then realization hit her and she felt her cheeks heat. "It was just a pickle."

"It didn't look like it."

"You have a dirty mind."

"You helped."

She couldn't smother the sound of frustration that bubbled up from her throat. "You were the one who insisted on watching me eat. I tried to make you leave."

"I know. Feel free to leave now," he said.

Offended by his abrupt dismissal, she scowled at him. "That's just rude."

He leaned closer to her. "I'm telling you to leave before me because it's going to take me a few minutes to get rid of this hard-on you've given me."

She blinked, feeling a conflicting surge of pleasure and embarrassment. "Oh," she said, willing her gaze to remain above his shoulders.

"Okay." She picked up her trash and stood. "Well, uh, goodbye."

"Goodbye." He paused then added in a low voice, "I missed you, Amelia."

Her heart turned over at the admission, but she

didn't like that she responded so strongly. She didn't like that her body reacted without her permission. "I think you already extracted most of the secrets I could tell you about Bellagio."

"Maybe," Jack said without batting an eye. "But I'd like to find out the rest of Amelia Parker's secrets."

His gaze made her feel hot all over. She wanted to give him a sizzling comeback, but her brain felt as if it were overheating, so she fell back on a phrase she'd been taught at the age of two. "No, thank you," she said and walked away.

THAT NIGHT, AMELIA WAS SO determined to get Jack out of her mind that she put on a yoga DVD and tried to meditate and lotus him out of her mind. The only problem was that the setting for the yoga lesson was a lovely beach, and when she thought of the beach, she thought of Jack.

The following morning, she worked with the Bellagio girl from the legal department. Although the young woman seemed scattered and easily distracted, Amelia thought she could be improved.

That afternoon, Amelia put together a training class for all Bellagio support positions. Like the rest of the Bellagio employees, she also attended a meeting called by Marc Waterson.

Standing behind a podium, he seemed at ease in

front of the large group. "Welcome, everyone. It's that time of year when we participate in the fund drive for the children's hospital. As you know, this is Alfredo's pet charity and he would be up here hounding donations from you, but he's taken some time off. It's up to me now, so I'm asking you not to make me look too bad in his absence."

A chuckle ran through the crowd.

"Through the years I've seen that the people who work for Bellagio share some great qualities. You take pride in your job and your company. You're hard workers. You're persistent. You keep working until the job is done. And you're generous."

"He must have missed his calling. He should run for political office," Jack said from just behind Amelia, startling the daylights out of her.

She jerked in surprise and threw a quick glance over her shoulder, putting her index finger in front of her mouth in a shushing motion.

"Bellagio will be contributing several items to the auction, including several wardrobes of Bellagio shoes, a weekend trip to Jekyll Island and a trip to Italy, home of the original Bellagio."

"And the grand prize," Jack said sotto voice.

"And this year for the first time, we're offering a pair of shoes designed by Jenny Prillaman for the highest bidder," Marc said, beaming with pride.

The crowd applauded.

"That's pretty good," Jack conceded.

"Who are you kidding?" Still clapping, Amelia turned to look at him. "It's awesome. Jenny's the best."

"Can't argue with her talent. Plus she seems like a nice person."

"She is."

"Unlike her husband."

"Maybe you just bring out the worst in him."

"Or maybe he hasn't given me a chance. Interesting that he didn't ask me if I wanted to contribute anything to the fund drive."

He had a point. Alfredo would shake down his mother to get a donation for the children's fund drive.

"Now I'm going to draw tickets for the formal auction. Just in case you didn't know, the event is scheduled for next Saturday night. I'll draw four pairs of tickets and I'm saving the last pair for the employee who brings in the most donations for the fund drive by next Wednesday. First winner," Marc said as he drew a piece of paper from a bowl. "Marylee Gearhart."

The crowd whistled and applauded as one of the executive assistants went forward to claim her tickets. Marc called out the next two winners and they too collected the coveted tickets.

Then Marc pulled out the last name. "Jack—"

He faltered and looked toward the back of the room. "O'Connell." Marc laughed uneasily. "Jack, I must have forgotten to tell you. All the board members get tickets. I'll have my assistant get yours to you tomorrow."

"Are you sure?" Jack said. "This sounds like the event of the season and I'd hate to miss it."

Marc smiled, but it looked more like he was baring his teeth. "I'm sure. I'll draw another name."

While Marc called out the final winner, Amelia glanced at Jack, who was now standing beside her. She looked at Marc and felt a weird sensation in the pit of her stomach. Marc had tried to snub Jack. The only reason the head VP was giving Jack the tickets was because he'd been publicly shamed into it.

That bothered her. It probably shouldn't have, but it did. She studied Marc and took in his dark wavy hair, his chiseled profile, his tall powerful stance and she saw, as Trina had, his resemblance to Jack.

Jack was just as confident, but he also possessed a humility that shined through every now and then, surprising her every time it surfaced.

Marc dismissed the group and Amelia found herself walking out of the room beside Jack.

"It looks like I have tickets to the auction, the event of the year. You want to go?"

"Not with you," she said cheerfully.

He chuckled. "Don't bottle up those feelings, Magnolia. Tell me how you really feel."

"Marc is currently the most powerful man in the company and he—" She broke off, reluctant to use harsh words. "He seems to dislike you."

"And you're afraid you'll be put in jeopardy if you associate with me."

"I wouldn't say I'm afraid."

"I would. Ever been to this bash before?"

"No."

"Another first? Tell you what, I'll give you the ticket with no strings. If you show, we'll have a drink and that's it. See ya later, Magnolia."

This time, he moved ahead, leaving her to digest his offer. And eat his dust.

CHAPTER FOURTEEN

"GIRLS' NIGHT OUT ON Thursday," Trina had told her. "Minus Maddie. Plus Chad."

Amelia wouldn't miss drinks and dinner at the trendy new restaurant with this group of people. As she entered the busy eatery in Buckhead, she spotted Trina, Liz and Chad. Liz and Chad, longtime friends of Jenny's, had invited Trina into their inner circle via Jenny. Trina had thrown a M.A.P party—also known as a *men are pigs* party—for Amelia last spring, when Will had broken up with her the first time. Liz had ushered Amelia into her first margarita hangover with some sage feminine wisdom. "The great thing about getting a hangover when your heart is broken is that your head hurts so much it distracts you from other pain."

Liz and Trina smiled and waved. "Come on over. Jenny's running a little late," Trina said. "Liz already ordered a drink for you."

Liz rose to give Amelia a hug. "You're looking

good, girl. I hear you finally left wishy-washy Will behind. I'm glad to hear it."

Amelia laughed. "Thank you. It was more like he left me behind. But I'm mostly over it."

"Mostly?" Trina asked.

"At least ninety-five percent."

"Good for you," Liz said. "We just need to find you a hot guy to help you with that last five percent."

Amelia felt a trickle of nervousness. Liz was a powerful woman. Not much scared her. If she put her mind to something, it usually happened. "I'm okay," she said. "I'm not in a rush to get into another wrong relationship. Chad," she said, turning her attention to the good-looking man seated beside Liz. "We haven't met, but I've heard so much about you."

"And I you," he said, shaking her hand. "Lovely manners. A true southern belle. I was told you were over-the-top conservative, but I wouldn't say that." He glanced at Liz. "Why did you lie to me?"

"Well, she *was* conservative. The girl hadn't even drunk more than one margarita before last spring."

"Just because she's not a lush or slut doesn't mean she's convent material."

"I didn't say she was," Liz protested.

"Quit squabbling," Trina said. "You're making Amelia uncomfortable."

Amelia felt Liz and Chad look at her expectantly.

"I was very naïve when Liz first met me. I'd spent most of my life doing everything to please my fiancé from the way I dressed and did my hair to where I lived and worked."

"I really like your hair," Liz said.

"I threw away my flat iron."

"Good girl," Chad said and lifted his martini. "So we're all agreed that we're glad Amelia dumped her loser fiancé."

Amelia bit her tongue to keep from correcting him. Will had done the dumping, and Will wasn't a total loser.

"To better days," Trina said.

"And better boys," Liz added with a wink.

"Hear, hear," Amelia said and drank a sip of her appletini.

Jenny rushed toward the table, giving everyone a quick hug. "Sorry I'm late. Between designing and Alfredo being out of the office and Marc—" She shook her head and took a gulp of the drink in front of her. "It's just crazy." She glanced at the martini. "Oops, is this mine?"

"Don't worry, darling," Chad said, putting his arm around Jenny like a comforting brother. "Liz has graciously offered to treat everyone." He waved toward the waiter. "Another round, please. Now, what's this about Alfredo being out? And what could possibly be wrong with perfect Marc? If you're done with him, I'll take him."

Amelia couldn't choke back a laugh. Trina had told her that Chad was a loveable gay mooch, but also incredibly loyal. She'd nailed him to a T.

"Alfredo is having heart problems," Trina said. "Marc is having board issues."

Jenny threw him a skeptical glance. "I know why you're digging. You just like some juicy gossip."

"Shame on you," he said and looked at Trina. "Board issues. What could that mean?"

"There's this venture capitalist guy who worked a deal to help out with the redesign for the activewear line. Thank God that's not my responsibility," Jenny said and took another gulp of her martini. "Part of the deal is that the investor gets a temporary seat on the board. Marc thought it was just for show until this guy showed up and wanted an office. And now he's—" She broke off, searching for words.

"Berserk," Trina finished for her. "Marc's great, but he's berserk. And if you repeat that, Chad, we'll never buy drinks for you again."

Chad made a face. "Damn, and it's such delicious dish. What's wrong with this guy?"

"He's good-looking and smart," Trina said.

"But he's not a Bellagio," Jenny added. "Marc doesn't want him messing things up." She paused.

"And I really pissed Marc off the other day when I agreed with Jack that Bellagio should start a more affordable line. He didn't speak to me for the rest of the evening."

Trina winced. "Big ego issues here."

Chad looked at Amelia. "What about you? Don't you work for Bellagio, too? What's the new guy like? Is he evil or is he good?"

Both, Amelia thought, but didn't want to say that. "I've been away from Atlanta for the past three months. I just got back last week." She decided to switch the conversation to a safer topic. "I thought Marc did a great job at the employee meeting yesterday. And the prize of winning a pair of shoes designed by Jenny just for the winner was brilliant."

Jenny smiled. "Thanks. That was Marc's idea." Her smile fell. "But he was in a horrid mood when he was pretty much forced to make sure Jack O'Connell gets tickets to the Children's Auction event."

Chad gasped. "That's the hottest event in town. I was counting on getting some help from you for my own tickets," he said to Jenny.

Jenny shook her head. "Marc and I are going, but he's being very tight-fisted with those tickets this year. Apparently we received less than usual because there's less room at the new venue."

Chad look at Liz, who shook her head. "Sorry

darlin', I've already bought my dress. I made sure my darling husband and I got two tickets, but you don't want to know what I had to do to get them."

"Yes, I do," Chad said, then glanced at Trina, who also shook her head.

"Sorry. Walker and I have to go."

Chad sighed then looked at Amelia. "And you?"

"I don't have tickets," she said, then paused. "Actually, I've been invited, but I don't think I'm going."

Everyone stared at her.

"The man who asked me," she explained. "I don't really like him."

"You don't have to bear his children," Liz said. "If he's a total Cyclops you could ditch him at the auction."

Jenny frowned. "No, that wouldn't be nice."

"Is he that bad?" Trina asked.

Trying not to squirm under their expectant gazes, Amelia struggled to come up with a suitable explanation. "He reminds me of Will," she blurted out, feeling her cheeks heat from the lie.

"Oh," Trina said sympathetically.

"Sucks," Liz said.

"Maybe you could suggest me as a replacement," Chad offered. "I'm a delightful escort or date. Ask anyone."

Jenny rolled her eyes. "He might not want to go with a guy, Chad."

"You never know," he said.

"I do know with this guy," Amelia said. She had firsthand experience with his preferences.

Chad made a sound of disgust and finished the rest of his martini in one swallow. "Well, if I can't go with him, then you should," he told her. "Buy something wicked and wonderful. It will be your Atlanta coming-out party."

"But he looks like her ex," Jenny said.

"I don't care if he looks like Shrek, this is a once-in-a-year if not once-in-a-lifetime experience. So buck up and move on. I'll even do your hair," he offered.

"You gotta go now," Liz said. "He's great with hair."

Jenny nodded. "He should have done it professionally."

"I'm an artiste. I never could have done hair for money," Chad said. "If, however, you feel compelled to repay me, I enjoy a good lobster dinner and a trip to Versailles—or I could even make do with Provence."

Amelia blinked. "I don't think I can afford—"

"He'll be happy as a clam if you cover his martinis one night," Liz assured her.

Chad grinned. "I always aim high," he said. "I must do your hair for this event. I already have a vision. *You* will be a vision."

He sounded a little scary to Amelia, but from the

expressions Trina, Jenny and Liz wore, Chad's vision was a good thing. "Thank you," she said tentatively.

"Call me," he ordered, giving her a colorful card with his photo on it.

IN ORDER TO AVOID JACK, Amelia skipped her favorite deli for five days and took the stairs. *I'd better be getting a great rear end out of this,* she told herself.

By Thursday, she got another assignment with a distant relative of a Bellagio employee, and she needed a pickle fix badly. She could skip the club sandwich, but she needed the pickles.

Arriving at the deli, she checked the back room before she ordered. Finding Jack absent, she ordered her favorite with two extra pickles this time and carried the meal to the back.

She crunched down one and a half pickles and ate the half-sandwich interspersed with half a pickle. Just as she started on the final pickle, a man with long legs wrapped in black slacks appeared in front of her. She didn't need to look above or below his belt to know it was Jack. Statistical probability was not operating in her favor.

"I'm starting to think you have a thing about pickles. I didn't know this about you."

"You didn't eat with me that often," she said, closing her eyes so she wouldn't think about the time he'd unzipped his slacks and thrust inside her... She took a bite, determined to enjoy her last pickle spear.

"Why don't you just buy a jar and eat them?"

"I have jars, but it's not the same as getting just one pickle spear at lunch. Two is considered a splurge. And three is over the top."

"How many have you had today?"

None of your business. "This is my third."

"Rough day?"

"I haven't been here in a few days. The deprivation got to me."

"Better be careful," he said. "What happens if you're depriving yourself of more than pickles?"

She finally met his gaze and immediately felt a kick inside her. Damn.

He took a sip of coffee. "Just a guess, but I'm betting you keep running into incompetent distant family members of Bellagio employees who were hired because they were related." He took another sip. "But you don't have to confirm or deny."

"I *won't* confirm or deny," she said, but curiosity got the better of her. "Don't tell me I told you this that night I drank too many hurricanes."

He chuckled and shook his head. "No. Marc is so determined to keep me away from his pet projects that it gives me plenty of time to observe. Amazing what you can learn in the employee workroom if you're busy taking notes or appear to be working on your laptop."

"That's sneaky," she said with as much disapproval as she could muster.

He shrugged and sat across from her. "I'm in plain sight and I speak the truth."

"Sometimes," she said.

"When I know people can handle it," he corrected. "Sometimes when they can't."

She would have to think about that later. Although Jack presented himself as a selfish, superficial man, she knew different. She knew there were layers. It would have been a lot easier for her if she could paint him a total bully, but she knew too much. Yet, at the same time, she knew too little.

"How do you distinguish between when to tell the truth and when to withhold it?"

"Instinct," he said. "Most times I'm right. I'm rarely wrong."

She bit her lip. "And with me?"

He sighed and looked away. "Jury's still out. I never wanted to offend you." He looked at her again. "You going to meet me at the charity auction on Saturday night?"

"I hadn't decided," she said.

He nodded. "On eBay the tickets are going for four figures minimum."

"I'm not surprised. I just wish I knew why you're so insistent that I join you."

He leaned forward. "You can't tell, Magnolia? I have a terrible crush on you."

Dictionary Definition:
Flip-flop: *Noun*. A type of sandal, usually a thong with a lightweight foam sole that makes a "flip-flop" sound as you walk.

Amelia Parker's Definition:
Flip-flop: *Transitive verb*. What a really hot guy makes your heart do.

CHAPTER FIFTEEN

JACK SAT IN HIS OFFICE, aka former skinny file room, comparing the best-selling shoes at Bellagio with other brands. Bellagio was a clear winner among special occasion shoes.

Jack liked the whole ad campaign of using a glamorous *Desperate Housewives* theme, showing a celebrity going from her Bellagio special occasion shoes to her Bellagio activewear shoes.

Guys were easier. They all wanted to feel like they were the next great basketball player.

He heard a brisk tap at his door before it opened. Marc Waterson entered and closed the door behind him.

Jack was surprised as hell, but he didn't show it. Instead, he leaned back in his desk chair and nodded. "Hello."

"Hello," Marc returned, glancing at Jack's computer. He tossed a pair of tickets onto Jack's desk. "Here they are."

Jack saw they were the tickets for the charity auction. "Damn. I was hoping you were going to invite me to a Braves game."

Marc shot him a deadly gaze.

"To what do I owe the pleasure of your charming presence?" Jack asked. "You could have sent your assistant's assistant or the janitor's assistant to deliver these to me."

"I like those people. Why would I want to ruin their day?" Marc returned.

"Hey, I can be a nice enough guy."

"I realize you're a short-timer, but with Alfredo out for a while, people are looking to me for leadership and stability. What you pulled yesterday in the employee meeting—don't do that again."

"If someone had informed me that the board members automatically get tickets, I wouldn't have needed to do that, would I?" Jack asked.

"You created unnecessary awkwardness in front of all the employees."

"I didn't draw the name."

Marc clenched his jaw. "Even so, I'm asking you not to pull anything like that again." He turned to leave.

"As long as you make sure I'm kept informed, it shouldn't be a problem."

Marc stopped with his hand on the doorknob. "Are you suggesting that I report to you?"

"I'm suggesting that you keep me informed, just like you do the other members on the board. If you want to do that through your assistant, via e-mail, fax, voicemail or singing telegram, that's your choice."

Marc turned around and narrowed his eyes at him. "If you weren't such an ass, this wouldn't be so difficult."

"There's where you're wrong," Jack said. "I could be God, Mother Teresa, Donald Trump, take your pick. I could be the nicest guy in the world, but since I'm not a Bellagio, my ideas are worthless, my suggestions are ridiculous. I'm a carpetbagger. And you're so scared shitless that I'm going to do something terrible to Bellagio that you can't even hear when I say something worth considering."

"It's safe to say that your intentions aren't clear. You've put several companies in caskets," Marc said.

"Companies that were dying and needed to merge or consolidate, and none of those companies were as large as Bellagio," Jack said. "But I'll agree that a certain level of paranoia is healthy."

"You haven't been in the business of building a company that will last after you die. You've been in the business of making money. That's all. Money. I'm not going to let you come in and mess up what it's taken generations to create. And while I'm at it, don't drag my wife into our debates. It upsets her."

Jack cocked his head to one side. "Looked to me like it bothered you more than it did her."

"Don't bother Jenny," Marc said again, and left.

"And have a nice day to you, too," Jack said to the door. "Sure. I'll be happy to join you for a beer sometime." He laughed at himself in gallows humor. He'd had no idea how much they would hate him when he'd put together this plan. Turning back to the computer, he shrugged off Marc's attitude and continued working the numbers. It would be interesting to see if the green money would win over red Bellagio blood.

EVEN THOUGH AMELIA PUT the ticket Jack left on her desk on Monday deep in her purse, it might as well have burned a hole through the material to her hand.

The auction was black tie. Women would be dressed to the hilt in long gowns. Champagne would flow freely. No doubt it would be a first for her to attend such an event.

She'd bought a couple formal dresses for proms, but not for anything like this. The prospect made her feel both nervous and excited.

She decided to call Chad for a consultation. She would feel as if she were imposing if she asked him to do her hair, but asking his opinion wasn't too much in her mind.

He gave her an earful. "Ignore all shy, conservative, ladylike instincts. They'll just get in your way. You need to wear something head-snapping. Head-turning isn't enough. Show skin, bare your cleavage, get something with a slit. And for God's sake if you buy something black, white or pastel, I'll burn it before you get out the door. I'll be over to do your hair at five Saturday night. This is going to be so much fun. Make sure you have vodka for martinis."

So Amelia shopped during her lunch hour on Monday, Tuesday and Wednesday. By Thursday at lunch, she was starting to get nervous and seriously reconsidering. "Maybe I shouldn't go. I can't find anything to wear except black," she confessed to Chad. "Everything else is too—" She shook her head. "Just too—"

Chad snorted in disapproval. "Ridiculous. Okay, I guess I'll have to do it myself. Give me your measurements."

She blinked. "Excuse me?"

"Your measurements," he said impatiently. "If I'm going to find something, I need to get to work immediately."

Her mouth worked, but she couldn't push out a sound.

"Amelia, you have nothing to worry about. I'm not after your body. I just want complete and total credit for turning you into the most beautiful woman at the auction." He paused. "And I won't object to dinner and cocktails at the new Italian restaurant, either." He waited another half-beat. "So get over the southern church girl thing and cough up your measurements and shoe size."

Feeling as if she were jumping out of a plane, she closed her eyes and told him her measurements.

"Very good," he said briskly. "I'll have the perfect dress and accessories for you on Saturday."

"But what if that one dress isn't really perfect?" she asked, already second-guessing her leap of faith.

"I'll bring a selection, but the perfect one will be obvious. Ciao, darling."

Amelia stared at the receiver before she hung up. What had she just done? Had someone slipped some crack in her coffee this morning? Dazed, she went to Trina's office.

"Do you have a minute? I just did something really crazy," she said as she entered the office of Bellagio's PR guru.

Trina juggled her red-haired toddler daughter on her hip. "I was just getting ready to take Maddie back to the office nursery, but I have a few minutes." She glanced at Maddie and smiled. "We had lunch with Daddy at Burger King, didn't we?" Maddie beamed. So did Trina.

"I can't tell which of you is happiest," Amelia said, thinking their joy was infectious.

Trina laughed. "It's a tie. Okay, so tell me about your crazy thing. Is it so deliciously shameless and juicy that I need to cover Maddie's ears?"

"No. I just agreed to let Chad dress me for the charity auction event. How do I call him back and say thank you, but I was temporarily insane?"

Trina shook her head. "You don't. I know it's scary, but Chad is awesome. He could be a professional stylist. You're going to look great." She paused and frowned. "In fact, I'm jealous. Why is he doing that for you and not me? I wonder if he's dressing Jenny." She made a sound of disgust. "Left out in the cold again. I'll see you at the event, but you still need to take pictures. This is something you won't want to forget."

"Are you sure?"

"Have I ever misled you?"

Amelia shook her head.

"Good. Gotta tell you, I wasn't a hundred percent sure when you temporarily moved in with my mother, but that seemed to go okay."

"That was exactly what I needed when Will dumped me," Amelia said. "The first, second *and* third times."

Trina scowled. "I'm so glad you're done with him."

Maddie started to squirm and make noises.

"Oops, she wants to walk," Trina said. "Can't have that in the office. I need to scoot. Enjoy the star treatment with Chad. And I want to meet your mystery man. Later," she called as she rushed out of the office.

"Never ever," Amelia murmured to Trina's back. The prospect of trying to explain Jack to Trina made her even more hysterical than letting Chad outfit her for the biggest event she'd ever attended.

SATURDAY ARRIVED and Amelia talked to her mother and sister. They were getting antsy about wanting her to come home for the weekend. Amelia hadn't been able to bring herself to go home after that last breakup with Will. She was afraid memories of Will and the dreams they'd shared would totally engulf her. She didn't want to hurt her family's feelings, but she just didn't feel ready to face all that. She felt as if she'd successfully crawled out of a hole and was enjoying the sunshine.

She painted her fingernails and toenails a neutral color since Chad had refused to give her any hints on the color of her dress. He arrived promptly at five armed with a plastic barrel full of various electric hair utensils, styling products and a makeup kit.

He stopped and studied her face as he walked into

her condo. "Just washed. Good. I like to start with a fresh palate. You did moisturize, didn't you?"

She smiled at his imperious tone as he set down his equipment. "I did. Where's the dress?"

"In due time," he said, pulling smaller containers from the barrel and setting them on her sofa. He removed the shade from a lamp and pushed the curtains to the sides of the windows. "Light, I need lots of light," he said with the tone of a true artiste.

He swept to her side again and lifted her hands. He made a clucking sound. "The color is fine for your fingernails, but you could definitely use some more moisturizer. Do you moonlight as a dishwasher?"

"I wash my hands a lot. My mother was big on cleanliness."

"A southern Lady MacBeth," he said and lifted an eyebrow.

She studied his face, entranced by his rakish features, dark, sultry eyes and dark hair. He really was gorgeous. "Shame," she murmured, appalled when she realized she'd spoken her thought aloud.

He smiled, revealing white teeth. "I'm a great dancer, too."

"I know. Trina told me. You're perfect."

He puffed up his chest. "It's good that you recognize this. I know how to make every heterosexual guy in that place want to be with you."

Amelia felt a kick of excitement and apprehension. And terror. She bit her lip.

"Stop," Chad said. "It's just for one evening. Feel the power. Enjoy it."

He started with her toenails, replacing the neutral shade she'd chosen with a vibrant reddish coral. Although she'd discovered in Florida that she liked bright toe-polish, she got a funny feeling about his color choice. He did her hair, using the hot curling iron to exaggerate her waves. He left most of her hair down, but pulled back a few tendrils with rhinestone-enhanced bobby pins. Then he did her makeup, all of it except her mouth.

"Time for martinis," he said cheerfully. "Just try not to dribble on the chin. Where's the vodka?"

"Kitchen counter," she said and headed for the bathroom. "I want to see what you've done."

"No. Absolutely not. I don't want you looking in the mirror until the transformation is complete. Totally complete." He moved to the kitchen. "I'm in the mood for lemon drops. Do you have fresh lemons?"

"Yes. I drink iced tea with lemon."

"We'll skip the house wine of the South tonight," Chad said.

She joined him. "House wine?"

"Iced tea," he said, opening the vodka. "No caffeine for you. I want you relaxed."

Why? she wondered. Why did she need to be relaxed? She felt her nerves jiggle and jump. "I want to see the dress."

"After a lemon-drop martini. It will give those lips a lovely pucker." He dampened the rims of two of the martini glasses she'd bought that day, pulled out her canister of sugar and rolled the rims in it.

"What does it look like?"

"I can't do it justice with words."

"Please try," Amelia said.

Chad mixed the concoction, added ice and shook. "It's glamorous and beautiful, sumptuous. A head-snapper."

"Can you be a little more specific? And what about the back-up dresses?"

He shook his head and poured the martini into her glass. "Oh, I didn't bring any. After I saw this, I knew everything else would pale beside it."

Amelia felt her anxiety shoot through the roof. "But—"

"Here," he said, pressing the martini into her hand. "Try this. Tell me you don't love it."

She took a quick sip and her lips puckered at the lemony taste. "It's tart," she said. "But just a little sweet." What if he'd brought a slut suit and she was going to have to tell him she couldn't wear it?

"Perfect," he said and mixed another martini. He

glanced at her and sighed. "You look like you're getting ready to face the guillotine. You're going to love the dress, but you must work on your diva attitude."

"I don't have a diva attitude."

"Then pretend. Drink up," he said, waving at her martini.

She took a few more sips. "The suspense is killing me."

Chad rolled his eyes. "Okay, I'll bring it in, but keep sipping and no peeking."

As soon as he left, Amelia considered throwing the rest of her drink down the drain. Had he put two shots of vodka in this? Conflicted, she poured a little into the sink and took a few more sips. Dying of curiosity, she raced to the powder room and flicked on the light.

She stared into the mirror, but saw another woman with hair that fell in a combination of sexy waves and curls that evoked an image of a temptress or an angel. He'd applied her makeup with a light touch. Her cheeks were flushed with just a hint of sparkle, her eyelids dusted with sheer iridescent color, her eyelashes darkened with mascara. Wow, Trina had been right. He was good.

Hearing the front door open, she rushed out of the bathroom, carrying her martini glass toward the front room.

"Turn around," he instructed. "I don't want you to see it piecemeal. It's all at once or nothing."

Amelia turned around and tapped her glass with her finger. She heard the rustle of plastic as Chad hummed a bluesy tune.

"Now," he finally said. "You may look."

Amelia took one last sip of her martini and turned around. "Wow," she said, blinking at the color, a combination of red and coral. The material was softer than satin, with a hint of sheen. The low-cut halter top had gathers below the bodice and the skirt featured two slits in the front. The slits might have pushed the dress into the slut category except the edges had the slightest hint of a ruffle, making them appear more girly.

"It's beautiful," she said.

"I know," he said smugly. "Now finish your martini, brush your teeth carefully and use the powder room. After that I'll give you the foundation garment and you can put on the dress."

"Foundation garment?" she echoed, imagining a long-line bra connected to a control bottom that would smooth her belly, hips and thighs.

Chad held up a thong. "Here it is."

CHAPTER SIXTEEN

SHE BLINKED. "That's it? What about a bra?"

"Won't need it," he said.

"But—"

"Go on now. I don't have all night if I'm going to mooch my way into the event."

Within ten minutes, Amelia had pulled the gown over her nearly naked body. She stepped into the silver sandals Chad had brought for her. He applied her lip color and gave her the gloss for touch-ups, then guided her to the full-length mirror.

"Well?"

"You're amazing. Thank you."

"You're very welcome. If I have it my way, I'll see you later tonight at the auction."

"How will you get inside?"

He waved his hand. "There's always a way. Heads are gonna turn and hearts are gonna roll. Think of all the money I could make off of the whiplash victims tomorrow morning if I were a chiropractor."

"That may be an exaggeration."

Chad shook his head. "You'll see. Ciao, my dear. Would you mind if I take your vodka with me?"

AMELIA COULDN'T LIE. She felt like Cinderella at the ball. She'd splurged on valet parking, so she wouldn't work up a sweat hiking from some faraway spot in the parking lot. That was a first. Will had always been too cheap to use valet parking.

She walked into the luxury hotel and found her way to the line to get into the ballroom. When she arrived at the front, the tux-clad ticket-taker stamped her hand.

"Alone?" he asked.

"Sorta," she said, because Jack had told her she only needed to have one cocktail with him.

The ticket taker smiled. "Sorta? Does that mean you're hoping the status will change during the evening?"

"Not really."

"Well, if I get a break later, maybe I can change your mind. Have a good time."

Blinking, Amelia walked into the ballroom, unable to stop a giggle. She'd just been hit on. Okay, that was fun.

A waiter carrying a tray of flutes filled with champagne breezed past her, then paused and looked at her. "Champagne?"

"Thank you, yes," she said, feeling a little bubbly on her own from the attention.

"Amelia! Oh, my God, look at her."

Amelia turned at the sound of Trina's voice. Trina was joined by her fiancé, Walker Gordon, and Jenny and Marc Waterson.

Jenny squealed, and she and Trina broke away from the guys to rush toward her. "You came! Where's the guy?"

"I don't know. I just got here," Amelia said. "And he promised I don't have to spend the evening with him. Just a drink."

"Well it sounds like he's being very accommodating," Trina said, raising her eyebrows. "A motivated man is not a bad thing."

"We'll see," Amelia said vaguely. "You both look gorgeous."

"Who'd notice us next to you? You're a total vision," Jenny told her. "Your hair, your dress…" She nodded in realization. "Chad did you, didn't he? He's awesome, isn't he?"

"Totally. I feel like he waved a magic wand and transformed me. I don't recognize myself in the mirror."

"Don't underrate yourself," Trina chided. "He had some great material to work with. You look beautiful."

Jenny nodded, grabbing two glasses of champagne from a waiter carrying a tray. "Thanks," she said with a smile. "I need to get Marc started. He's wound tight tonight."

"Have you thought about slipping him some kind of relaxer?" Trina asked.

"You mean drug him?" Amelia asked.

"That's a harsh way of putting it," Trina said.

"If he doesn't calm down soon, one or both of us is going to have to be medicated," Jenny said, downing a gulp of champagne. "The very presence of Jack O'Connell makes him crazy."

Amelia paused a second, then gave into her curiosity. "Is Jack that bad?"

"No," Trina and Jenny said at the same time.

"But you didn't hear that from me," Jenny said.

"Or me," Trina added. "Jack actually has some good ideas."

Jenny nodded. "He does."

"But he's not a Bellagio," Trina said.

"And the Bellagios don't like outsiders. They're very territorial. If Marc were a dog, he'd pee the perimeter of the building to mark his territory."

Amelia laughed. "This is a problem on the lower level, too. Relatives get hired, but they're not necessarily qualified or motivated."

"Tell me about it," Trina said. "I had to deal with

an assistant last year who was distantly related. I was so relieved when she quit."

Jenny gave a helpless look. "I wish I could get through to him…."

"I think you should just try to get through the night and have a good time," Amelia said.

Jenny sighed. "I think that's the sweetest thing anyone has said to me in ages. I should scoot and give Marc his champagne starter."

"Then you can move onto the manly drinks. Scotch, bourbon," Trina said and turned to Amelia. "I should probably go, too. The auction is starting with the Bellagio donations. They wanted to start with a bang. Enjoy being the most gorgeous woman here."

Amelia laughed. "Thanks."

She wandered through the crowd, spotting lines at several tables where attendees waited to register and receive an assigned number card shaped like a peach fan.

"You're not bidding on anything?" a male voice said from behind her.

Her heart jumped in her chest. She turned to look at him and immediately got distracted from his question. He wore a black tux that fit him to perfection. His white shirt was crisp, his dark hair contrasting with his blue eyes. She blinked. "Um, I think most of this is going to be out of my price range." She glanced at the number card he held. "I see you're ready."

"It's for a good cause." He paused a half-beat. "You take my breath away."

She fought the giddy sensation, but felt her cheeks warm anyway. "Thank you. It's all due to Chad."

"Chad?"

"He's friends with Jenny Prillaman and Trina Roberts. He could be a professional stylist, but he says he's too much of an artiste for that."

"You look beautiful. You're going to see every guy here following you around with his tongue hanging out of his mouth and all but barking at you like a dog. But just remember, I knew you were beautiful the first moment I saw you." He took her hand for a couple of seconds and touched his thumb to the inside of her wrist where her pulse raced. "I'll buy you that drink later. I want to bump up the bids for the Bellagio items if necessary. Meet me at the bar on the other side after the end of the auctions for the Bellagio donations. Okay?"

He stepped away and she felt wobbly. She rubbed the inside of her wrist against her dress, trying to rub away his effect on her, but she still nodded. "Okay," she said and watched him walk toward the seats.

"Welcome to the twelfth annual Auction for Children's Health," a junior league–looking woman an-

nounced from the stage. "It's my pleasure to introduce the mayor of Atlanta…."

The preliminaries began. The mayor encouraged everyone to be generous for the good cause.
The head of the auction committee spoke, and
finally the male auctioneer, a good old boy wearing
a tux that didn't hide his beer belly, introduced the
first item up for bid—a shoe wardrobe of Bellagio
shoes.

The bidding started off at a healthy clip. Every time
it began to slow, Jack lifted his card, launching another
round. The wardrobe finally sold for the equivalent of
a small but new car, Amelia noted and was glad she
hadn't registered. Everything in this auction was definitely going to be out of her price range.

She sampled a couple of appetizers while she kept
an eye on the auction. The bidding to receive the pair
of individually designed shoes by Jenny went
through the roof. Amelia caught sight of Jenny
standing next to Marc and saw the delight on her face
as Marc gave her a squeeze of congratulations.

"We have two more items donated by Bellagio.
They came in at the last minute. Men, get your
engines ready. Ladies, if you want to give the man
in your life the gift of his dreams, here it is. Two
season tickets to the Braves games. Seats are behind
home plate. VIP room privileges and one meal with

one of the players. All I can say is, somebody at Bellagio has connections."

Amelia glanced at Jack, who was slouched too casually against a column. She looked at Marc, who was staring at Jack with narrowed eyes.

The bidding began. Jack didn't need to lift his card because the bids became, in Amelia's humble opinion, crazy. Finally the insane winner of the tickets gave a loud whoop of joy.

"Don't be upset if you didn't win that last auction," the auctioneer said. "If you're a football fan, I have a nice consolation prize. Season tickets for the Atlanta Falcons, fifty-yard line VIP seats and one meal with the quarterback of the team."

A roar went through the crowd. This auction created even more havoc than the previous one had, with the final bid going into the stratosphere. Amelia walked toward the bar at the far end of the room, ready to fulfill her duty of having a drink with Jack.

Amelia took a seat at the back of the semicircular bar so she wouldn't be as visible. Several moments passed and she began to wonder if Jack had forgotten or changed his mind. Just as she rose to leave, he entered the area wearing an expression of disgust and disbelief.

"Whiskey," he said to the bartender. "The best you've got."

"That'll be fifty bucks a shot," the bartender warned him.

"I'll probably want three." He turned to Amelia. "What would you like, Magnolia? Hurricane? Margarita?"

"I don't really—" She saw something dark and almost lonely in his eyes she stopped herself. "Uh, lemon-drop martini."

"There you go. Sorry it took me so long."

"Problem?"

"Marc Waterson came up to tear a strip off of me for making Bellagio donations to the auction without consulting him."

The bartender poured Jack's first shot and he tossed it back. He replaced the shot glass on the counter and gave the bartender a nod.

Amelia was confused. "Why would Marc mind if you make donations in Bellagio's name? It's just going to make Bellagio look better, isn't it? And it's for a good cause."

"My thinking," he said, and drank the second shot. "But not his."

The bartender placed her martini in front of her. "Thank you," she said and watched him fill Jack's shot glass one more time. "How many of those does it take for you to feel it?"

"Apparently more than two," he said. "You didn't tell me Marc Waterson was a lunatic."

"He wasn't one before you came. Well," she said, pausing, thinking back to some rumors she'd heard about his pre-Jenny days. "I heard that Jenny really helped him mellow out."

She took a sip of her martini and looked at his shot of whiskey. "What does that taste like, anyway?"

He chuckled. "You want to taste it?"

"I don't know. Do I?"

"Another first. You can say you've drunk fine whiskey." He lifted the shot glass to her. "Drink up."

She took a quick gulp and gasped, feeling as if fire were pouring down her throat. She pushed the glass back toward him. "That's vile. How do you drink it? You must have burned away all your taste buds."

He laughed. "No, I haven't. It's an acquired taste."

"But why bother?" She thought of something Trina had said earlier. "Because it's a manly drink, right?"

He shrugged. "My uncle introduced me to whiskey in moderation," he said. "Nice guy. Took me to a few ballgames when he was in town."

"Is he alive?"

Jack nodded. "Got a family. I see him every now and then."

"Holidays?"

"Nah," he said. "Wouldn't want to intrude. So how many men have you beat off with a stick tonight?"

"Just three during the auction and four here in the bar."

"I'm surprised. I would have expected twenty or more."

"You're doing that blarney thing again," Amelia said, but felt her heart squeeze tight at the way he looked at her.

"No. I'm not."

His gaze was so intense, filled with a mix of emotions that made her confused. She forced herself to look away.

"Jack?" a familiar female voice called. "Jack O'Connell?"

Amelia glanced up, shocked to see Jenny and Trina coming toward them. She bit her lip, wondering how she would explain sitting with Jack.

"Oh, hi, Amelia. You still look gorgeous," Jenny said, then turned to Jack. "I must apologize for my husband's behavior. He's being a jerk and I've told him that. What you did, donating the season tickets, that was amazing and wonderful—"

"And who do you know?" Trina interrupted.

"I had a few connections. One of those friend of a friend things," he said with a shrug. "I've done a few favors."

That sounded familiar, Amelia thought. He'd done a favor for Ian, too, she recalled.

"Well, if I'm ever in dire need of a contact, I'm coming to you," Trina said.

Jack laughed. "I'll do what I can."

"But I'm sorry Marc was a jerk. You did a good thing," Jenny said. "I wish he would be reasonable instead of insane."

Silence followed.

An idea occurred to Amelia. "Maybe you could invite him to a ballgame," she said. "Seats on the fifty yard line, VIP privileges."

"That's brilliant," Jenny said. "I just need to get him drunk enough to say yes. If you could throw in a meeting with Marcus Vick…"

Trina threw Jack a sideways glance. "I bet that could be arranged by your friend of a friend."

"The only thing," Jenny said and looked Jack dead in the eye, "is if you hurt Marc or Bellagio, I will call in all my favors and someday somewhere someone will chop you into little pieces and feed you to the fish in some skanky, dirty river."

Jenny was so cute that it was hard for her to look menacing, but her eyes looked crazed enough to be believable.

"Consider yourself warned," she added. "And if

you decide to ask Marc to a game, let me know so I can loosen him up first."

Trina suddenly threw Amelia a curious glance. "What are you doing back here with Jack?"

"I'm not with Jack," Amelia said, grabbing her lemon-drop martini. "I just wanted to get away from the crowd and he happened to come back here after I'd been sitting awhile. I'm actually ready to go. It was nice meeting you, Jack. I hope you enjoy the rest of your evening."

His eyes full of a wickedness that terrified her, he took her hand and rubbed his forefinger over her pulse, as he'd done earlier. "My pleasure, Amelia. Same to you."

Amelia stumbled backward, wincing when she nearly spilled her martini. "Yikes," she muttered to herself and strode out of the bar area, certain her entire body had suffused into a blush. Her skin probably matched the color of her dress, except it would be splotchy.

"I think he likes you," Trina said, stepping beside her.

Amelia shook her head. "No. He was giving another woman the eye just before you two got there," she lied, hoping she wouldn't get struck by lightning.

"I think you're wrong. I didn't see any other woman," Jenny said.

"You were too upset to notice. She left after the two of you came," Amelia said, feeling even worse for embellishing. "Have you guys eaten any of the food? They have these great little crab quiches. Do you know if there's any chocolate?"

"There has to be chocolate," Trina said.

"I haven't been able to eat a thing with the way Marc has been acting," Jenny said. "That's what I'll do. Food and hard liquor."

"Perfect," Amelia said. "And I'm getting another of those crab quiches." She darted toward one of the food areas and gulped down half her martini, then set it on a tray. She felt as if she'd spent the evening drinking half or less of everything.

Taking some deep breaths, she indulged herself in one more crab quiche, still wondering where the chocolate was located. A waiter approached her carrying a tray of champagne and she shook her head. "Thank you, but I've really had enough for now."

He handed her a folded cocktail napkin instead. "A gentleman asked me to give this to you."

Intrigued, she opened the napkin and read a message written in a black masculine print. "Meet me outside on the back verandah, Magnolia. You still owe me a cocktail."

CHAPTER SEVENTEEN

SHE SHOULD IGNORE HIM. But she didn't. Amelia argued with herself for ninety seconds until she couldn't stand her internal debate.

Making her way to the verandah, she didn't see him until she walked away from the entrance. He looked isolated as he stood alone, leaning against a column and staring into the night.

She felt a twinge of something and tried to dismiss the feeling with debatable success. "I don't owe you a drink. You had two going on three and I had one."

He turned to look at her. "Nice to meet you again, Miss Amelia Parker," he said in a mocking voice. He shook his head. "Afraid to admit you even know me in front of your friends?"

A slice of guilt cut deep. "It's more about my job. You're obviously not going to be here forever and if it got around that you and I—" She broke off, searching for the right words.

"That you and I had a wild affair when you were down in the Keys and that you spilled information about your company—"

"Because I didn't know you were planning a takeover," she reminded him, frustrated.

"I never said I was planning a takeover."

"No, but that's what everyone is afraid of."

"Including you?"

She met his gaze. Her mind told her one thing while her gut told her another. "I don't know. I don't know how much of the real you I got to know in Florida."

He paused for a moment. "Fair enough. So why did you come out here? When you're ashamed of your association with me?"

Rolling her eyes at his added dig, she leaned against the railing. "I'm not ashamed of you."

"You didn't answer my first question," he said.

"I don't know," she said. "If I think about it too much, I'll probably have to go back inside."

He slid his arm around her back, drew her to him and kissed her firmly on the mouth.

Her breath stopped and her heart raced. "Why did you do that?"

"Aside from wanting to?"

She moved her head in a circle that she hoped resembled a nod.

"To distract you. Did it work?"

The way he looked at her made her bones feel as if they were melting. "Yes."

"Do you know how beautiful you look tonight?"

She smiled. "Yes, as a matter of fact, I do. I've been told by several men, most complete strangers. I've been given a slew of business cards. Want to see my collection?" she asked, opening her tiny purse.

He laughed and put his hand over her purse. "So I'm one of many."

She glanced away, finding it more difficult to joke. "Depends. Congratulations on the success of your contributions for Bellagio's donations to the auction. You got the crowd on their feet. Huge success. Now, tell me how you did it."

He waved his hand. "I told you back in the bar. Friends of friends. Someone I did a favor for."

"That's what you said about Ian. What did you do? Invest in a football team?"

"Once or twice," he said. "I have different kinds of investments. Clear winners, but every now and then I'll invest in a wild card. I've also been known to match up an investor with an investment that turns out well. In that case, the investor is grateful."

She smiled. "See, this is why I don't feel like I know you very well. You don't give specifics. You didn't give me one name."

He sighed. "If you really want to know me better, you're going to have to spend more time with me."

She looked at him, unable to deny that he fascinated her. He could be tough and cold, but she'd glimpsed a tender side. "Still waiting for an answer to my first question."

"Okay. I helped one of the Falcons coaches get involved in an investment deal that went well."

"How well?"

"I'll put it this way. The deal netted him a high six-figure return. He's very grateful." He picked up her hand and toyed with her fingers. "How's your Dad's gout?"

She shouldn't have been surprised that he'd remembered that little fact. "I haven't heard any complaints lately, so that's good."

"How much longer will you be able to dodge going home?"

"I don't know. My mother and sisters are starting to gang up on me. I love them and miss them, but I just haven't felt like facing their disappointment. It's crazy, but it's almost like a divorce. They had a relationship with Will, too, so they probably miss him."

"Do you?"

"Not so much anymore. Every once in a while when I need to make a decision, like what color towels to buy, I find myself reaching for what he would choose. So I have to stop and ask myself what color towels *I* want."

"And what color towels does Amelia like?"

"Depends on what mood I'm in and the bathroom décor. Sometimes I freeze a little when I need to make a decision. What do I want? What if I don't know what I want? What if I change my mind tomorrow about what I want? And the answer is, it's okay if I change my mind tomorrow. For today, I just need to choose what I want this moment."

He lowered his head close enough to kiss her. "And what do you want at this moment, Magnolia?"

Her throat tightened. "I thought we were talking about towels."

"That what you want? Towels?"

He was bad the same way chocolate was, the same way triple fudge ice cream was, the same way a hurricane was. Sometimes a girl just wanted some bad chocolate, bad ice cream and a bad mixed drink that could knock her on her backside.

Giving in to a bad urge, she lifted her hands to pull his mouth to hers and slipped her fingers through his hair. She slid her tongue over the seam of his lips until he opened his mouth and then she indulged herself in the male equivalent of a big chocolate brownie.

"Let's get out of here," he muttered against her mouth.

He felt so good, smelled so good. He slipped his hands around her back and pulled her flush against him.

"I'm not sure that's a good idea."

"Come out to my car with me," he coaxed and she felt a wicked thrill at the thought.

"I *know* that's not a good idea."

"Why? Are you afraid? Think of this as another first. I bet you've never done it in the car."

"Actually, I have," she said, pulling back slightly.

Jack looked at her in surprise. "Well, damn that Will."

She couldn't quite stifle her own laughter at his disconcerted tone.

"I bet I could do better."

She bet he could, too, but she wasn't going to say it. "I'm not messing up my dress and my hair for a romp in the backseat."

"Feeling prissy, are we?"

She was feeling hot and bothered, but she knew better than to go all the way down that road with him. "I should go back in."

He nodded. "Okay." He reached into his pocket for something. Then he leaned toward her, took her hand and pressed a key to her palm at the same time he kissed her. "I'll send you a text message with my address."

She pulled back, offended. "If you think I'm coming to your place for a booty call, you're insane."

"You're not giving me much choice. Since you won't be seen with me in public, I need to provide a private place. I want to see you. I want to be with you. That's about as honest as I can get, Magnolia. Can you be that honest?"

She opened her mouth, but she couldn't think of anything to say.

"How am I supposed to get your attention?"

His request was unbearably sexy, and at the same time it tugged at something deeper inside her. He was a complication she didn't need, but couldn't resist. "You're a creative guy. You'll think of something," she said and turned and walked away.

LILLIAN BELLAGIO ARRIVED at the office on Monday morning. Jack saw her stride down the hallway outside his pseudo-office toward the executive wing. He wondered what was on her mind. According to gossip, one could never be sure if Lillian's visits were social or business-related until she got around to announcing her intentions.

Ten minutes after she'd arrived, his phone rang and he was invited to Marc's office via Marc's assistant.

Jack rubbed his hand over his mouth, feeling a kick of humor. This should be interesting, if nothing else. He pulled on his suit coat and straightened his tie because he knew Lillian appreciated appearances, then he walked to Marc's office. Marc's assistant immediately paged her boss and opened the door to his spacious, luxuriously furnished corner office.

He entered the room and nodded toward Lillian first, then Marc. "Hello, Mrs. Bellagio. Marc."

"Good Morning, Mr. O'Connell," Lillian said. "I decided it would be nice to have tea with the two of you this morning. It should arrive in just a few—"

Another knock sounded at the door. "Oh, that's probably it already. Do you mind opening the door, Mr. O'Connell?"

Jack opened the door and two assistants carried in trays of sandwiches and scones and hot tea. Jack stole a glance at Marc and saw a long-suffering expression on his face. Marc looked at his watch and sighed.

Jack suspected this impromptu treat had blown the hell out of Marc's schedule. Jack decided to savor every minute. "Looks good," he said cheerfully and enjoyed the fleeting look of disbelief on Marc's face.

"Okay, choose your tea bag and I'll pour," Lillian said.

Jack had never had formal tea in his life, so he did what he'd done on several other occasions. He waited for Lillian to start and followed her actions. The tea was watery and tasteless, the sandwiches and scones drier than the Sahara, but he soldiered through.

"I've been hearing that you two boys aren't getting along," Lillian said. "Why is that?"

His expression pained, Marc visibly swallowed and took a drink of tea. He looked at Jack, then plastered an innocent expression on his face. "I can't imagine why anyone would say that Jack and I don't get along. We don't cross paths much since I have a full schedule every day and he doesn't have any real duties except to attend board meetings if he chooses."

"That's right," Jack said helpfully. "I've offered my expertise, but Marc hasn't taken me up on it. He did set me up in an office on the other side of the building. I could show you—"

Marc cleared his throat and threw Jack a glance of censure. "Everything's fine."

Lillian wrinkled her brow in confusion. "But I heard Jack almost didn't get tickets to the Children's Auction."

"A little mix-up. My assistant forgot to give Jack his tickets," Marc said, leaning back in his seat.

"Jack, I heard about your last-minute donation of the season tickets. Very generous of you," Lillian said, then glanced at Marc. "Don't you agree?"

Marc nodded, but Jack could tell it nearly killed

him. "Very generous. So you see, there are no problems between Jack and—"

"The only thing I can imagine as being a problem is that I don't think Marc likes my idea of introducing a less expensive line of shoes to gain a larger market share," Jack said, not about to pass up this opportunity.

"Really?" Lillian said. "Why is that, Marc?"

Marc cleared his throat. "Bellagio has always been sold as a luxury brand for the discriminating buyer. We don't want to taint the image we've worked so hard to foster."

Lillian frowned. "I see that, but couldn't we call it something else? Market it differently. The way we're marketing the activewear line."

Marc sighed. "I suppose, but Alfredo's never been fond of this idea, either."

"But have you ever studied the numbers?" Jack asked. "Or have you always killed the discussion at the idea stage without research?"

"Our decisions are almost always backed up by research, aren't they, Marc?" Lillian asked.

He nodded slowly.

"I don't recall the board discussing this. Perhaps we should put it on the agenda."

"But Alfredo—"

"I know," Lillian said. "It's sad, but Alfredo may need surgery. We're hoping that he won't, but I'm afraid it doesn't look good. In that case, all of us need to continue to make sure Bellagio stays on course. We should give Jack's idea consideration." She brightened. "Now, wasn't this a wonderful idea? A little tea goes a long way."

"I couldn't agree more," Jack said, taking another sip of the tasteless, lukewarm brew.

Lillian made small talk for a few more minutes and Jack noticed Marc surreptitiously checking his watch.

"I've enjoyed our visit," Lillian said. "We should do this again sometime. In the meantime, I think you two boys should set up a luncheon date."

Marc looked at her with a blank expression. "Luncheon date," he echoed.

"Yes," Lillian said in a brisk, positive tone as she rose.

Jack and Marc immediately rose to their feet. Jack decided to take pity on his nemesis before Lillian recommended a place where they could have tea again.

"Maybe you know a place where we can grab a quick burger," Jack said to Marc.

"Yeah, good idea. Lillian, it was good to see you, as always," Marc said, ushering her to the door.

"And my pleasure to see you, Mrs. Bellagio," Jack added.

"Thank you." She looked at both of them with a

nod of approval. "You know, you're both handsome, intelligent men. A credit to Bellagio."

"Thank you," Jack said quietly.

"Thank you," Marc quickly added, looking confused. "Shall I walk you downstairs?"

"Oh, no, I'm fine. I'll be back," she said and walked out the door.

With a fierce expression on his face, Marc closed the door behind her and turned toward Jack. "She likes you. What do you have on her?"

Jack shook his head. "Have on her?"

"She likes you and you're not a Bellagio. You must have something on her. Are you blackmailing her?"

"No," Jack said. "Lillian Bellagio is perfect. What kind of dirt could I possibly have on her?"

Marc narrowed his eyes. "No one is perfect. No one is completely clean. You must have something. She must be afraid of you."

"With all due respect, Marc, you're psycho." Jack headed toward the door and grabbed the doorknob. "Have a nice day."

"Wait a minute," Marc said.

Jack turned slowly.

"I don't trust you one millimeter. I still think there's something not right about you. Not right about how Lillian treats you. She usually turns up her nose at outsiders. I don't trust you," he repeated.

"But I'll have lunch with you. Italian or sports grille?"

"Sports grille," Jack decided.

"Thursday at one o'clock okay?"

"Yeah," Jack said.

"Okay. I'll send you an e-mail confirmation."

"I'll look forward to it," Jack said.

"No need," Marc returned. "I just want to be prepared for whatever you present in a board meeting regarding a street line of Bellagio shoes."

Jack stifled a sigh. "And a nice day to you, too, Marc," he said and headed back to his pseudo-office.

CHAPTER EIGHTEEN

JACK DOUBLE-CHECKED the address Amelia had given him in her voice message. Yep, the street address matched the old, worn three-story community center.

Shaking his head as he parked his car on the street, he wondered if the tires would still be attached to his vehicle after he went inside the building. This wasn't Atlanta's nicest neighborhood.

She'd instructed him to dress casually to join her as she crossed something off her list, and to come *only if you dare*. The message had sounded sexy and too inviting to miss.

That sweet southern girl had tricked him. Smelling a do-gooder activity, he went against his usual instincts and decided to join her anyway.

Walking inside, he heard the sound of voices coming from a gym on the right. He entered the gym and saw a few adults and a large group of elementary school-age children.

Spotting him, Amelia waved and moved toward him. "I'm glad you could make it," she said.

"When you said it involved your list, I imagined something else," he said.

"That's because you added the word *naked* to everything on my list. I've added a few things of my own since you saw it."

"You should let me see the updated version," he told her. "So I can help you with your progress."

"That's what you're doing tonight," she said.

"We'll see," he said. "I'm undecided. Looks like you have more boys than girls."

"They're desperate for male volunteers," she said.

"And you thought you could sucker me into volunteering."

"I wouldn't say sucker. I issued an invitation, hoping to appeal to your better nature."

"And that's why you mentioned your list," he said, not believing a word.

She moved her head in a noncommittal circle, her expression slightly guilty. "Well, it's not as if it will hurt you."

"Can't guarantee the same about my car," he muttered. "Let's negotiate. You let me come over to your place and fix breakfast on Saturday and I'll stay."

She shot him a suspicious look. "Breakfast?

How early? Does breakfast include a sleepover the night before?"

"What a dirty mind you have," he scolded, although he wouldn't have turned down the sleepover invite. "It's just breakfast, and I'm fixing."

She blinked. "No male has ever fixed breakfast for me. Unless you count the Cheerios my dad poured in a bowl when my mother was in the hospital after giving birth to my two younger sisters."

"There you go. Another first."

Her lips played with a surprised smile. "Can you really cook?"

"I'm great with breakfast and get by with everything else. Deal?"

She paused a moment, considering, then nodded. "Yes."

"What's the game plan?"

She brightened. "Vigorous physical activity for the first thirty minutes. Arts and crafts the second thirty minutes."

"You really think you're going to get those guys interested in arts and crafts?"

"No. So we need someone to keep wearing them out during the second half."

"That's me."

She smiled and impulsively hugged him. "Thank you. It really means a lot."

He inhaled her scent and felt a twist of something inside him. He'd felt it that night she'd come to Ian's house and slept with him. It had bothered him so much he'd left town the next day. But Amelia had haunted him, and that twist in his gut had never gone away.

That was why he was willing to run the little animals congregating in the gym ragged. In the hour that followed, Jack broke up four fights, confiscated three pocket knives and gave a lesson on chivalry to a little boy who thought it was okay to trip a little girl. He gave pointers on shooting baskets and promised gum as a prize to the kids who exhibited the best sportsmanship. When three of the kids' parents didn't show for pick-up, he took them home. His car had been left intact, after all.

Returning to the community center, he slumped in a chair next to Amelia and leaned back against the wall. "How bright is my sucker light flashing?"

"It's not. You should feel good about what you did. Those boys loved you."

"It's a good thing I work out at the gym every now and then."

She snickered. "Yeah." The lights flickered. "Oops. They're closing up. Time to go."

He walked her to her car and she looked up at him just before she turned to get inside. "Thanks," she said. "You could have turned around and left."

"Breakfast on Saturday," he reminded her.

She nodded, hesitated, then rose on her tiptoes and kissed his cheek. "G'night, Jack."

His hands itched to hold her, but he balled his fists instead. Soon, he would have her again. Soon.

DYING OF CURIOSITY about Jack's true culinary abilities, Amelia opened the door to him as he carried two bags of groceries.

"Good morning, Sunshine."

Her stomach took a little dip as she looked into his killer blue eyes a little too long to maintain her equilibrium. "Good morning to you," she said. "The kitchen is this way. Those bags look pretty full. How many are you cooking for?"

"Just you and me," he said and pulled out a carton of eggs, grated cheese, ham, tomatoes, an onion, fruit, buttermilk…

"Can I help?"

He shook his head. "Just relax and watch."

Although it went against her nature, she sat down and did just that. Watching Jack wasn't difficult. He looked good in jeans, just as he'd looked good in a tux, suit and Tommy Bahama shirt. And naked. He'd looked great naked, she thought as she recalled that night in the pool. Fabulous chest, wonderful pecs…

He gave a loud whistle. "Amelia, hello? I've asked you the same question twice already."

She blinked and told herself not to blush. He didn't know what she was thinking. "I'm sorry. I was distracted. What did you ask?"

"Are you allergic to any foods?"

She shook her head, watching him sauté vegetables in one pan while he fried potatoes and onions in another. He mixed pancake batter and took the lid off a bottle of pure maple syrup and placed it in the microwave. Her kitchen should have looked like a disaster area, but he rinsed and cleaned utensils with each step.

"I'm stunned," she said. "When did you learn this? Did you work in a breakfast place?"

"One of my jobs when I was a teenager, but I learned before that," he said as he poured pancake batter mixed with blueberries onto a hot griddle. "Way back in the day, my uncle taught me what he called the fine art of making breakfast. He said it was a survival skill and later on, chicks would love it."

She smiled. "Your uncle sounds like a character."

"Yep," Jack said.

"Why don't you see him more often?"

"I think I remind him of his sister and that he couldn't save her. When I was growing up and she was alive, he always had a little hope, but now she's gone."

His explanation bothered her. It made her stomach and chest tighten. "Are you sure—"

"Don't try to fix it, Amelia," he said before she could finish. "I like that about you, the way you try to fix things, but this isn't something you can do anything about. Omelet time," he said and broke some eggs. He lifted a well-used spatula. "My secret weapon," he said. "This is the perfect tool for flipping."

Within minutes he served her more breakfast than she would normally eat in a month. She shook her head at the plate crammed full with a three-egg omelet, breakfast potatoes, too many blueberry pancakes and fruit. "I'm amazed. The only thing missing is grits."

He looked at her with a wary expression on his face. "Grits? You don't really eat those, do you?"

She laughed. "I'll have to fix them for you sometime."

"Not necessary."

"Oh, have I finally found a first for you? A never-been-done? I'll *definitely* fix grits for you."

"No, thank you," he said. "Really."

"Hmm. I dare you."

His forkful of pancakes stopped mid-lift as he shot her a dark look. "Don't do that," he said. "Don't dare me."

"You do it all the time with me."

"I don't dare you about grits."

"I double-dare you."

"Okay," he said, defeated. "I'll eat grits. Let's not ruin the meal with this discussion anymore."

Just as Amelia was stuffing in one last bite of blueberry pancake, her doorbell rang. She glanced at her clock. "Who could that—"

The doorbell rang again and she looked at Jack and shrugged. "Excuse me. I'll be back in a minute." She went to her front door and looked through the peephole.

"Oh, God." She just wasn't quite ready for this. Maybe in another week. Or two. She slowly opened the door.

"Surprise!" her mother and youngest sister Gwendolyn called.

Her mother's eyes were bright with determination. Her sister's face was full of dread. Something was up.

"The mountain wouldn't come to Mohammed, so Mohammed came to the mountain," her mother said in a cheery voice and immediately pulled Amelia against her warm, chubby form. "I've missed my little chick. Do you realize it's been over three months since you've been home?"

Her mother pulled back and scrutinized her from head to toe. "You're thinner," she said with a frown. "But I smell maple syrup, so that's good."

Gwennie stepped forward and gave her a hug. "We've all missed you terribly."

"And we haven't stopped worrying about you," her mother said. "Especially since—" She broke off and put her hand to her chest. "Well, we won't discuss it right now. Gwennie and I want to see your new place."

Amelia felt as if she were watching the beginning of a train wreck. "Um, Momma, it's good to see you, too, but—"

"This seems like a good neighborhood. The man at the gate almost wouldn't let us pass until I told him we wanted to surprise you. Then, I'm sorry sweetheart, but I had to give him one of your pies. I left the others in the car. We'll get them in a few minutes."

Amelia felt a stab of alarm. She knew that her mother baked pies when she was upset. "Is something wrong with Daddy?"

"No. He needs to lose some weight, but he says I don't help with my cooking."

"What about Rose and Valene?"

"They're fine."

"And the kids?"

"Growing like weeds, but you wouldn't know that because you haven't been around."

Amelia dodged the guilt. "I know they're growing. I sent gifts for their birthdays."

"Which was very nice, but not the same as you being there. Now, show us the rest of your little place here."

Amelia thought of Jack in her kitchen. There was no way she could hide him, no way she could dodge the questions she would be asked. Might as well get it over with. "I have a guest. He's in the kitchen."

"A guest?" her mother echoed, her eyebrows flying upward.

"He?" Gwennie repeated.

Stifling a groan, Amelia led the way to the kitchen, where Jack stood at the sink washing a frying pan.

"Jack, my mother and sister decided to surprise me with a visit. Shelley and Gwennie Parker, this is Jack O'Connell."

"He does dishes," Gwennie said in amazement.

Jack set down the frying pan and dried his hands. "Pleasure to meet you," he said, moving toward them and extending his hand. If he felt awkward about meeting Amelia's family, he masked it well. "Mrs. Parker, Gwennie, I've heard so much about you."

"You have?" her mother asked, shaking Jack's hand and casting an inquisitive look at Amelia. "We haven't heard a thing about you."

Jack smiled wryly. "Amelia's always talking about her family. You can tell she cares a great deal for you all."

"Well, that's true," her mother said. "She does. I'm…sorry we interrupted."

"No problem. We'd just finished the breakfast I fixed."

Her mother and Gwennie gaped at him, then Gwennie looked at Amelia. "He cooks, too?"

"Breakfast," Amelia rushed to say, then saw her mother's gaze turn suspicious. "And probably Chicago-style hot dogs, since he's from Chicago."

"Oh," Gwennie said.

Her mother cleared her throat. "Are you visiting Atlanta, Jack?"

"No. I live here," Jack said. "At least temporarily."

"Uh-huh," her mother said. "Do you live close by?"

Amelia knew where her mother's questions were headed and decided to save both her mother and Jack the long, awkward trip. "Jack came over this morning and fixed breakfast. He didn't stay here overnight, Momma."

Her mother pushed a strand of her brown bob behind her ear and nodded. "Of course he didn't. Listen, why don't you and Gwennie go get our stuff out of the car? I'll help Jack with the dishes."

"I'm okay," he said.

"Nonsense. I can help you clean up in no time. Run along, girls."

Amelia really didn't want to leave her mother

alone with Jack. She cringed at the questions she knew her mother would ask, but Gwennie tugged at her arm.

"C'mon, Me-Me," Gwennie said, and Amelia allowed herself to be led to her mother's '85 El Dorado Cadillac. "Momma made three pies for you. We gave the apple one away, but you can still have the chocolate chip and cherry pie. We got some of your favorite bath gel and uh, I got you a bear," she said, holding up a collectible bear clad in a frilly dress and holding a parasol.

Amelia's heart squeezed tight in her chest and she gave her youngest sister a hug. "Oh, she's darling. You shouldn't have. You're so sweet."

"We've really been worried about you," Gwennie continued, pushing her straight, shoulder-length blond hair behind her ear nervously. "I've wanted to talk to you, but it seems like every time you call, I haven't been there."

Amelia watched her youngest sister bite her lip and knew something was off-kilter. "Sweetie, you seem so nervous. What's wrong?"

Gwennie sobbed and covered her face. "I'm just so sorry. I know it's terrible timing." Gwennie sobbed again.

Alarm shot through Amelia and she pulled her sister against her. "Gwennie, what is it?"

"I'm getting married," Gwennie wailed.

Amelia was confused. "To Robert?"

Gwennie nodded.

"Do you love him? Do you want to marry him?"

"Yes," she said in an uneven voice.

"Then you should be happy. Why are you crying, sweetie?"

"Because you should be getting married to Will."

"Oh," Amelia said, finally understanding her sister. Gwennie clearly felt guilty that she was getting married instead of Amelia. "Listen, Gwennie, Will and I shouldn't get married. I don't *want* to get married." To her relief, she realized she spoke the truth.

Gwennie looked at her in surprise. "You don't?"

"I would have to be nuts to want to marry someone who doesn't want to marry me, Gwennie."

"But what if he did want to marry you?"

"He doesn't," Amelia said firmly, propping the bear under her arm and carrying one of the pies. She nudged the car door closed with her hip. "So there's no need to discuss it or even think about it. This is part of the reason I put off coming home."

Carrying the bath gel and other pie, Gwennie walked with her to the condo. "Why?"

"Because it was hard enough for me to move past my relationship with Will without having to help the rest of you get over it, too."

Gwennie stared at her. "Well, that's a different way of looking at it."

Amelia put her hand on the doorknob.

"There's something else I need to tell you," Gwennie said, nervousness creeping back into her voice.

Amelia turned toward her youngest sister. "What's that?"

"The wedding is next month."

"Wow." Amelia paused. "Are you pregnant?"

"No. I just didn't want to tell you I was getting married when you were a mess over Will."

Amelia nodded. "Okay, I can understand it. But I'd like to know the date so I can put it on my calendar, if that's okay with you."

"Sure," Gwennie said with a smile. "I was kinda hoping you would be my maid of honor. You're the reason I finished college before getting married."

"What a nice thing to say," Amelia said, touched that she'd had such a positive influence on her little sister.

Gwennie's smile faded. "There's just one other thing."

"Is this the last thing?" Amelia asked wryly.

"Robert insisted that we ask Will to the wedding. They're good friends and—"

Amelia shook her head. "It's no problem. You

should feel free to invite whoever you want to your wedding."

"Are you sure?" Gwennie asked uncertainly.

"I'm sure. I'm also sure I need to get cracking on plans for a wedding shower and bridesmaid party."

"I don't want anything wild," Gwennie said.

"Of course not," Amelia said, but in light of her recent experiences, she felt compelled to make sure Gwennie had at least a few wild single-girl memories. But that was for later. Right now, the only thing she felt compelled to do was rescue Jack from her mother.

She headed for the kitchen and found the two seated cozily at the table. Jack met her gaze and smiled.

"I told her," Gwennie said.

"How'd she take it?" her mother asked.

"Great. We probably could have told her before." Her mother sighed in relief. "Thank the Lord."

"The pies were a dead giveaway," Amelia said. "You always bake pies when you're upset or worried."

Her mother smiled. "You do the same thing. How many did you bake when you and Will broke up?"

"Too many," Amelia said, sneaking another glance at Jack. "But that's in the past. Do I need to go shopping for a bridesmaid dress?"

"We already ordered it," her mother said.

"It sounds like it's going to be the wedding of the season in your town," Jack said. "I can't wait to see it."

She met his gaze again. He looked amused and slightly smug. "Pardon?"

"Your mother invited me. I believe this will be the first southern wedding I've ever attended."

"Then you're way overdue," her mother said, looking from Jack to Amelia to Jack again.

Amelia felt a sharp twist of desperation. Was her mother *matchmaking?* Heaven forbid. "Momma, I can't believe Jack would be interested in attending the wedding of people he's never met."

"But I have met them, Me-Me," he said, using the nickname that only her family called her. "Through all the stories you told me. Remember when I gave you a ride to the post office so you could mail a package to your three-year-old nephew Ricky? You sent him books."

"She's always sending books," her mother said. "She's good about that."

"And your father's gout and his golf game. His biggest wish is to attend the Master's Golf Tournament in Augusta, right?"

Her mother nodded. "A dream come true."

"You've told me over and over how proud you are of Gwennie for finishing college before she got married. You made her believe it was possible."

"That's right, and if Will hadn't broken your engagement, then—" Gwennie stopped, biting her lip.

"Then I wouldn't have gotten to meet her, and that would have been a damn shame," Jack said.

"Aww," Gwennie said in a soft voice.

Amelia glared at Jack. She knew what he was doing. He was seducing her mother and sister. "You have an amazing memory," Amelia said. It came out as an accusation.

"Well, you impressed me from the first time I met you."

Yeah, right. Because you encouraged me to blab everything I know about Bellagio. If that wasn't bad enough, I kissed you like there was no tomorrow.

Jack rose. "I should leave so you can enjoy your visit with your sister and mother. Pleasure meeting both of you."

"It was our pleasure," Amelia's mother said, rising to her feet and giving Jack a hug.

Gwennie murmured her agreement.

"I look forward to seeing you ladies at the wedding, if not before." He slid his hand down Amelia's arm. "Call me later, sweetheart."

Sweetheart. Amelia felt the situation spiraling out of control. "Let me see you to the door."

She walked outside with him and closed the door behind her. "Have you lost your mind? *Sweetheart?* You don't know the meaning of pressure until you've met my mother trying to marry off her daughters."

"Oh, she's a lovely lady. You're exaggerating."

"You have no idea what you've gotten yourself into. What you've gotten *me* into," Amelia told him. "She will hound the living daylights out of me every time I talk to her to ask how my relationship is progressing. My mother is from the old school and she won't feel that her job is complete until I'm married." She sighed. "Why did you do this?"

"I didn't do anything. She invited me. Should I have turned her down?"

"Yes," Amelia said.

"You haven't helped the situation," he told her.

She looked at him in confusion. "What on earth do you mean?"

"I've had to bribe you to spend more than five minutes with me since you came back to Atlanta."

"That's because you tricked me. The same way you're tricking my mother and sister with your flattery and pretend interest."

"I'm not pretending interest. Your family sound like nice people."

"They are, but you're really not interested in them. The same way you weren't really interested in me down in Florida. And that's okay. I accepted that."

"Wrong," he said with a wry expression. "Wrong that I wasn't really interested in you. Wrong that I'm not really interested in your family. And wrong that you accepted that I wasn't really interested in you. How many pies did you bake after I left?"

"Only three," she said.

"Amelia," he said patiently. "I'm coming with you to the wedding. Will is coming, too. I can take some of the heat off of you."

She opened her mouth and stopped, because what he said was true. She hated the idea of everyone pitying her because Will had dumped her. "Is that why you accepted my mother's invitation? To make it easier for me?"

"That would suggest that I'm not a selfish bastard who's only after one thing. You in my bed."

"Right. So that would be really silly to even consider," she said, but she wasn't so sure.

He dipped his head and slid his mouth over hers. "You still taste like maple syrup. I wonder how you would taste with maple syrup on some other parts of you."

She felt a rush of adrenaline at his wicked suggestion. "I would taste sticky."

"Yeah. It would probably take a long time to lick off that syrup," he said and grinned. "I'm up for it. Are you?"

She felt her cheeks heat and pushed away from him. "I need to go see my mother. Thank you for breakfast."

"You're welcome. Call me."

"Have a nice day," she said, determined to remain noncommittal, and returned to the kitchen where her mother and Gwennie sat.

"He's a hottie," Gwennie said.

Her mother nodded. "He's very nice, for a Yankee."

As full as she still was from breakfast, Amelia decided that now might be a very good time to dig into one of her mother's pies.

CHAPTER NINETEEN

"I DON'T HAVE MUCH TIME," Marc said as the waiter delivered their burgers for lunch. "I've already told you that I don't think an economy line is the best way to go for Bellagio. Why are you so insistent?"

"Thanks," Jack said to the waiter, then looked at Marc. "Because it could be good for Bellagio. Have you looked at the numbers?"

"Have you examined the adverse effect on the couture line?"

He swallowed his first bite of the burger. "This is good. Hits the spot."

"Not as good as The Vortex, but it's pretty good," Marc agreed. "But—" His cell phone rang and he picked up. "Hey, sweetheart, I'm in a business lunch. What can I do for you?" He paused and smiled. "Thanks. This is the best call I've received all day. I love you, too. I'll stop in and see you after lunch. Okay?" He closed his phone and glanced at Jack, his smile falling. "About your idea," he said.

"You can't ignore the financial boost a bigger share of the market would give Bellagio. You could call it something else, put it under a different umbrella. Hell, put it under a different name. You don't even need to call it Bellagio. Just give it some half-decent quality and a hip design and you'll take the company to the next level."

Marc frowned. "Alfredo will never go for it. The old guard is big on offering the highest quality."

"Bellagio can still offer high quality. We'd just simplify the designs. Even Jenny agreed with me."

"Don't bring Jenny into this," Marc warned.

"Why not?" Jack demanded. "She's a Bellagio employee. Intelligent, creative. Why shouldn't her opinions count?"

"She's my wife," Marc said. "Don't go there. Alfredo will never go for this." His cell phone rang again. "Excuse me," he muttered. "Marc Waterson." He sighed. "Not again. You tell his people that we have a contract and he has agreed to make public appearances. We'll sue if he doesn't fulfill his end of the agreement. I'll talk to you later." He put the phone down again. "That was my assistant. We're having problems with one of our sports celebrity endorsements."

"Have you already done all the ads?"

"No. Why?" Marc took a bite of his burger.

"Professional sports players aren't always the most dependable guys."

"Tell me about it."

"It'll be little more expensive, but you might want to feature more than one guy so if he flunks out, you're still covered."

"I'll think about it," Marc said grudgingly.

His cell phone rang again and he swore. "Can't get down half of my burger." He flipped it open. "Marc Waterson." He pursed his lips. "Okay." He closed the phone. "Alfredo's going into bypass surgery. They're asking for donations. He has a rare blood type."

"What is it?" Jack asked.

Marc looked at him. "Doesn't matter to you. You're not a Bellagio. You can't help."

"Just satisfy my curiosity."

"AB negative."

Jack nodded, but said nothing.

"That's not your blood type," Marc said. "Is it?"

"Crazy coincidence," Jack said, but he knew better. "I'll head off to the hospital after I finish eating."

"Yeah," Marc said. "I don't trust you."

"You're paranoid," Jack said. "That's not a totally bad quality for someone in your position. Just don't let it get in the way of making the best decision for the company."

"Who the hell are you to give me advice?" Marc demanded.

"I'm a board member," Jack said smoothly. "And your company owes me money."

AFTER HIS LONG, CRAPPY DAY, Jack pulled his curtains and sat in his dark den with a beer and surfed his wide-screen TV in search of a ball game featuring a team from anywhere but Atlanta.

His cell phone rang. Amelia's number flashed in the caller ID, surprising him. "You left your pancake-flipper spatula here. Do you want to come and get it?"

"Now? Aren't your mom and sister there?"

"No, they went home once they realized I wasn't dying of heartbreak. They still have a lot of details to plan for Gwennie's wedding. Is this an inconvenient time?"

"What did you have in mind?" Jack asked. "Were you going to leave it on your porch in a bag or beat me over the head with it? Gotta tell you, I'm not in the mood to get in line for anymore abuse today."

Silence followed. "Tough day?"

"You could say."

"You want to come over for a little while?"

She sounded almost compassionate. "Yeah."

"Bring your beer because I don't have any. All I've got are little bottles of sissy wine."

He smiled at her description. "Okay."

"But I have two homemade pies and I'll share."

"Ah, so you're inviting me to help you get rid of the pies," Jack said.

"Something like that."

"Too much pie and I'll turn into a fat boy."

"I don't think there's any danger of that. Not with your body," she muttered.

"What do you mean by that?"

"You don't need me to tell you that you have a hot body."

"There's need and there's want, but sometimes the line between the two gets smudged. I'll be right over, Me-Me."

AMELIA PICKED UP JACK'S special pancake-flipper and swatted it through the air. She probably should have just put it in a bag and left it in his office. Her mother would say she should return it to his home with a pie as a thank-you for the breakfast he'd made for her.

The personnel administrator had told Amelia something today that bothered her. Amelia swatted the pancake-flipper through the air again and frowned. She had some questions for Jack and she wanted to see his face when she asked them. The shark could be darn tricky to read.

She poured herself a glass of pink wine and sat down in the den while she tried to concentrate on reviewing the training class she was putting together for support staff. Impatient, unable to concentrate, she kept glancing at the clock. When the doorbell finally rang, she felt ready to burst.

Instead she forced herself to calmly walk to the door and open it. Jack stood there, carrying a carton of beer, his hair mussed, his eyes a little more dangerous than usual. He looked too good in his jeans and the black T-shirt that emphasized his muscles.

Her heart rate picked up. "Hi."

"Hey. I brought the beer. Show me to the pie."

Amelia turned around and headed for the kitchen. "On second thought, I'm not sure pie really goes with beer."

"Everything goes with beer," he said.

Her lips twitched. "Spoken like a guy."

"And what would a girl say, Me-Me?" he asked.

She felt a little kink of irritation as she pulled down a couple of dessert plates from the cabinet. "Only my family calls me Me-Me."

"Did Will call you Me-Me?" he asked.

She stopped to think. "No. Never."

"There are so many names I could call you. Amelia. Magnolia. What about Jezebel?"

She felt her cheeks heat. "Jezebel met her demise

when she was eaten by a shark. Which do you want? Chocolate chip or cherry?"

"Both."

"Big appetite," she murmured and cut and served the slices.

"Just trying to keep up with Jezebel," he said.

"If you were a gentleman—"

"Which we've established I'm not," he interjected.

"If you pretended to be a gentleman, you could just forget Jezebel."

"Not in a million years," he said and stuck his fork in the cherry pie. "But I like the idea of adding more names, so how would you like to be addressed?"

She met his gaze dead-on. "'Your highness' would be a nice change."

He laughed and she felt a zingy crackle between them. "Your highness, you never answered my earlier question. If a guy says everything goes with beer, what does a girl say?"

"That's easy. Chocolate goes with everything."

"I'll remember that."

She nodded and served herself a small piece of chocolate-chip pie. "We can eat in the den. There's something I want to ask you."

"Okay." He set his carton of bottled beer on the counter, opened one of them and followed her to the den. He sat next to her on the sofa. "What's up?"

His intensity made her nervous. She set her dessert plate on the end table. "I was wondering if you had anything to do with my job."

He took a long draw from his beer. "What do you mean?"

"I mean did you use your influence to get me the job I have now?"

He moved his head in a motion that was neither up and down nor side to side. "First, you're assuming I have influence. Everyone knows Marc Waterson doesn't trust me and is suspicious of everything that comes out of my mouth."

"You're hedging. Can you say that you had no influence on the creation of my job and the offer made to me?"

Sighing, he leaned back and took another long draw of beer. "I may have mentioned the idea to the personnel director in a way that made her think she had come up with it herself. And some people may have come up with your name when she asked who would be a good candidate for this kind of position. It so happened that some of those people were noisy in their support of you."

She didn't know whether to slap him or— "You engineered the whole thing."

"That's a gross exaggeration."

"They wouldn't have offered me that job if you hadn't finagled it," she said.

"Finagle," he said with a grin. "I haven't heard that word in a while, Magnolia. If they were smart, they would have formed that position and given it to you a long time ago. People who worked with you were fighting to keep you in their department. You don't want to let that kind of employee get away." He set down his beer and moved closer to her, capturing her hand in his. "Everyone wanted you. They just needed to figure out the best position for you. If you hadn't been so good at what you did, it wouldn't have happened."

"Are you sure?"

"I'm sure."

"And *I'm* sure you would also say that you weren't being nice by facilitating this career move for me," she said. "You would just say you were doing it for the company, protecting your investment."

"Right," he said.

"And there were no personal motives," she said.

"None except I wanted you in Atlanta."

"Did you really think I would fall back into bed with you?"

He looked away, giving a short humorless laugh. "I just wanted to see you again, Magnolia. I missed you," he said, returning his gaze to her and stopping her heart.

"Then why didn't you visit me in the Keys?"

"I was your transitional guy down there. I wanted us to meet again in a different place."

The expression on his face freaked her out. "You're not saying you would want a real relationship with me, are you?"

"And if I were?" he asked, studying her.

Panic shot through her. "I'm not ready for anything serious or permanent, Jack. I'm better than I was, but I'm just not ready for—"

"Slow down, Magnolia. I brought over a six-pack, not a diamond ring."

Taking a shallow breath because she couldn't manage a deeper one, she nodded. "Good, because I did some reading about breakups and one of the columns I read said you should wait one week for every month you were involved before you get into another relationship. If I follow that to the letter, then I think I'll be retirement age before I can really get involved again. I don't think I'm going to wait that long, but—"

He pressed his finger over her mouth. "I just want to be with you. Is that okay?"

Her throat tightened with a knot of emotion she would have to examine later. She couldn't remember when she had felt so safe and so free at the same time. "Yeah," she whispered.

"Good," he said and nodded toward her half-glass on the end table. "You need some more girly wine?"

She smiled. "Yes, thank you. Bottom of the refrigerator."

She watched him get her wine, admiring the graceful but masculine way he moved his body. He returned with her wine and she noticed the bandage on his arm.

"What's that from?" she asked.

"Oh, I donated blood today. Alfredo Bellagio's scheduled for surgery tomorrow. He has a rare type of blood. Turns out I have the same type."

"Really?"

"Yeah. Apparently the doctors think the stents aren't doing the job, so they're going ahead with the bypass. Poor guy."

"And you have the same blood type?"

"Yeah. You should have seen Marc's response when I mentioned it at lunch. He looked at me like this was some part of my big conspiracy plot." He lifted his hands. "I'm not responsible for choosing my blood type."

She laughed and took a long sip of wine. "I guess you're not."

He tugged her closer to him.

"What are you doing?" she asked, feeling light-headed again.

"I need to make it clear that I'm not having sex with you tonight."

She blinked. "You're not?"

"No. So don't try begging me or seducing me. I'm not having sex with you."

She couldn't stop a smile. "Okay."

"But I'm going to kiss you," he said, lowering his head.

Her heart bumped and stuttered. "You are?"

"Uh-huh." He pressed his mouth against hers and nibbled at her lips with his. "I'm gonna kiss you until you wish I would tear off your clothes and take you."

And he did.

AMELIA PICKED UP her cell phone when it rang the following day, but she didn't recognize the number on the caller ID. "Amelia Parker."

"Anna Jones here, aka Brooke Tarantino, your partner in crime. I'm in town. Your idea to take a trip with Lillian worked. We went to California. She visited her son. I shopped. I've met Ian three times on the road. Omaha, Detroit and Boston. Have lunch with me today," Brooke demanded.

Amelia had to smile. Brooke was clearly her usual breathless self. "It's already twelve-thirty. When did you want to get together?"

"Oh, two-ish. Or three. Maybe we could stretch it out with a few martinis." Brooke giggled. "I have some stories for you."

Amelia shook her head. "I'm sure you do, but Brooke, there's this little matter of my job. I'm working today."

Brooke sighed. "How annoying. Then let's meet for dinner, but make it early. The second you get off work. Four?"

"Five," Amelia corrected. "I'm delighted to see you, but what's the rush?"

"I've actually been out of Lillian's incarceration a couple of weeks now and part of the deal was that I had to start doing something like finding a job or working for a charity. I was hoping you could help me figure something out."

"Okay," Amelia said slowly, wishing Brooke had exhibited just a sliver of interest in finding something herself. "Let me think about it and make some calls."

"Thanks," Brooke said. "Can you tell me what you find out at dinner? My dad's starting to push."

"I'll do what I can."

"Great," Brooke said. "Dinner's on me. I'll call you when I decide where we should go. Ciao."

Amelia hung up the phone and clicked on the website for local charities. She remembered her own time at the community center. She personally felt that Brooke could benefit a great deal from spending some time with people who hadn't been given a fraction of the advantages she'd received growing up.

She heard a tap at her door. "Yes?"

Jack poked his head inside. "Hi," he said and walked into her office and closed the door behind him. "Don't worry. Your reputation is still safe. No one saw me come in."

Her heart gave a little jump. "You didn't ask permission to enter," she said, even though she was way too happy to see him.

"You gave permission after I knocked. You said yes. I've been thinking about it, and I think you should have an entire day when you say yes and not no. And you should spend that day with me."

She laughed. "The things you think of. *I* think you have a little too much time on your hands."

"You can help with that," he said, leaning over her desk and allowing his gaze to linger on her mouth so long her lips burned and she felt as if she'd been kissed. "Think of me as a delinquent. Make your contribution to society by keeping me off the streets tonight."

"Very tempting," she said. "But I'm already booked. Brooke Tarantino called. She's out of jail and needs to get a job or volunteer and she wants my help."

He gave a low whistle. "Hey, why don't you do something easier? Like climb Mount Everest."

"Thank you for the encouragement," she said dryly.

"You really think she can work?" he asked. "At an actual job?"

Amelia winced. "I think she could, but she's not motivated to operate on anyone's schedule but her own. Or Ian—Snake's."

"They're still seeing each other?"

"Apparently. She's met him on tour several times. She sounded giddy."

"Did she ever tell him who she really is?"

"I have this feeling that she hasn't gotten around to it."

"Ian's not going to like it when he finds out. He likes to surround himself with people he thinks will be real with him."

"He doesn't like to be tricked," Amelia said, identifying with the singer. Every once in a while it still pinched that Jack hadn't told her the truth about himself and his motives.

"You always knew my name," Jack said, clearly reading her feelings.

She pushed her thoughts aside. "I can encourage her to tell him the truth, but Brooke's going to do what Brooke's going to do." She glanced at the computer screen and clicked the command to print.

"I found a volunteer interest questionnaire I can give her, and I'm going to get a few contact names and e-mail addresses."

"Problem-solving again," he said.

She glanced up at him. "What do you mean?"

"Someone gives you a problem and you feel compelled to solve it. You did the same thing in the Keys. Were you always that way?"

Amelia paused and thought for a moment. "Mostly," she said. "Gwennie left her favorite doll out in the rain, so I gave her mine. My oldest sister set up a lemonade stand, and I suggested giving free samples of popcorn. Whenever we had a fever, my mother gave us salty popcorn so we would get thirsty and drink a lot of liquids."

"So you came by the fix-it gene honestly from Shelley?"

She smiled. "Maybe. What gene were you born with?"

"Scrapper. Survivor. Bastard," he said a little gruffly, and shoved his hands into his pockets. "Call me if you need a nine-one-one rescue from heiress wonderland."

"She's buying dinner. I should be okay."

"Save tomorrow night for me," he said.

"I'm not really supposed to be seeing you."

"I know. Makes it even more fun, doesn't it?" he

said and gave her a two-fingered salute before he left her office.

Closing her eyes, she inhaled deeply and caught just a hint of his aftershave. She remembered how he had kissed her senseless the other night. If he was just a little more callous or possessive or pushing her to be serious or determined not to commit, then maybe she could find it in herself to turn away from him.

But she saw flashes of vulnerability and she knew he had a good heart even though he would deny it to death. He wanted her, but he wasn't going to push her—for the most part, anyway. She suspected that he wouldn't fight her if she invited him to sleep over, although she knew there would absolutely be no sleep. *Which wouldn't be all bad,* she thought, remembering how his lips had felt, remembering how his mouth had felt on her breasts and lower... She remembered the wicked things he'd whispered in her ear when he'd slid inside her in Florida, the way he'd praised her, how sexy he had made her feel.

And how stupidly turned-on she was at this very minute. Amelia took a deep breath and picked up a file to fan her face. "Insane," she muttered to herself. "Totally insane." She forced herself to look at her computer screen, but unfortunately, finding volunteer options for Brooke wasn't nearly as interesting as thinking about Jack.

BROOKE DECIDED TO make use of her chauffeur, so she picked up Amelia and they were driven to a trendy upscale restaurant. "See? I'm wearing black, so I won't draw attention to myself," Brooke said and flipped her long red hair behind her shoulder, her diamond earrings sparkling like disco balls.

The hemline of Brooke's skintight black dress was well above the knee with a slit and she wore a pair of platform sandals. The dress also featured two slits on the chest, one that revealed her cleavage.

"I'm pretty sure that dress has already caused some serious whiplash, Brooke."

"You think?" she asked, clearly pleased. "I haven't worn anything like this for Ian yet."

"Speaking of Ian," Amelia said. "Have you told him your real name?"

Brooke sipped her martini. "There hasn't been a good time."

"You might want to go ahead and find a way. The longer you wait, the harder it's going to get."

Brooke sighed. "I know, but it's so nice not living up to the Brooke image. Did you find a volunteer position for me?"

"I brought a questionnaire and some contact names." She gave Brooke the folded papers she'd printed off.

"I need to take a test?" Brooke murmured, looking at the papers. "You can't just tell me?"

"I think you need to make this choice," Amelia said. "If you choose your volunteer activity yourself, I think you'll find it more fulfilling."

"Hmm," Brooke said, tilting her head as she glanced through the papers. After a moment, she glanced at Amelia. "So what's up with you? Are you dating again?"

"A little," Amelia said. "I'm getting settled in my apartment and my new job."

"You like it? What about your ex? Do you ever see him or hear from him?"

Amelia shook her head. "He lives somewhere else, but I'll probably see him at my sister's wedding in a few weeks."

"Your sister's getting married? How old is she?"

"Twenty-two."

Brooke grimaced. "What a waste. That's so young."

Amelia laughed. "In my family, getting married is very important."

"But you didn't," Brooke said. "Thank goodness. You need to have some more fun before you settle down."

"And you?"

"I've found my soul mate. I don't need a marriage certificate to be committed to Ian."

"Even though he doesn't know who you really are?"

Brooke scowled. "Names aren't important when souls connect. Plus, he's amazing in bed. Amazing. Trust me, there's more than one reason he's called Snake."

"You've just told me more than I ever wanted to know."

Brooke giggled. "Okay, what about Jack? Ian's hottie friend? Did you ever hear from him again?"

Amelia didn't want to talk about Jack to Brooke. She didn't want to talk about Jack to anyone. Her relationship with him was indefinable and trying to explain it would give her a headache. "I told you he was temporary."

"Yeah. Ian told me more about him. He had a rough upbringing, but he's successful and isn't stingy with his wealth. He likes to keep that on the down-low, though. Ian says he's a good guy."

"Men have different ideas than women do about the definition of a good guy."

"True that," Brooke said and glanced at the volunteer information Amelia had given her. "I always thought Habitat for Humanity sounded like a cool thing, but I bet it's hell on manicures."

Amelia could only sigh. Some things, it seemed, never changed.

CHAPTER TWENTY

THE FOLLOWING AFTERNOON, Jack stopped by Amelia's office again.

"How'd you manage this covert trip?" she teased.

He shook his head and raked his hand through his hair. "Sorry, that didn't even occur. I just thought I should let you know I won't be coming over tonight. I gotta head back to Chicago."

Her stomach sank. "Oh." She told herself she shouldn't be surprised. She told herself she shouldn't feel anything. Jack was just a distraction—one who could make great pancakes and kiss her so that she felt like melted syrup. "Tired of Bellagio and Atlanta?" *And me?* Okay, where did that come from?

"No. It's my uncle. Apparently he was in an accident. He's in bad shape and there's a screw-up with his insurance. His wife, Cindy, called me, which she ordinarily never does, so she must be pretty upset."

"I'm so sorry," Amelia said, concerned. "Do you know anything about his condition?"

"He's stable, but he's got a concussion, broken bones. He's unconscious. It doesn't sound good."

"Is there something I can do?"

"Nah, I've already booked a flight. I'm going back to my apartment to grab some clothes, then straight to the airport."

"Can I give you a ride to the airport?"

"No. Thanks, though." He leaned toward her to cup her jaw and brush his mouth over her forehead. "I'll be back when I get things straightened out. Meanwhile, Marc Waterson's office has the contact info of the hospital my uncle's staying at. I'm not sure I'll be allowed to keep my cell phone on while I'm there, so I left what numbers I could in case anyone needs to reach me."

"Okay," she said, and bit her lip. She impulsively put her arms around him and hugged him. "Would you call me when you get a chance? Let me know how he's doing—and how you are?"

He looked surprised. "Yeah."

She watched him leave and felt a terrible tightness in her chest. She'd never seen Jack look so shell-shocked. She knew his uncle had been a bright spot in an otherwise dark childhood. If she'd heard Jack correctly, then Thomas was his only living relative.

She, on the other hand, had relatives coming out of her ears. She tried to imagine how she would feel if the life of her only other living family member was in danger.

Jack almost always gave the impression of being okay with no commitments, but if that were one hundred percent true, then why had he memorized so much about her family? She'd been certain she'd bored him to death with stories about them, but maybe not.

Amelia tried to refocus on her work, but her mind kept straying. She wished he had let her take him to the airport. That night she surfed the TV and watched her cell until she couldn't sit still. Then she gave in and baked two pies.

She didn't sleep well and when she went to work, she struggled with feeling distracted all day long. It just felt wrong for him to be dealing with this crisis alone. Later in the afternoon, she gave in to an urge to check airfares to Chicago, certain everything this late would be priced through the roof. One airline, however, offered a low-cost last-minute weekend rate.

She was insane to even consider such a thing. It wasn't as if he'd invited her. He hadn't even hinted that he'd wanted her around. But he wouldn't ask even if he did want someone with him. He was too tough, too accustomed to handling everything on his own. It wouldn't occur to him to ask.

Her internal debate raged as she stared at the blinking cursor on the travel website. She and Jack didn't even have a real relationship. What was wrong with her?

Every rational cell inside her told her to say a prayer for him and his uncle and drop it. But some crazy instinct made her click that mouse.

AFTER BEING UP for thirty-nine hours straight, Jack's eyes felt like sandpaper and he'd chewed an entire pack of gum to get rid of the taste of stale coffee in his mouth.

His entire day had been spent by his uncle's bedside urging Tom to wake up, comforting Cindy or alternately chewing out either the personnel representative at the company where Tom had just begun working or his previous employer. Both of whom had stonewalled him until he'd promised legal action.

The tide had started to turn when the old company buckled and admitted Tom had fifteen days left on his policy. More important, Tom had awakened twice in the past hour. He couldn't talk with the tube in his throat, but he'd been lucid enough to blink his eyes in response to the doctor's instructions.

Cindy sat with Tom while Jack walked down the hall to a small waiting area. He hated hospitals. He couldn't count how many times he'd sat and waited with one of his mother's so-called friends to find out if she would survive another overdose. The memory called up a bitter taste in his mouth and he tried to replace the thought with something else. Something sweeter. Like Amelia. He closed his eyes and could swear he almost smelled her.

"There you are," he heard her say and he opened his eyes, certain he was hearing things. But she was there in front of him, her hair mussed, her blue eyes wide with concern. Dressed in work clothes, she carried a large tote bag and a box. It was almost as if he'd conjured her with his mind or some other part of his anatomy that he'd been certain didn't exist. He suddenly felt as if the sun had come out from behind a cloud.

He blinked, still wondering if he was hallucinating. "What are you doing here?"

"How's your uncle?"

"He's taken a turn for the better. He won't recover in a week and he's not out of the woods, but he regained consciousness. That's good news." He shook his head. "What are you doing here?"

She bit her lip. "It's gonna sound crazy, but I realized I'd never taken an impulsive trip anywhere, especially to Chicago, and I decided that would be a good thing for my list and—" she broke off, allowing her tote to slide to the floor "—and I made pies."

Something inside him cracked. He'd figure out

what it was later because he couldn't remember ever having the sensation before. He saw her bite her lip and realized she was nervous. He pulled her toward him and slid his hand through her wavy hair. "You just made my year."

She stared at him for a long moment that stretched into some kind of deep dangerous territory, then took a breath. "I didn't realize you liked pie that much," she finally said with a smile.

He laughed in relief and kissed her cheek. "How long are you here? You can stay at my place."

"Are you sure? I'm just here till Sunday morning. I had to take whatever flights were open."

"Yeah, it's a one bedroom with an office with a pullout couch. I'll—"

"I'll take the office," she insisted, anticipating his words.

"No way. I should probably hang around here awhile longer. I can give you the key and put you in a cab if you want to go ahead—"

"No. I came to be here," she said. "With you."

"Jack?" Tom's wife said from the doorway. She looked at Amelia with curiosity in her weary gaze.

"Cindy, this is Amelia Parker. She lives in Atlanta and she came to bring us some pie."

Cindy wrinkled her brow in confusion. "Pie from Atlanta?"

Amelia bit her lip again and her cheeks colored. "I wanted to make sure Jack and his uncle were okay. How are you doing?"

"It's been a rough ride, and not one I want to repeat. Jack really came through," she said, meeting his gaze. "Thank you again."

"Tom has always been important to me," he said.

"Yes, I see that," Cindy said, with a hint of regret in her eyes. "You can get some rest if you like. I'm going to stay the night."

"Are you sure that's a good idea?" he asked. "You need rest, too."

"I think I would do better here. My mother has the kids and the nurse said she would give me a cot." Her eyes watered and her voice caught. "I just can't leave him yet."

Amelia made a sympathetic sound and moved toward her. "You've had a tough time, haven't you? Why don't we see if we can get a few things to help make you a little more comfortable, at least for the night?"

In true Amelia form, she procured toothbrush, toothpaste, washcloth and towel and other assorted toiletries for Cindy. Amelia also talked the nurse's aide into finding a gown without a hole in the back and soft blankets. She negotiated the use of the microwave to heat the pie and someone rounded up

Dixie cups of vanilla ice cream to put on top. Amelia bullied Jack into eating a piece, too.

"Where did you find her?" Cindy asked Jack as she ate her piece of pie.

He looked at Amelia and smiled. "At a tiki bar in the Keys. She was drinking a hurricane."

Amelia glowered at him. "Thanks for helping me create a great first impression."

"I didn't want Cindy to feel intimidated. She already knows you make great pie and work wonders with nurses and aides," he said.

"True," Cindy said and looked at Amelia again. "You're not who I would have expected for Jack."

"I didn't think you knew me well enough to have expectations," Jack told her.

She gave him another look of regret. "You're right. I didn't. I'm sorry I've kept you away from Tom. He was so torn up when your mother died. I wanted to shield him from any reminder of her. I was wrong." She sighed. "I'd like to try to make things different."

"We can talk about that another time," he said. "You've got enough to think about with Tom right now. Are you sure you don't want me to stay?"

"Sure," she said. "I'm going to try to sleep a little here. Maybe you could take over tomorrow and I can go home for a little bit to see the kids."

"Call me for anything," he said.

She smiled and hugged him. "Thank you for coming, Jack. I don't know what I would have done without you."

Surprised at how tightly his uncle's wife clung to him, he squeezed her in return. "I'll see you in the morning."

After Cindy left the waiting area, Jack picked up Amelia's tote bag. "Are you ready?"

"You're sure you don't mind me staying with you?" she asked as they took the elevator down to the ground level.

"Wouldn't have it any other way." He looked at her again and felt a lightness after a day of unrelenting heaviness. Hailing a cab, he gave the driver his address and allowed his head to fall back against the seat. "This isn't what I pictured when I thought about you and me getting away from Atlanta."

"I didn't know you'd thought about that."

"Yeah," he said.

"What did you picture?"

"Somewhere tropical."

"Like the Keys?"

He shook his head. "Less accessible. More Caribbean or Mexican. Somewhere I'd be able to talk you into going topless."

"That place would be exclusively in your dreams. Can you imagine what my family would—"

"They wouldn't have to know," Jack said. "You could put it on your list and mark it off."

She was silent for a moment. "Have you noticed that many of your suggestions for my list involve me not being fully dressed?"

"I think it's an area you've neglected. I'm trying to help you catch up."

She laughed. "How generous of you."

The cab stopped in front of his building and he paid the driver and helped her out of the cab. They took the elevator to his tenth-floor apartment. "It should be clean. I pay a cleaning lady to come every two weeks whether I'm here or not. Sorry, but I don't think there's anything in the refrigerator but beer, Coke and water."

"Water's fine," she said. "You look tired. Why don't you go on to bed?"

"Shower first. You go ahead and take the master. No argument," he said when she opened her mouth. He took a shower, brushed his teeth and thought about drinking a beer, but he was too tired.

He entered his office and found Amelia asleep on the sofa. Sighing, he picked her up. She opened her eyes. "What are you doing?"

"Putting you to bed," he said, carrying her to his king-size bed. He liked the idea of her there. He would like knowing she had slept there even after she'd returned to Atlanta.

He put her down on the bed and pulled the covers over her. "Sweet dreams, sweetheart," he muttered and turned to go.

She caught his hand. "Stay."

His heart stopped. He didn't know what she was inviting him to do, sleep or more. But she had to be nuts to think he wouldn't want more. "Can't sleep with you in the same bed."

"Betcha can," she said. "Tonight."

Too weary to fight, he turned out the lamp and slid beneath the covers. "I'll give it ten minutes. If I don't fall asleep, I'm going to the sofa bed."

She folded herself around him, her front to his back, her hand curled against his arm. "You'll be gone in less than three minutes."

No chance, he thought, too aware of her breasts against his back, too aware of her softness.

"Close your eyes," she whispered. "And stop thinking."

He felt the tension of the day ease out of him, and damn if she wasn't right. He took about ten breaths and slid off to la-la land.

The next morning, he woke up with an erection, but not with Amelia. He'd dreamed about her. Blinking awake, he smelled fresh coffee and food. Unable to distinguish what kind of food from scent alone, he rose and headed for the kitchen.

Fully dressed, Amelia stood next to the kitchen bar sipping a Starbucks coffee. Another cup was on the counter next to a paper bag.

"Good morning," she said with a smile. "Coffee?"

He lifted the cup and took a sip, staring at her over the rim. "Thanks. When did you get up?"

"About twenty-five minutes ago. You were totally out, but I was afraid you would wake up while I was gone. I got a breakfast sandwich for you, but I'm warning you, it's nowhere near as good your pancakes."

He dug into the bag and pulled out the sausage-and-egg sandwich, taking a big bite. "This'll have to do. But it's a big letdown. I was planning on having you for breakfast."

"You were too tired."

He shot her a dark look. *Like hell.* Maybe last night, but not this morning. His cell phone rang and he picked it up from the kitchen counter. "Hello." He smiled. "Good, good. Thanks for letting me know. I'll be over as soon as I can." He glanced at her as he ended the call. "Tom's awake."

"That's great."

"Yeah. I'm going to the hospital, but you don't have to."

She looked at him as if he were crazy. "Yes, I do. That's why I'm here."

"You sure you don't want to do something fun?" he asked. "Shopping on Michigan Avenue?"

"I can shop anytime."

She stayed with him or Cindy the entire day, bringing coffee and juice and soda. She ordered a couple of pizzas for lunch and Cindy decided to take one of them home to share with the kids.

When Tom fell asleep and Jack felt restless, she dragged him outside for a short walk, then shared her iPod with him when they returned to Tom's room.

"You didn't bring a coloring book and crayons for me?" Jack asked, mocking her efforts to keep him occupied.

"They have some down in the gift shop. Would you prefer Disney princesses or SpongeBob Square-Pants?" she asked, giving it right back to him. "You don't have a gift for idleness."

"I hate hospitals," he admitted. "Spent too many trips coming and going as a kid."

"Your mother?" she asked.

He nodded.

"I think this trip will have a happier outcome," she said, looking at Tom, who was sleeping peacefully.

"Yeah. You don't strike me as the type that likes to sit still, either," he said.

"No, but one of my sisters was in a bad bicycle accident when we were kids and my mother, oldest sister and I took turns sitting with her. I learned that when you can't fix it, there's value in being the equivalent of a human grease spot sometimes." She looked at him. "I can stay if you need a break."

"No, he's my uncle."

She nodded. "I could get your laptop from your apartment."

Escape into work, he thought, without letting anyone down. "That's not a bad idea."

She opened her palm. "Keys?"

Cindy returned late in the evening with a promise to leave by midnight, so Jack and Amelia left just after ten. He picked up a bottle of girly wine for her on the way to his apartment. Tired, but restless, he took a short run and showered afterward.

Feeling like a deprived animal, he watched her sip her wine while he downed two beers. She sat on the sofa. He sat in a chair.

"You seem moody. Are you worried about your uncle?"

"Not too much. He's a lot better."

"What's wrong?"

"You came to Chicago and I didn't even take you out to dinner."

"That wasn't the purpose for this trip. It's okay."

"It's not okay with me," he muttered, standing.

She followed him to her feet, studying his face.

"You're going to have to sleep by yourself tonight. I'm not tired enough not to take advantage of this situation."

She met his gaze for a long moment that seemed to stretch into forever, then she took his beer from his hand and set it on the kitchen counter. She slid her hand through his and tugged. "Let's go to bed."

"Amelia," he began.

"Just trust me."

She led him to bed and kissed his cheek and stroked his head. It was nice, but he wanted more. She took his mouth with hers and he slid his hands underneath her pajama top to her breasts. She helped him pull off her top.

Sucking his tongue deep into her mouth, she lowered her hands to his waist, slipping them under the waistband of his boxers. She touched him and he felt the blood surge to his crotch. The combination of her soft sweet mouth and relentless hands made him sweat. She made him so hard he wasn't sure he could control—

Pulling her mouth from his, she flowed down his body, planting a trail of open-mouthed kisses on his chest, his ribcage, his abdomen.

He felt his need ratchet up another notch, stronger than before. He needed to tell her that he didn't have much restraint. He didn't have control.

She pushed down his boxers and he swore. "Oh, Amelia."

"Trust me," she whispered and took him into her mouth.

The pleasure and eroticism left him speechless. He loved the sight of her hair splayed over his thighs, her mouth taking him intimately.

The wicked massage of her lips on him was too much. His release roaring through him like a freight train, he pushed her mouth away and she shocked him by pulling him against her, catching his release with her breasts.

"Holy—" He struggled to catch his breath, staring at her. She looked like a combination of an angel and his most seductive dream. He slumped on the bed.

She searched his face. "First time you—"

"Not all of it," he said. "But the end…"

"Oh," she said, her lips lifting in a pleased smile. "Well, that's kinda fun."

"I'm a selfish dog."

She shook her head. "I'll let you make it up to me another time."

He would consider it his mission, he thought as he fell asleep minutes later. He rose before dawn and argued with her about driving her to the airport.

"It's crazy for you to waste time driving me to the

airport, especially when you're going to spend most of the day in the hospital. I'm totally okay with a cab."

"I'm not," he said and turned a deaf ear to the rest of her squabbles and drove her to the airport. As he neared the drop-off point, he turned to her.

"Thank you," he said, touching her hair and feeling something inside him sink like quicksand.

"You're very welcome. Would you call me to let me know what's happening?"

He nodded. "I'll call." He put the car in Park and slid his hands to the back of her nape, pulling her to him. He took her mouth, totally, completely.

When he pulled back, he saw a combination of emotions in her eyes, something deep and warm… and fear. He bit back an oath at the last one. She was afraid of him, he realized, afraid of what she felt for him. And with her heading back to Atlanta and him staying put in Chicago for the time being, there was nothing he could do to reassure her.

CHAPTER TWENTY-ONE

JACK STAYED IN CHICAGO for another week, but he
called Amelia every day. She tried to use the distance
to get her head screwed on straight, but she thought
about him much more than she knew her should.

She wondered what would happen between them
when he returned. Would he take over her bed?
Would she let him?

He must have sensed her hesitation, or maybe he
had his own, because he didn't rush her into bed
when he returned to Atlanta. Which, of course,
made her question her ability to arouse him to the
point of insanity.

He took her back to kisses. Long, drawn-out,
bring-her-to-the-edge-of-madness kisses. Every time
she saw him, he left her hot, wet and bothered and
wanting more. For some reason, though, they both
resisted taking the next step.

The weekend of her sister's wedding arrived and
she took Friday off and left Thursday afternoon to

join the festivities. Jack joined her, pleased with his assignment to play golf with her father.

"Just so you know," she told him as he drove his Porsche Boxter toward her hometown, "everyone will be insane."

He glanced at her. "Everyone?"

"Everyone," she said with a nod. "It's an emotional time. People reflect and make it all about themselves, what they have, what they don't."

"You, too?"

"I'm usually a little less insane than everyone else, but I don't make any guarantees. You may surprise yourself and go a little nuts, too."

"I have an escape hatch. I'm playing golf. Nothing insane about that."

"Right," she said dryly. "Swinging a club and trying to get a tiny ball into a tiny hole hundreds of yards away isn't the least bit insane."

"You're not a golfer."

"I always wanted to be a jock, but it just didn't happen. One of my sisters could run like the wind. Not me."

"You have to settle for being the brains of the family."

She shot him a dark look. "Is that your way of saying I'm the geeky, not particularly pretty or sexy sister?"

He slowed the car down to a crawl, then pulled

over to the side of the road. "Not at all," he said. "Would you like me to show you what I think?"

His expression was dangerous and edgy. During the past week, though he'd asked for nothing more than those drugging kisses, she'd had the feeling that he was a whisper close to seducing her and ravaging her body. She was a whisper close to letting him.

Amelia spotted a police cruiser driving past. "As inviting as that sounds, I'd rather not get arrested before Gwennie's wedding. She would never forgive me for messing up her wedding photos by wearing an orange suit and handcuffs."

"Chicken," he said and pulled back on the road.

She couldn't disagree. Not this time, anyway. "You're not worried about this at all, are you?" she asked, amazed because she would think that most men would be terrified.

"Why should I be?"

"Because it's a wedding and I've told you my family will be insane. My ex-fiancé will be there. And everyone will be watching you to see how you act toward me. Some of my aunts will be giving you the wink-wink-nudge-nudge about marrying me."

He gave a slow smile. "Really?" He laughed. "I could be Jack the Ripper and these people would try to marry you off to me."

"Pretty much," she said. "For a Parker woman,

marriage is the ultimate achievement. Spinsterhood is the ultimate failure. Even though this is the twenty-first century," she muttered.

"Hmm. Do you want to pretend to be engaged?"

She shook her head. "That would be even messier. They would start planning the wedding immediately, book a place for the reception, ask someone to make the cake…"

"How did you get out of all that when you were engaged to Will?"

"He proposed while we were still in college and I made it perfectly clear that we were both going to graduate and he was going to get his career off the ground. It helped that I was three hours away from my family."

"I wouldn't want to be Will. I'm surprised he's got the nerve to attend the wedding."

"I'm not sure I'd call it nerve. He's very convinced of how lovable he is. To be honest, I'd bet my family is hoping he will come to his senses and come back to me."

Jack was silent for a long moment. "What would you do if he asked you to take him back?"

She sighed. "That would really suck, because then I would have to be the one responsible for our break-up. Now he is and although I don't enjoy the pity thing, dealing with my mother's disapproval would be a major pain." She laughed dryly to herself. "When he broke up with me for the third and final time, I never would have dreamed I would be thankful to him."

Jack didn't say anything. He took her hand and lifted it to his mouth. "So what are your words of wisdom for me?"

"Compliment everything and you'll be safe."

"Your mother likes me."

"Maybe," Amelia said.

"Maybe? She begged me to come to this wedding within minutes of meeting me."

"My mother is a complex woman," Amelia warned him.

"What do you mean by that?"

"I mean, don't be surprised if she finds some diabolical way of using you to try to get Will and me back together."

"Shelley wouldn't do that," he said.

"If it suited her, she would. Consider that a warning."

He shot her a wary look. "What about your father?"

"If you take him away from all this to play golf, he will worship the ground you walk on forever."

"And what does it take to win over your mother?"

"Time and commitment. Being there for the rough moments."

"Like you were for me in Chicago."

That had been more for her, but she couldn't explain it to Jack. She hadn't been able to stand the idea of Jack dealing with his uncle's crisis by himself.

Amelia pushed the subject aside and returned to pressing pre-wedding plans. "The big sticky time for you is going to be tonight and maybe the wedding rehearsal. I'm sorry I have to bail on you tonight, but I consider it my duty to give Gwennie a real girls' night out before she gets married."

"Don't people usually do the bachelor and bachelorette thing the night before the wedding?" he asked.

"Usually. That's what my mother expects and she usually nixes the bachelorette party by appealing to female vanity. She insists that the bride needs her rest so she doesn't look like a hag on the most important, most-photographed day of her life. The fear of having a hundred photographs with baggy undereye circles and a dull green complexion was enough to scare my other two sisters into going to bed early."

"Clever," Jack said. "But you've got a plan to get around Shelley. It'll be interesting to see if you succeed."

"Oh, I will. I have the perfect cover. I've contacted the other bridesmaids, including my sisters, and told them I think we should hold a special brides-maids-only dessert party for Gwennie. Cake and punch is what I'll tell my mother. We're to meet at the church."

He chuckled. "At the church. Amelia, aren't you afraid you're going to be struck by lightning?"

"No, because we're not going into the church at all. I'm going to use Valene's van to carry us to three bars over the state line."

"How did you find out about the bars?"

"I have one wild aunt. Tammy. My mother always tried to supervise any visits we had with her because Tammy wasn't shy about sharing her adventures. Your part of the mission is to distract my mother by being a demanding guest. Ask for extra towels. Tell her you have a headache and need aspirin. Hint about what your favorite food is and she'll feel compelled to make it. And when you just can't take it anymore, go to bed."

"I don't suppose she'll mind if I sleep in your room."

Amelia choked at the ridiculous statement. "If you don't mind her going after you with my daddy's shotgun."

"Have you ever had sex in your bedroom at your parents' house?"

"No, and I don't think this is a good weekend to start."

"You could put it on your list—"

She felt an outrageous shot of adrenaline. "My list is long enough right now. You need to concentrate on surviving the night with my mother."

"You act like this is going to be difficult for me."

She thought about it for a moment. "Now that you mention it, you're excellent at keeping secrets and fooling people, so it shouldn't be a problem."

"Give me a minute while I pull the knife out of my side," he said.

"The only thing is that my mother has eerily well-honed instincts about her daughters, sometimes about everyone. She may try to dig for information from you."

"That's easy. If she gets upset because I won't talk, I'll tell her what I tell everyone. I'm a bastard."

She laughed because that statement would make even Shelley Parker pause. "You know, I think I like that about you. You are unapologetically a bastard. It's like you give clear warning not to count on you for decency. The problem is that underneath your bastardness—"

"Don't say lies a heart of gold."

"No, but you can be a very decent man. I've seen it."

He sighed. "Don't spread it around."

"What I don't understand is why in the world you agreed to do all this in the first place."

"I told you. It means I get to spend time with you."

"But you've already been spending time with me."

"Your family expects you and me to be involved. I get a break from being your dirty secret," he said.

That jolted her. "You're not a dirty secret," she protested, but felt like a hypocrite. She still hadn't told anyone at work that she and Jack were involved. Most of their dinners consisted of take-out eaten at her condo or his apartment.

"Don't take it so hard. I'm a bastard," he said. "I've always been the dirty secret."

But it bothered her. She suddenly realized that with the exception of her visit to Chicago, she'd been totally concerned about her own feelings. Not his. After all, like he said, he was a bastard. That didn't sit well with her at all and she had a difficult time pushing it from her mind.

An hour later, Jack pulled into her parents' driveway. The sight of the white two-story home where she'd spent most of her growing up years smoothed over jagged edges she hadn't realized she felt. Her mother had finally surrendered to her father's request to switch to vinyl siding last year, and it was clear Shelley had ordered a good power wash and clean windows. Hardwood trees dotted the green lawn surrounding the house and two rocking chairs and a swing offered seating on the front porch.

"That's nice," Jack said, pulling to a stop. "You grew up here?"

She nodded.

"Looks pretty close to a Norman Rockwell painting to me," he said.

She'd wondered what he would think of her family home. After all, Jack was loaded. Her parents weren't. "I had a pretty nice upbringing."

"You did," he said and she wondered if he was thinking about where he'd lived when he was a child.

"Let's go inside. I'm sure my mother has dinner ready."

He glanced at his watch. "At a quarter to six?"

"She has a sixth sense about these things. Actually, she has a sixth sense about a lot of things," she added. "Which is why I'll need you to help distract her while I get Gwennie out of the house."

"At your service," he said and they walked to the house.

As soon as the screen door closed behind them, a short-haired dachshund bounded toward them, barking.

"That's Priddy," Amelia said, bending down to pet the excited animal.

Jack joined her. "Priddy?"

"Daddy gets Momma a new dog whenever the old one dies. This is actually Priddy Three. Priddy One and Priddy Two have gone to doggy heaven."

"Took the final dirt bath," he said, petting the excited, wiggly animal.

Amelia shook her head. "Don't say that kind of thing around Momma. She's very sensitive about her dogs."

"Thanks for the warning."

Shelley appeared in the hallway. "Hi, Sunshine. Come on in. I'm just getting dinner on the table. Hello there, Jack." She yelled in a different direction. "George, come inside. Amelia and her friend are here."

Gwennie poked her head around the corner and squealed. "Amelia!"

Jack watched the two sisters hug.

"Are you ready?" Amelia asked.

"I think so. I'm crossing my fingers that nothing will go wrong at the last minute, like one of the kids getting sick. I have Ricky pulling Emily in a wagon. Rose promises she's been coaching him, but you know what a terror he is."

"It's going to be beautiful. I can't wait to see your dress. Jack, you remember Gwennie."

"Good to see the beautiful bride-to-be again."

Gwennie lifted her shoulders and beamed. "Thank you. I'm so glad you could come."

A man of medium height with a slight pot belly and a long-suffering expression on his face moved toward them. "Hey, little girl, you've been away too long," he said, giving Amelia a hug and kissing her cheek. "It's good to see you." He turned toward Jack. "I'm George. I understand we're supposed to play golf tomorrow. What's your handicap?"

Just like that, he was brought into the fold. Both Amelia and her mother watched over him and his dinner plate, making sure he got refills even when he didn't need any.

Jack took in the sights and sounds of a real home. It was, in some ways, like visiting a foreign country for him.

After dinner, Amelia excused herself to help Shelley with the clean-up. George invited Jack outside to stroll around the backyard then sit on the back porch with a beer.

"I've been to Chicago a couple of times," George said. "It's cold. No ocean, no mountains. Why would you want to live there?"

Jack shrugged. "Cubs, Bears, Chicago hot dogs and pizza."

George nodded. "I guess I can see that. Nothing like a good hot dog." He paused. "How long have you known our Amelia?"

"A couple of months. She's an amazing woman. I'm sure you're proud of her."

"Yep," George said. "She's the most ambitious of the four. It's gonna take a strong, smart man to keep up with her. I think Will was always a little threatened by her. She may have tried to hide it, but she was always a smart girl. The boy can't help it, but Will's just average."

Jack enjoyed hearing George's assessment. "I bet you've had your hands full raising four daughters. How did you manage it?"

"Make the money, give them hugs, get out of Shelley's way and realize that after about age twelve, I have very little control."

Jack chuckled. "Smart man. Diplomatic, too, I'll bet."

"In a house full of women, you bet. It's necessary for survival."

Amelia peeked through the sliding glass door. "Anyone want coconut cake or peach pie with ice cream?"

George slid a wily glance at Jack. "Shelley made the coconut cake for me. She thinks I get upset about the wedding fuss."

"Do you?"

"I get upset enough that I need coconut cake."

Jack laughed. "I'll go with the peach pie then.

Wouldn't want to get between a father-of-the bride and his coconut cake."

"I'll let you have a piece," George protested. "The problem is once you have one bite, you'll get greedy. Go ahead and get us a little slice of both," he said to Amelia. "You know what I mean by a little slice of coconut cake for me, though, don't you?" He winked.

Amelia smiled at Jack. "I know, Daddy. A small slice means you want one-fourth of the cake instead of half." She scooted back inside.

"Sassy girl," George said, but Jack could tell he loved her. And Jack could tell George loved being the hen-pecked lion surrounded by females.

Amelia returned with the dessert and chatted with her father about her job and her desire for a new car. Instead of telling her to stick with the practical Honda, George said he would try to come up with a few suggestions for her.

Amelia kept checking her watch. Shelley and Gwennie joined them on the back porch.

"Oh, my goodness," Amelia said brightly. "I just remembered that I need to get some shoes."

"Shoes?" Shelley echoed. "But you told me you already had some silver sandals."

"I did, but when I pulled them out of my closet, one of the straps was broken."

"Your daddy could fix it."

"I didn't bring them."

Her mother looked at her in a mixture of consternation and disbelief. "Amelia Louisa, have you lost your mind?"

"I figured I could get some here. Payless or Wal-Mart."

Shelley made a tsk-ing sound. "I don't believe this. You work for a shoe company and you can't get a pair of silver sandals?"

Gwennie bit her lip. "Do you think you'll be able to find something? Robert's family from out of town is coming in tomorrow, so it's gonna get busy."

"Let's go out now," Amelia said.

"Now?" Shelley echoed, glancing at her watch. "It's almost eight o'clock."

"I bet if we hurry, Gwennie, you and I could find some shoes."

"You know, I did see some silver Nine West shoes a few days ago that I really liked," Gwennie said.

"I love Nine West shoes," Amelia said.

"Make sure Marc Waterson doesn't hear you say that," Jack muttered.

"Who's Marc Waterson?" George asked.

"VP of Bellagio," Jack said.

George nodded and grinned. "I got you."

"Well, I can't just go shoe shopping," Shelley said. "I've got a ham in the oven."

"That's okay, Momma. Gwennie will help me. We're on a mission, right?" Amelia asked, standing.

"Well, Gwennie shouldn't be staying out late," Shelley said.

"Won't be a problem," Amelia said. "The stores close at nine. Gwennie will be in bed by ten, dreaming of Robert."

Shelley cocked her head to one side and twitched her nose as if something didn't smell quite right.

"Can we take your car?" Amelia asked Gwennie. "Jack has a Porsche and I've only had one lesson."

"This is good," Gwennie said, standing. "We'll get this taken care of tonight and then we won't have to worry about it tomorrow."

"Well," Shelley began. "You better not stay out too late."

"Make sure you can dance in those shoes," Jack said, and everyone stared at him. He glanced at Shelley. "You don't mind if I dance with your daughter, do you, Mrs. Parker?"

Amelia chose that moment to pull Gwennie toward the door leading out of the house. She shot him a big smile of victory.

"I think I need another piece of coconut cake," George said.

"You can wait. Jack asked me a question and I'm going to answer him."

"Oh, no," George muttered.

Shelley glanced at her daughters' retreating backs, then back at Jack. "It depends on what kind of dance you plan to do with my daughter. I'm most concerned with how she's treated, especially since she recently had her heart broken. Amelia is a precious girl and she deserves to be cherished. If some randy guy comes along thinking he can take advantage of her and dump her like yesterday's news, then I would probably have to demonstrate—"

"Here it comes," George muttered.

"—that I not only own my daddy's shotgun, I know how to use it."

DESPITE SHELLEY'S WARNING, Jack held true to his word to distract her. He helped her make ham biscuits for a while, then when over an hour had passed, he developed a headache, followed by a stomachache, followed by a request for warm milk, which he surreptitiously poured down the sink.

Just after eleven o'clock, however, Shelley made calls to Amelia's sisters and learned, to her consternation, that none of them were home. Jack immediately went to bed.

At thirteen minutes after twelve, the sound of his

cell phone jolted him awake. He picked up the phone immediately.

"Jack, this is Amelia. I need your help. We're in jail."

Dictionary Definition:
Tongue: *Noun*. The flap under the lacing or buckles of a shoe.

Amelia Parker's Definition:
Tongue: *Noun*. Using it the wrong way can get a girl into big trouble.

CHAPTER TWENTY-TWO

WITHIN TWO MINUTES, Jack snuck out of the house. Speed was his friend. He heard Shelley calling after him just as he slammed the door to his car and reversed out of the driveway.

He called the police station across the state line where the Parker sisters, two other members of the wedding party and several other patrons of The Red Eye bar had apparently been taken.

As he entered the small facility, he heard singing in the background. He approached the harried-looking uniformed man behind the desk. "Sheriff, I'm here to escort some ladies from Georgia home."

The guy rubbed his face. "I'm not the sheriff. Who are you here for?"

"Six women celebrating the wedding of Gwendo-lyn Parker, which is scheduled for tomorrow."

The man cast him a wary look. "Oh. *Those* women." He glanced at papers on the desk. "Charges include public drunkenness, lewd behavior, nudity and resisting arrest."

"May I speak with Amelia Parker, please?"

"I'll bring her out," the officer said and a couple minutes later, he steered Amelia out in handcuffs.

She appeared delighted to see him. "Jack, thank God you're here," she said, batting her hands at him.

"Are the cuffs necessary?" Jack asked the officer.

He gave a disgruntled look. "They were rowdy."

"I'm sure you can handle one small unarmed woman," he said and the policeman reluctantly removed the cuffs. Amelia had looked sexy in them and Jack was tempted to ask for a set for future use, but he stuck to the immediate task.

"Oh, Jack," Amelia said, throwing her arms around his neck.

She felt so good he was almost sidetracked, but he realized that if he'd lit a match in front of her mouth, he would have burned down the small building. "Amelia, sweetheart, the sheriff says there are some charges against you and your sisters."

Amelia sighed. "It's all a big misunderstanding."

"Drunk in public," the officer said.

She hiccupped. "Well, that one may be right, but just about everyone at The Red Eye was loaded."

"That's why they're in jail," the officer said. "Lewd behavior."

"Gwennie and her two school friends were singing a rap song."

"Banned on most radio stations," the officer added.

"Gwennie is the bride-to-be," Jack said. "And I'm sure this is their first offense."

The officer sighed. "Public nudity."

"Rose got a little carried away. She was just trying to show us some of the moves she learned from the pole-dancing video she ordered."

"The woman is an officer in the parent-teacher association, the mother of three children and teaches Sunday School," Jack recited, recalling Amelia's description of her oldest sister.

"Resisting arrest," the officer said, continuing down the list.

"Valene is pregnant, so she wasn't drinking," Amelia said. "She refused to leave without the rest of us."

Jack met the officer's gaze. "These are all first-time offenses."

"They're still loaded. Look at her."

"I'll take full responsibility for getting them home." He looked at Amelia. "Just tell me they haven't impounded the mini-van."

The bridesmaids were released, but it took several minutes to stuff them into the van. Gwennie and her friends kept singing, while Amelia tried to cover her youngest sister's mouth.

Rose hugged Jack several times. "It's so nice of you to come get us."

Jack offered to drive the van, but Valene insisted on getting behind the wheel. "I'm totally sober. Besides, they would drive you crazy."

"Are you sure? It's late and you're pregnant."

She leaned toward him with a light of mischief in her eyes. "The truth is I don't want to miss it. I can hold this over my sisters' heads for years to come. It's been so much fun. And just think, we can blame it all on sweet little Me-Me."

He followed the mini-van back to town and helped each of the inebriated bridesmaids to their respective homes. They would need to pick up their cars from the church parking lot tomorrow.

The last stop was Amelia's parents' home. He helped Amelia and Gwennie to the front door. Gwennie kept trying to sing the nasty rap song and Amelia kept trying to cover her mouth.

No chance for a quiet entrance with Priddy III announcing their arrival with a stream of barking. Shelley stormed into the hallway wearing her housecoat.

"Hi, Momma," Gwennie sang, throwing her arms around her mother. "We had the best time tonight. Do you know they'll let anyone use the microphone to sing a song at The Red Eye?"

Shelley glared over Gwennie's shoulder. "You took the bride-to-be to The Red Eye?"

Amelia gave an exaggerated nod. "It was my sisterly duty."

Shelley rolled her eyes. "Well, it's too late for a lecture tonight. I suspect you both will suffer enough for this in the morning. I'll make sure to wake you up early, Amelia."

Amelia sighed. "Okey dokey." She kissed her mother's cheek. "G'night, Momma."

Shelley just threw her hands in the air, then helped Gwennie to her room.

Amelia turned to Jack. "Thanks for rescuing us." She smiled. "Bet that was a first."

He helped her toward her room when she stumbled. "Unfortunately, I've been called to the police station for my mother before."

Her face crumpled. "I'm sorry. I didn't mean to call up a bad memory."

"Trust me. This wasn't anywhere near the same," he said, grinning, and ushered her into her bedroom.

She sat on her bed and fell backward. "That's good." She kicked off her shoes and smiled again. "You want to stay in here with me tonight?"

"Yes, but I'd want you awake and you're going to sleep soon."

She shook her head. "No, I'm not. I'm just a little dizzy. It'll pass."

"I'll be back in a minute. I'm getting a bottle of water and aspirin for you to take in the morning," he told her, just in case she fell asleep before he returned.

He went to the kitchen and got the bottle of water out of the refrigerator and the aspirin out of the cabinet Shelley had shown him earlier when he'd asked for something he didn't need in order to keep her distracted.

When he returned, Amelia was asleep. He scooted her body so her head rested on a pillow, but resisted the urge to remove her clothes. The thought of Shelley's shotgun made him pause. No need to push his hostess over the edge tonight. They would be here at least one more night. He still had time to take Amelia in her girlhood bedroom.

MOMMA LIED ABOUT GETTING Amelia up early the next morning. Just after nine o'clock, Amelia woke with a terrible taste in her mouth, feeling rumpled from sleeping in her clothes. Spotting the bottle of water on her nightstand, she unscrewed the top and chugged half of it in no time. She noticed the little pill and swallowed it.

Unable to bear the icky sensation of slept-in clothes and make-up, she grabbed her robe and darted down the hall to take a shower. After a thorough cleaning, she felt much better and retreated to her room to get dressed.

Momma was waiting with a cup of coffee. She pushed the cup into Amelia's hands. "I do not approve of you getting your sisters inebriated, but if you were determined to party, at least you had the good sense to do it two days before the wedding instead of the night before."

Amelia nodded, sensing that more was coming.

"However, I am not pleased at all that you got your sisters put in jail."

"That wasn't my fault. Gwennie was singing dirty rap songs with her friends over the microphone and Rose was starting to pull off her clothes in a pole dance."

Shelley put her hand to her forehead. "Oh, my Lord. With all of you drunk, you're lucky nothing worse happened."

"Actually, Valene wasn't drunk because she just found out she's pregnant."

Shelley brightened. "Really? I thought something might be going on with her. Another grandbaby." She beamed, then seemed to remember she was supposed to be fussing at Amelia. "I'm surprised that you did this. You're usually very sensible."

"I know, but sometimes I just need a break from

it. I can only hope that if I ever get married, my sisters will do the same for me."

Shelley's lips twitched. "I'm not sure The Red Eye can survive the Parker sisters again." She cleared her throat. "I decided to let your sister sleep a little longer. You and your boyfriend can go pick up her car after you get dressed."

Amelia did as instructed, although the task took a little longer than necessary because she and Jack started kissing in the church parking lot and forgot about the time. Something about the fact that Jack had rescued her and her sisters last night and hadn't run screaming from her mother made her want to get as close as possible to him.

It was, however, a busy day filled with family and activities. Jack and her father played a round of golf. Then Amelia and Jack joined the rest of the wedding party at the church for the rehearsal. And that was when things started to go downhill for Amelia.

Gwennie met her in the back of the church, wringing her hands. "I really meant to tell you this earlier," she began.

"Tell me what?" Amelia asked, moving toward the double doors into the sanctuary.

"I didn't tell you who the best man is."

Amelia smiled. "Usually the groom's dad or brother."

"Or best friend," Gwennie said, biting her lip.

Amelia's stomach sank. "Not Will."

"I'm sorry, Me-Me, but I couldn't talk him out of it. Do you think you'll be okay?"

Amelia took a deep breath. This had been such a nice visit until now. She'd barely even thought of Will. "I'll be fine. This is your special time. Don't worry about me."

"You're the best, Amelia. I knew you'd understand." Gwennie hugged her, pulling back with a smile. "If it's any consolation, Robert told me the other day that Will's not dating that awful girl he dumped you for anymore. Sidney. Apparently she fell in love with someone else and dumped him. How's that for just deserts?"

Amelia realized that she'd forgotten all about Sidney's existence. But a part of her was still glad that things had worked out for Will the way they had. Even so, though, she wasn't looking forward to seeing him tonight.

She waited a long moment after Gwennie retreated into the church, feeling Jack's gaze on her. "This sucks."

"Yeah. You want me to kidnap you, so you don't have to do it?"

She smiled. "No." She sighed. "This was really going well up until now."

"You want me to knock him out so he can't be in the ceremony?" he asked.

Her lips twitched. "What if I said yes?"

"I'd do it. Remember, I'm a bastard. This is the kind of thing I do best."

"That's a big fat hairy lie," Amelia told him. "And we'll talk about that more later. After I get through this."

"You're going to introduce me to him, aren't you?"

She gave him a double take. "You really want to meet Will?"

"Yes," he said, straightening his tie.

She studied his face, wondering if the warrior look in his eyes was a product of her imagination. "Okay. After the rehearsal…"

"Now," he said.

She blinked. "Now?"

"Now."

He was very firm, she thought. "Okay, then let's do it."

She put herself into pretend mode. It was a game she'd learn to play to help her overcome uncomfortable situations, such as when she'd given the valedictorian speech at her high school commencement. She pretended she was a queen and these were her subjects, so she had to act with great decorum. It was a crazy way of faking it, but it worked for her.

She led the way up the center aisle of the church, smiling and waving at relatives of Robert. Will stood at the front with the groom and two of the bridesmaids. Her mother and sisters stood a few feet away.

Amelia felt her mother's gaze on her as she moved toward the groom. "Hi, Robert," she said, hugging him. "Congratulations on snagging the best girl in the county, state, country. I hope you know how lucky you are."

He hugged her in return. "Yeah, I do. I wanted to commit her before she had a chance to reconsider. It's good to see you, Amelia. You look great."

"Thank you. I'd like you to meet my friend Jack O'Connell. He's from Chicago, but he's living in Atlanta right now."

Jack shook Robert's hand and gave him his best wishes while Amelia greeted some of the other people standing close by.

She noticed Will start to slither away and she took a quick breath. "Will, how are you?" she asked, but didn't give him time to answer. "I'm sure you're enjoying your new job. Jack O'Connell, this is William Farley."

"Good to see you, Amelia. You look nice." Appearing incredibly uncomfortable, Will stuck out his hand. "Nice to meet you, Jack."

"My pleasure," Jack said. "Amelia told me about you, and I have to thank you."

Will looked at Jack in confusion as the small group grew quiet. "Why?"

Jack slipped an arm around Amelia's waist. "Your loss is my gain."

Jack had just delivered the almost-civilized equivalent of a punch in the nose. Amelia bit her lip to keep from wincing or laughing. She heard a soft gasp and her father's low chuckle. Jack just smiled like the shark he was.

Long after the awkward but wonderful moment, Amelia couldn't stop looking at Jack and smiling. She couldn't believe what he'd said to Will. He couldn't have said anything more perfect, whether he'd meant it or not.

After the rehearsal, Robert's parents hosted dinner at a nice little Italian restaurant the next town over. Amelia offered a toast to the bride and groom and teased Gwennie by asking her to do a rap number for the crowd. Gwennie blushed like a rose bush.

Between courses, when Jack slid his arm along the back of Amelia's chair, she moved closer to him. She inhaled and caught a hint of his aftershave.

"You smell delicious," she whispered in his ear.

"How much have you had to drink?" he asked, studying her.

"One glass of champagne and one-half of a glass of wine. Are you inferring that I'm drunk?"

"No. You just seem more affectionate than usual."

"I feel affectionate. Should I stop acting the way I feel?"

"No," he said and slid his hand behind her neck and lightly rubbed her with his fingertips.

Amelia was filled with the wildest thoughts and cravings. She wanted to slide her hands inside his coat and press herself as close as she possibly could. She wanted to kiss him, more than once, long open-mouthed, sensual kisses that got her hot and him, too.

She sighed and slipped her hand below the table to his knee. The muscles in his leg immediately contracted beneath her touch. Struck with a wicked urge to rev him up, she allowed her hand to slide higher on his thigh. She moved her hand in a light massaging motion. Oddly enough, her secret caresses began to affect her.

Her breasts grew heavy and sensitive. Hyper-aware of him, she felt restless almost to the point of being achy. The intense feeling of want burned through her bloodstream. She wasn't interested in food.

Her lack of interest, however, didn't stop the waiters from serving the main course. Reluctantly moving her hand from his leg, she curled her foot just inside his ankle.

He lifted a shrimp from his seafood platter. "It's good. You want to try it?"

"Yeah," she said and he extended his fork and she took a bite. She ate a couple more bites of her own dinner, then stopped.

"Full?" he asked in a low voice.

"Tired of eating," she said in an equally low voice. "Tired of being here."

He met her gaze and she could see that he read her mood. She was aroused and having a hard time hiding it. She slid her hand over his thigh, glancing his crotch, and was surprised when he opened his thighs further.

She should stop before things got truly insane, but she was feeling a little insane herself. She took another sip of wine and slid her hand intimately over him. He was hard. A shot of sexual adrenaline ran through her.

He lifted his water glass and took a long drink. "I hope no one asks me a question where I'm required to provide an intelligent answer," he murmured to her.

She lifted her glass again and licked a drop of wine that clung to the edge. "Want me to stop?"

"How much do you think your family would mind if I put you on this table and have you for dessert?"

She couldn't hold back a breathy laugh. "I hate to deprive you of the tiramisu they make here. It's wonderful."

"I can do without tiramisu," he said and met her gaze.

Her heart flipped over itself and she felt a rush of heat. "I want to leave," she told him in a low voice that she knew didn't hide her need.

"Then let's go."

"We need an excuse. I feel like I have sludge for brains." She closed her eyes. "Your uncle. How's Tom?"

"He's doing well."

"Actually, his wife called and asked you to return the call. We should leave so you can call her back. I'll tell my mother," she said and rose to walk toward her mother, feeling Jack's gaze on her the entire time.

Her mother was so totally sympathetic that Amelia felt a sliver of guilt, which was extinguished when Jack rose to join her to leave. They thanked Robert's parents and as soon as they got into his car, he took her mouth in a mind-blowing kiss.

"Tell me that wasn't for show for Will," he muttered, sliding his hand possessively over her breast.

She shivered. "Will who?"

He gave a rough chuckle and kissed her again. "Where are we going?"

"To my bedroom," she said, and she might as well have waved a red flag in front of him. He started the car and the tires of his Porsche screeched as he backed out of the parking spot.

With the convertible top locked in place, the car felt more intimate. At every stoplight, he reached over and kissed her, sweeping his tongue over hers.

By the time they arrived at her parents' home, she was so hot her hands shook when she unlocked the door. They dashed past Priddy III to her bedroom. Jack closed the door and locked it.

She immediately pulled him against her and kissed him. She tugged at his tie and the buttons to his shirt.

"What's gotten into you tonight?" he asked.

"You," she said. "I want you everywhere, every way at once."

"What an invitation," he murmured and unzipped the back of her dress and pushed it off her shoulders. He unfastened her bra at the same time he kissed her and immediately began to touch her nipples.

The caresses made her even more restless and she shoved off his jacket and pushed his shirt aside to feel his bare chest against her. She slid her hand down to his crotch. "I want to hurry, but I want it to last."

"If you keep touching me like that, there's no chance of me lasting." He pulled her hand away.

"But—"

"But nothing." He pushed her panties down her thighs and they slid to her feet, pooling with her dress above her sandals. He surprised her by picking her up and carrying her to bed. Her clothes seemed to dissolve and he was sliding his wicked and wonderful mouth down her throat, pausing at the hollow there, then moving down to take her nipple and work it into a tight bud.

She couldn't keep herself from wriggling beneath him. She felt restless and needy all over and all under. He skimmed his lips over her belly and lower until he took her intimately in his mouth. She felt seduced, devoured and cherished. His tongue provided the most delicious friction against that most sensitive part of her.

Feeling herself spiral suddenly out of control, she climaxed in a mega-wave of pleasure that left her breathless.

Lifting up, he pulled a condom from his pocket, shucked his slacks and underwear and thrust inside her.

She wrapped her legs and arms around him, wanting to feel every inch of his flesh against hers.

"Closer," she whispered. "As close as you can."

He rocked inside her and the way he rubbed and stretched her got her going again. He slid his hands beneath her bottom and squeezed her.

"You feel so good I almost can't stand it."

She instinctively flexed around him and he took a fierce indrawn breath. "What are you doing?"

She flexed again. "Nothing, I—"

He began to pump inside her, obliterating every thought except him. She forced herself to acknowledge the sensations of feeling him everywhere, his chest and belly against hers, his pelvis locked with hers, his thighs between hers. She felt herself reaching for more of him, more of her, more of them at the very needy core.

She saw a flash of his climax on his face before she felt it. The intense pleasure and something more, an ultimate connection she'd never felt before that echoed way deep inside her. Sensation and emotion sent her over the edge with him.

For several seconds, all she could do was try to breathe. The sound of his labored breaths mingled with hers. He rolled onto his side and pulled her with him.

"Why did you want to make love to me in my childhood bedroom?" she asked when her lungs and brain began to function.

He laughed. "You mean aside from the adrenaline rush I get from knowing your mother could show up any minute ready to blast me with buckshot from her daddy's shotgun?"

"There's that," she said, ducking her head into his chest at the image. "What else?"

"I wanted to give you a different memory."

She eased away from his chest and searched his face.

"You spent a lot of years dreaming of Will in this bed. I wanted to give you something else to dream about, and I'm enough of a bastard that I wanted that something else to be me."

He had helped to usher her away from the Will stage of her life, sometimes gently, sometimes with shocking lessons she learned about herself. One of the most shocking things of all was how free, yet safe she felt when she was with him.

She felt a lot of things with him, about him, and some of those things were so strong and complicated that it scared her.

"You're thinking too much, Magnolia," he said. He must have been able to read the fear on her face.

"Do I need to distract you?" he asked and slid his hand between her legs.

She felt a kick of adrenaline that knocked her sideways. "We don't have time. There's no way we have—"

He lowered his mouth and drew in one of her nipples. He toyed with her sweet spot and slid one of his fingers inside her. Switching his mouth to her other breast, he played her like a musical instrument.

It wasn't possible, she told herself. She'd already gone… It wasn't possible. But she felt herself sinking again, and he had her flying over the edge just as a car pulled into the driveway.

GWENNIE'S WEDDING went off without any major hitches. The ceremony was poignant and left Amelia with a lump in her throat. "Be good to each other," she told Gwennie and her beaming groom.

At the reception, Amelia danced with just about everyone except Will, but the most romantic dance of the evening for her was the one she shared with Jack outside the reception hall. The song playing was "At Last," and the way he looked at her made her heart skip every other beat.

Much to the disappointment of her sisters and mother, Amelia skipped the bouquet-throwing scene. She wished Gwennie well and blew bubbles with the rest of the guests as Gwennie and Robert drove away in a car decorated with shaving cream, balloons and tin cans.

Despite the ups and downs of the weekend, she

dreaded returning to Atlanta. She and Jack had
reached a new level. How were they going to keep
their relationship secret now?

CHAPTER TWENTY-THREE

Two days after Jack and Amelia returned to Atlanta, he showed up at her condo with chocolate. "Dessert," he said and watched her eyes widen with anticipation.

"Oooh, I can't wait." She reached for the box.

He pulled it from her reach and shook his head. "Oh, no. Didn't your mother ever tell you dessert is for after your dinner? Protein and vegetables before sweets."

She pursed her lips in the cutest, sexiest pout he'd ever seen in his life. It was so out of character for her that he almost gave her the candy. He bent toward her and brushed those sexy lips with his mouth. She was better than any candy.

"Let me take you out to dinner first," he said.

She tilted her head to one side and smiled. "That's a nice offer." She lifted her finger to rub his chin. "But why don't we stay in instead? It just occurred to me that there are some things with chocolate that I've never done."

"That's very tempting, but there's this place I've been wanting to go. Great reviews. I want to take you there."

She met his gaze, then gave a long sigh. "Oh, Jack, can't we keep it just between you and me a little longer?"

He felt an odd sinking sensation in his gut. "It wasn't just between us at your sister's wedding."

She grabbed his hand and tugged him toward the kitchen. "That was different. Come on. I'll fix anything you want. Or you can instruct me how to make a Chicago dog. How about that?"

He didn't care about a Chicago dog. He wanted to be able to take her out to dinner. But she clearly wasn't ready. He had the ugly feeling that she would never be ready. After all, she was the princess of light while he was the bastard of the night.

"Not ready to be seen with the bastard yet?" he taunted.

She sobered. "Don't say that. Please don't say that."

"Even if it's true, Magnolia?"

She bit her lip. "It's not true," she insisted. "It's just not—" She broke off. "It's just complicated."

"Yeah," he said, pushing back the bitterness that climbed into the back of his throat. "So, let's make those Chicago dogs. I hope you've got tomatoes and celery salt."

He fixed the dogs. She kept an ice-cold beer in his hand. The undercurrent of tension hummed between them like a live electrical wire, but she seemed determined to ignore it. There were moments when he almost felt as if he needed to yell to drown it out.

She fed him chocolate and then kissed him and took the treat into her mouth and gave it back. Her erotic experimentation made him hard. Soon enough, he pulled off her clothes and she pushed off his and they got hot. The chocolates melted from the rise in temperature and he brushed her nipples with some of the dark confection. He licked it off, not sure which was sweeter, the chocolate or the taste of her nipples or the way her body arched toward his as if she couldn't get enough of him.

He didn't have time to dwell on the sensual debate because she flowed down him, placing open-mouthed kisses over his chest and abdomen, then lower. And pure, sweet Amelia got incredibly creative with a melting chocolate and his hard, swollen…

He shot over the edge, but that wasn't enough for him. Using his hands and mouth, he turned the tables on her and took her to the top twice before sliding inside her.

She was the sexiest woman he'd ever met, but he woke up wanting more.

More than sex. Oh, Lord help him, he sounded like a woman.

He stared at her for five minutes before she awakened. Her eyelids fluttered and she curled toward him, like a flower to the sun. The natural movement undid him.

"Good morning, sunshine."

"Good morning, handsome."

Her hair felt soft against his chest. He touched her head. "I should go."

She groaned. "Bummer."

"You love your job, you love your job," he challenged.

She looked up at him and smiled. "Thanks for the chocolates."

He smiled back, but felt his throat close up because he knew he needed a break from this. It had gotten out of control. It had gotten stupid. "I'm not going to come see you at your condo for a while, Magnolia."

She looked at him in silence for a long moment. "It's because I won't go out in public with you."

He shrugged and moved toward the edge of the bed. "I don't want to ruin your career at Bellagio." He forced himself to get out of bed and pull on his clothes. "But I don't want to be your dirty little secret anymore, either. Let me know when you want to go out to dinner."

AFTER DELIVERING HIS ultimatum, Jack grew more irritated with each passing day. Marc Waterson was still as paranoid as ever and found ways to delay any discussion about expanding Bellagio into a value market. He and Amelia were at a stalemate. Even though he understood her concern about her job, he felt impatient with her insistence on keeping their relationship secret.

If his life were a song, it would feature Mick Jagger railing about not getting any satisfaction. He was tempted to blow off the rest of his time at Bellagio and head back to Chicago. At least there he didn't feel like a hated carpetbagger after the Civil War.

His bitterness intensified. Why was he even thinking about giving up already? Why did he care what Marc Waterson thought of him? It wasn't as if the man was his brother or a family member he'd known and cared about for years. Screw the Bellagios. If they didn't care about saving themselves from extinction, then why should he? As long as he got his investment back, he was okay.

And Amelia... Why had he let himself get involved? Why did he give a rip that she wanted to keep their relationship quiet when the sex with her was so good? He felt like ten kinds of a fool for caring, for wanting...

Jack was in such a nasty mood he almost didn't

attend Lillian Bellagio's semi-annual "Bellagio's Keys To Success Appreciation" cocktail party. All the board members, management and key personnel were invited. Amelia had been excited to be included, but she wasn't going with Jack. After taking a run around the complex of his temporary home, he took a shower and decided to go late to the party.

The event was held at Lillian's Atlanta home, which was listed in the historical registry. The beautifully decorated residence reminded him of a museum. Civil War artifacts along with Bellagio memorabilia covered the walls and were displayed in antique cabinets in the front rooms and hallway.

A waiter dressed in black and white approached him. "May I get you something to drink, sir?"

"Whiskey," he said, when he saw a large portrait of Dario Bellagio with his young son on his knee. Jack wondered if the portrait had been painted from a photograph. The painting captured the joy in Dario's eyes as he looked down at his young son. A smile wreathed his handsome face. The boy's face was turned sideways, looking at his father in a combination of awe and admiration.

Like a cluster of thorns, the image scratched at something inside Jack. Joy had been in short supply during his growing up years, unless he counted his mother's drug-induced euphoria, which he didn't.

He wanted some of that joy, and he was disgusted with himself that he did. It was his fault, though. He'd chosen to get involved with Bellagio, Inc., where everything he'd never had was rubbed in his face on a daily basis.

Ignoring the raw ache inside him, he turned away from the painting and entered two large connecting rooms filled with Bellagio employees. Standing with Jenny Prillaman, Trina Roberts spotted him and waved in his direction. Jenny also waved and smiled.

Jack lifted his hand in a return greeting, getting a cynical kick out of the fact that Marc's wife refused to allow her husband's antipathy for Jack to get in the way of her being her polite, friendly self.

He saw Amelia enter from a back hallway and felt his gut clench at the sight of her. As if she felt him looking at her, she looked up and met his gaze. He saw conflicting emotions in her eyes—passion, frustration and the one he hated the most, fear. He lifted his glass in a silent salute and she slowly smiled and waved.

Lillian entered the room with Marc Waterson by her side. Dressed in a winter-white suit that emanated wealth and good taste, she also wore reading glasses and carried a couple of sheets of paper.

"Attention, attention everyone," Marc Waterson said. "I know we'd all like to thank our generous hostess for this gathering tonight." He clapped his hands and everyone joined him.

Lillian smiled and nodded.

"It's become a custom at Bellagio for us to give special recognition to employees who go above and beyond their job descriptions to make Bellagio a better company," Marc continued. "These employees represent the key to our success. Ladies and gentleman, I present Lillian Bellagio."

The small group erupted in applause again as Lillian smiled. "Thank you so much for coming tonight. I have the pleasure of presenting fourteen-karat gold key holders with the Bellagio emblem to four of you tonight. Thank you for your contribution to Bellagio's continued success." She picked up her piece of paper. "William Foster, our sales representative for the U.K., who has doubled sales in the past year. Thank you, William," she said and led the group in a round of applause.

Another key holder was presented to a designer who was putting in extra hours on the activewear redesign.

Lillian smiled as she glanced at her paper again. "It was my pleasure to have this young woman as my assistant."

Amelia, Jack thought, feeling a surge of pride. He glanced at her and saw a flush of surprise and pleasure suffuse her face. She'd earned the recognition even though she preferred to keep a low profile.

"From the first week," Lillian continued, "I knew she wouldn't be staying with me very long because she was destined for bigger things at Bellagio. Even when she was with Bellagio as a temp, she solved crisis after crisis. Now, she's revamping our employee orientation so that many crises can be prevented before they interrupt precious productive hours. Ladies and gentlemen, Amelia Parker."

The applause rang with sincerity and Jenny let out a little whoop. Amelia's cheeks looked like roses. Jack knew she felt self-conscious as hell as she shook Lillian's hand and then impulsively hugged the grande dame.

After Amelia stepped aside, she looked at him and smiled. A moment passed, her smile fell, and she mouthed the words, *I miss you.*

His heart squeezed tight at her admission. He wondered how much she missed him. One-tenth as much as he'd missed her?

He distantly noticed Lillian clearing her throat. "This may come as a surprise." She paused and gave a soft, wry laugh. "Oh, that's too much of an understatement. This will *definitely* come as a surprise. We've recently added a new member to Bellagio, Inc. This man hasn't been received all that well. He is not the type to accept the status quo. He has vision, drive and experience gained the hard way. We're lucky to have this individual looking out for Bellagio's future, pushing for ways to continue to build the Bellagio name. Even though he doesn't bear that name, he is indeed a Bellagio."

Jack looked at Lillian in disbelief. *What the hell…* Why was she doing this now? They had agreed…

Lillian took a deep breath and met Jack's gaze. "I am pleased to introduce you to another member of the Bellagio family. Jack O'Connell is my husband's son. His father would be very proud of him. I am, too."

The room went completely still. Jack felt every eye on him. He couldn't meet Amelia's stunned gaze. He felt waves of shock, disbelief and suspicion. *Oh, Lillian, what have you done?* Sighing, he took a sip of his whiskey. How could he fix this?

"Does this mean he gets a Bellagio key holder?" Amelia suddenly asked, and her sweetly voiced ridiculous question broke the tension.

"We might want a DNA test first," Marc said. His wife gasped and jabbed him with her elbow.

"What?" Marc demanded. "How do we know he hasn't pulled one over on Lillian? Someone has to look after things."

"He hadn't pulled anything over on me," Lillian began.

Jack heard the strident tone of her voice, the beginning of a bitter argument. In that moment, that ugly moment when everyone was staring at him with doubt and suspicion, Amelia walked toward him and hugged him.

She felt like heaven. "What are you doing?" he whispered, holding on.

"You looked like you could use a hug," she said and then shocked him again by kissing him. "And just so you know. You've got a helluva lot of explaining to do about this."

A COUPLE OF DAYS LATER, Marc Waterson came into Jack's office and closed the door behind him, wearing a solemn expression. "I checked out your story with Lillian and a P.I. Sounds like you got the rough end of things, but climbed out of a bad situation."

"More like ran from it," Jack said, not at all surprised that Marc had hired a P.I. to make sure Jack was who Lillian said he was. "Listen, I don't expect you to be any more agreeable with me because Lillian announced that I'm part of the family."

"That's good," Marc said. "Because I'll still fight you 'til we're both bleeding if I think your ideas are bad for Bellagio." He paused. "However, I owe you an apology. My wife says I've been a paranoid ass."

Jack felt his lips twitch. "What do you say?"

Marc cleared his throat. "Let's just say I've seen

the error of my ways. One of those ways was my insistence to stick with one basketball player who we can't get to show up for appearances."

"Who is it?"

"T. J. Benson with the—"

"Detroit Pistons. Yeah, I know," Jack said. He pulled out his cell phone and hit one of his speed dial numbers. "T.J., Jack O'Connell here. How are ya?"

"Hey, man, I'm doing great. Thanks for that tip you gave me. I bought some more storage units and things are looking great." The charisma and enthusiasm of the rising star point guard came through loud and clear on the phone.

"Good for you. So what's this I hear about you making a deal for an endorsement for Bellagio Shoes?"

"Yeah. It'll give me a little more W.A.M.," T.J. said.

"Nice walk-around money, huh? So why the hell don't you get your dead ass to some of the appearances?" Jack asked.

"Hey, I got a new girlfriend. She's an actress. I gotta spend time with her to keep her happy."

"Why don't you bring her with you to these public appearances? She might get some publicity, too."

"Well, that'd be cool. Say, what do you care about it, anyway?"

"I'm on Bellagio's board. You gonna start showing up for the public appearances or not?"

"I'm cool. I'll be there. Don't want to get the man mad at me."

Jack shook his head. "Take care now," he said and turned off the phone. He looked at Marc Waterson, who was staring at him in amazement. "He should be okay now. If you have any more problems with him, let me know."

"You had him on speed dial."

Jack shrugged. "I met him when I was hanging out with one of his former coaches one night at a bar in Detroit. I gave him a few investment recommendations and they turned out well."

"Thanks," Marc said.

"You're welcome. What about my proposal for the economy line of Bellagio shoes?"

Marc made a face. "Okay, you're on the schedule for the next board meeting. But I'm still not sold on the idea."

Jack nodded. "I'll round up some numbers that will get your attention."

"Lillian wants a new position created for you."

Jack chuckled. "Really. What's that?"

"Pain in my ass," Marc said, but he smiled a little. "VP, long-range planning."

"I'll think about it. How do you think we would work together?"

"If we don't kill each other, I think we'd be okay."

"We should probably conduct all our meetings over burgers or hotdogs."

"I would be agreeable to that." Marc paused, then reached forward, offering his hand.

Surprised, Jack stood and returned his cousin's handshake.

"Welcome to the Bellagio family. Jenny says we're all a little nuts."

"I think I can handle it," Jack said.

"I think you can, too."

EPILOGUE

ONE MONTH LATER, after several dinners out, Jack took Amelia to Key West. As she slid her hand through his and watched the sun go down, she felt a sense of nostalgia so sweet it ached.

After that night at Lillian's, she'd told Jack that she'd seriously considered punching him for keeping secrets again. In response, he'd shown her photographs of his mother and father. The more she learned about his upbringing, the more she hurt for the little boy he'd been and the more she admired the man he'd become.

But he was determined to put the bad days behind him, and she found herself wanting to make his glory days as wonderful as possible.

The fact that he could make her heart stop and start again with just one look occasionally scared the poo out of her, but he was worth the fear.

She felt his chin rub against the top of her head and turned toward him, putting her arms around him. "This is so nice."

"Ready for the wet T-shirt contest now?" he joked.

She gave him a light, playful pinch. "Way to kill a moment. What's next?"

"I'm debating whether to get you loaded so I can talk you into getting a tattoo on your very nice bottom."

She shook her head. "This is turning into a quest."

"Nah, I just want you agreeable," he muttered and tugged her toward a wrought iron bench several steps away. The sun had slipped below the horizon, so the crowd began to drift away from the fence.

The wind slid over her and she snuggled against Jack.

"Cold?"

"No. You just feel good."

He put his arm around her and she felt his sigh of contentment. "I picked up a little something for you the other day."

"That's nice. Not necessary, but nice. Chocolate?"

He chuckled. "Not exactly."

"Another anklet?"

"No."

"Tickets to a ballgame I don't want to see?"

He laughed again. "No." He pulled back slightly and looked at her. "I love you, Magnolia," he said.

"I love you, Jack," she said. The words came easily because the feeling ran strong and free in her heart.

He lifted his hand to her cheek. "You are everything I never thought I could have in my life."

Her chest tightened at the force of emotion in his eyes.

"Sometimes I wondered if I dreamed you up, but I would have been too afraid to be that honest with my wishes."

Her eyes burned with unshed tears. "Oh, Jack—"

"Let me finish. I'm going to give you something and you can decide what you want to do with it. Whatever you choose to do is okay with me."

He pulled a jeweler's box out of his pocket and Amelia felt her heart stop. *Oh, no.* It was too soon for a ring. *Oh, yes,* the quieter voice inside her said. She'd never known she could love someone so much.

"Open it. Carefully," he added.

She did and found a small velvet bag inside. When she opened the bag, she saw something shiny and pulled out a loose stone. A diamond. She placed it in her palm. A large, beautiful diamond.

"You can put that back in the bag and think about it. Or you can get it set in a necklace." He paused. "Or you can get it set in a ring."

She felt nervous, but it was a good kind of nervous. "So, let me get this straight. You're giving me this diamond to do whatever I want with whenever I want."

"That's right."

"So you're not asking me to marry you," she said.

He stroked her cheek again. "I wanted to give you something to let you know that I want to be with you forever, and I'll wait."

"Oh, Jack…" She put the diamond in the bag and returned it to the box, then threw her arms around his neck. "You've just given me the most amazing and romantic things in the world."

"What's that?"

"Yourself and some time." She inhaled his scent and felt safe and so much more. Instead of feeling pressured, she felt a crazy but wonderful combination of freedom and commitment. It was so rare and amazing. *He* was so rare and amazing that she knew.

"That's a beautiful stone," she said mistily. "I think it might look best in a ring, but maybe next spring?" She looked up at him.

"Anytime, Magnolia," he said, meeting her gaze with that wicked grin she loved. "Anytime, any place." He bent toward her for a lingering kiss. "Now, about that tattoo…"

If you enjoyed what you just read,
then we've got an offer you can't resist!

Take 2 novels FREE!
Plus get a FREE surprise gift!

Clip this page and mail it to The Reader Service

IN U.S.A.	IN CANADA
3010 Walden Ave.	P.O. Box 609
P.O. Box 1867	Fort Erie, Ontario
Buffalo, N.Y. 14240-1867	L2A 5X3

YES! Please send me 2 free novels from the Romance/Suspense Collection and my free surprise gift. After receiving them, if I don't wish to receive any more, I can return the shipping statement marked "cancel". If I don't cancel, I will receive 4 brand-new novels every month, before they're available in stores! In the U.S.A., bill me at the bargain price of $5.24 plus 25¢ shipping and handling per book and applicable sales tax, if any*. In Canada, bill me at the bargain price of $5.74 plus 25¢ shipping and handling per book and applicable taxes**. That's the complete price and a savings of over 10% off the cover prices—what a great deal! I understand that accepting the 2 free books and gift places me under no obligation ever to buy any books. I can always return a shipment and cancel at any time. Even if I never buy another book, the 2 free books and gift are mine to keep forever.

185 MDN EFVD
385 MDN EFVP

Name	(PLEASE PRINT)	
Address	Apt.#	
City	State/Prov.	Zip/Postal Code

*Not valid to current subscribers of the Romance Collection,
the Suspense Collection or the Romance/Suspense Collection.*

*Want to try two free books from another series?
Call 1-800-873-8635 or visit www.morefreebooks.com.*

* Terms and prices subject to change without notice. Sales tax applicable in N.Y.
** Canadian residents will be charged applicable provincial taxes and GST.

All orders subject to approval. Offer limited to one per household. Credit or debit balances in a customer's account(s) may be offset by any other outstanding balance owed by or to the customer. Please allow 4 to 6 weeks for delivery.
® and ™ are trademarks owned and used by the trademark owner and/or its licensee.

BOB06R   © 2004 Harlequin Enterprises Limited

LEANNE BANKS

| 77052 | UNDERFOOT | ___ $6.99 U.S. ___ $8.50 CAN. |
| 77018 | FEET FIRST | ___ $6.99 U.S. ___ $8.50 CAN. |

(limited quantities available)

TOTAL AMOUNT	$ _____
POSTAGE & HANDLING	$ _____
($1.00 FOR 1 BOOK, 50¢ for each additional)	
APPLICABLE TAXES*	$ _____
TOTAL PAYABLE	$ _____

(check or money order—please do not send cash)

To order, complete this form and send it, along with a check or money order for the total above, payable to HQN Books, to: **In the U.S.:** 3010 Walden Avenue, P.O. Box 9077, Buffalo, NY 14269-9077; **In Canada:** P.O. Box 636, Fort Erie, Ontario, L2A 5X3.

Name: _____

Address: _____ City: _____

State/Prov.: _____ Zip/Postal Code: _____

Account Number (if applicable): _____

075 CSAS

*New York residents remit applicable sales taxes.
*Canadian residents remit applicable GST and provincial taxes.

HQN™

We *are* romance™

www.HQNBooks.com

PHLB0906BL